Hidden in a Heartbeat

PATRICIA McLINN

SILHOUETTE®

SPECIAL EDITION™

*Silhouette, Silhouette Special Edition and Colophon are
registered trademarks of Harlequin Books S.A., used under licence.*

*First published in Great Britain 2002
Silhouette Books, Eton House, 18-24 Paradise Road,
Richmond, Surrey TW9 1SR*

© Patricia McLaughlin 2000

ISBN 0 373 24355 3

23-0402

*Printed and bound in Spain
by Litografia Rosés S.A., Barcelona*

PATRICIA McLINN

says she has been spinning stories in her head since childhood, when her mother insisted she stop reading at the dinner table. As the time came for her to earn a living, Patricia shifted her stories from fiction to fact—she became a sports writer and editor for newspapers in Illinois, North Carolina and the District of Columbia. Now living outside Washington, DC, she enjoys travelling, history and sports, but is happiest indulging her passion for story-telling.

For the three Karens instrumental in putting
Far Hills, Wyoming, on the map—Karen Kosztolnyik,
Karen Taylor Richman and Karen Solem—
thank you!

Chapter One

He'd *have* to pay attention to her now.

Rebecca Dahlgren smoothed her tailored jacket and skirt, then pushed her hair behind her ears again in a futile attempt to control the wind-teased strands.

The man she'd tracked to this field eighteen minutes ago finally stopped cutting neat stripes in the long brown grass, exposing rusty-looking Wyoming earth. He'd seen her when she arrived, giving her a single, brief survey from head to toe. He'd shown no inclination to pause in his work, but now there did not appear to be a single blade left standing.

Now she'd have her chance.

He descended from the tractor, moving with a smooth, confident stride to where it connected to the even bigger machine that had rolled the grass—hay, she supposed—and left it in big rounds.

As she approached, walking on the balls of her feet so the heels of her pumps didn't sink into the clinging dirt, she saw him shifting levers, the movement emphasizing the muscles across his shoulders and back that the thin material of his faded plaid shirt did little to hide. Because he was slightly bent over his task, the worn material of his equally faded jeans stretched taut over hard, rounded—

"Stand back," he barked.

She halted so abruptly that both heels sank into the dirt.

He flipped another lever and the hay rolled out the back of the second machine, raising a cloud of dust. He locked up more levers then strode toward the front of the tractor, where she stood. His jeans were worn nearly white, making the zipper area and what was under it stand out in stark contrast. Her throat was suddenly desperately dry. Must be the wind, she decided. She licked her lips.

She shifted her weight, pulling one heel free from the clinging dirt, only to sink the other one deeper.

"Is it okay now?"

From his movement, she thought he flicked her a look, but she couldn't see his eyes under the brown cowboy hat. What she could see were a narrow nose that might have been perfect before it lost an encounter with a fist or some other immovable object and a jaw too square for strict good looks. A thin scar started just below the left corner of his mouth and hooked under his jaw like a misplaced dimple. Stubble all around it made it stand out in stark relief.

"Yeah." There was something warm and a little rough in that syllable—or in her imagination.

"Thank you. I'm—"

He walked past her toward the gate where her car stood. She had to pry her heels loose, turn and follow. Waiting to talk to him, she'd been standing heel-deep in dirt while the wind pelted the area beneath her skirt's dignified below-the-knee hem with grit until she feared her shins would resemble the surface of a golf ball.

The sensation was not conducive to being charming. And

she very much wanted to charm the man in the cowboy hat, jeans, boots and tough work gloves, because she wanted something from this foreman of Far Hills Ranch, Luke Chandler.

She needed something from Luke Chandler.

She intended to get it.

"Go back the way you came," he said. "Past the deserted house down by the red barn, then turn right."

He was telling her to leave? If she couldn't fulfill this small mission, how could she hope to succeed in her larger goal? Dismay dropped her stomach at the same time determination straightened her spine. She wouldn't fail, that's all.

"I beg your pardon? I've been waiting here to—"

"Getting the haying done comes before giving directions. Rain soon." It was an explanation, but not in any sense an excuse or an apology. "After you turn right past the old house, that'll take you to the highway. Go left for the town of Far Hills, right for Sheridan."

"But I don't— Oh. No, you misunderstood. I'm not lost."

"Have it your way. I'd've figured it was hard to get lost round here when there's only one road. Folks like you manage it just the same."

Folks like you. He'd barely looked at her, yet he was making judgments. She swallowed down irritation at that.

"One road or not, if you don't know where it's going, it's easy to get lost."

She said it with a cultivated smile, though an edge worked into her tone. How many times had Grandmother reprimanded her for that? What if he—

He tilted his head back, raising the shadow of his hat brim enough that light caught his eyes. And in that instant, she caught a flash of respect, perhaps a little amusement.

Simon, her most frequent escort back in Delaware, might have said *touché*. This man said nothing, just dropped his head so the shadow cut across his face again.

"If you're not lost, what're you doing here dressed like that?"

It wasn't hard to translate the movement of his head into a dismissive survey of her clothes, lingering on her dirt-dappled pumps.

She wore a perfectly dignified suit. Not what she would have worn if she'd known the business meeting she'd scheduled with the ranch owner was going to turn out to be a tromp through the mud with the ranch foreman. Yet the suit was a classically conservative choice.

So where did he get off making comments about her being *dressed like that?* Especially dressed the way he was, why it was nearly indecent the way those jeans— Not that that really mattered. She had to stop thinking of how he looked or how she might look to him.

She smiled coolly and held out her hand.

"I'm here to see you, Mr. Chandler. My name is Rebecca Dahlgren, I'd like to talk to you about—"

"Marti Susland's who you should be talking to." He gave his still-gloved hand a slight flip as if to indicate that was why he didn't shake hands—again, it was no excuse and certainly not an apology. "She owns Far Hills Ranch, along with some other family members. And she's in charge."

Darn cowboy hat. She wished she could see under it. It left her at a distinct disadvantage—while she couldn't see his eyes, she sure could feel them. Watching her, gauging, *judging?*

Her voice gave away none of that. "Ms. Susland said I should speak with *you*—that you would decide—"

"Why'd she say that?"

That threw her off. "I don't know."

"Maybe you should find out. I'm just the foreman. You won't be getting any commission out of me."

"Commission? I don't get a commission. The fee is flat and—"

"I wouldn't sell, but I don't own it, so I *can't*. Got it?"

Yeah, she got it, the arrogant, rude—

Rebecca reined in her temper with a deep breath. She dredged up another smile. "Mr. Chandler, I think you are under a misapprehension. I am not here to buy the land. I want—"

"You're not a real estate agent?"

"No." Exasperation seeped into that short answer, which didn't seem to bother Luke Chandler any.

He rubbed the side of his gloved thumb against his chin. She followed the movement as the faint sound of leather against stubble thrummed across her nerve-endings. When his thumb stilled against his jaw, her gaze rose. He'd raised his head enough that his light-colored eyes glowed out at her like embers about to spring to life with flame.

She looked away, studying the spray pattern of dirt her travels had added to the side of her car since morning.

"So, you're not from Denver or Salt Lake or Cheyenne."

"No, I live here, in Far Hills. The town," she added, then wished she hadn't. Of course he'd know she lived in the town, not on the ranch of the same name, since *he* lived here. "I only recently arrived here."

"Is that a fact?"

It was too polite to be mockery, but barely.

He looked her up and down again. This time she almost felt as if he were circling her, like a predator.

She clenched her teeth and held her position without flinching.

"You're not living in Far Hills—the town—to scout ranchland to buy? You're not with some real estate company?"

"Real estate? No. I have a contract with the Fort Big Horn Historical Site Commission to select, install and implement a computer system there. It will not occupy all my time, however, and Ms. Susland indicated there might be a position here that would supplement that work.''

She'd had eighteen minutes to practice the speech she'd formulated on the drive from the owner's house, and it came out just the way she'd planned it. "However, she said that your approval would be necessary before we could proceed. She directed me to this pasture so we could—''

"Pasture?'' He leaned back against the side of her car, one booted foot across the other ankle, arms that strained the faded shirt's seams crossed over a broad chest, his male arrogance not the least dimmed by the film of pale dust that clung to him. "Where you from, Rebecca Dahlgren?''

"I don't know what difference that could possibly make.''

She was an outsider, she didn't need it pointed out. She had been an outsider in Delaware, where she'd lived her entire life; it was unlikely to change here, where she was a newcomer.

"I'm wondering where people think that somebody who doesn't know a pasture from a field would be any use on a ranch.''

"I know how to customize a computer and I would be consulting on a computer system for the ranch,'' she pointed out with admirable calm—if she said so herself, "not branding cows.''

"Good thing,'' he muttered. "So how do you choose the right computer system to run a ranch without knowing anything about ranching?''

An astute question that pegged the consultant's challenge perfectly.

"It would be a system to *help* run the ranch, so I'd track the people who are doing the job now. From the information Ms. Susland supplied, a great deal of the operation funnels through you. Therefore I would begin with you. We'd start with an overall interview, leaving the in-depth work for—''

He was shaking his head. "No time. Besides, don't you know about Far Hills Ranch?"

Her heart jolted. He couldn't know anything...could he? No, no, of course he couldn't.

"Know what?"

With his gloved hand, he notched up the brim of his hat, setting it on the back of his head. The lift of his brows showed that he hadn't missed her reaction.

And she realized the hat alone didn't hide his expression. It was his eyes. He had sleepy-looking eyes that weren't sleepy at all; half-mast eyelids that gave away so little, while entirely capable of taking in more than she would have liked.

"Far Hills and the Suslands are cursed."

"Cursed?" she echoed in disbelief.

"That's what people say."

"Superstition is nonsense."

He shrugged, shifting the shirt's material against his shoulders, moving his open collar to show a different patch of strong, brown neck. "Have it your way."

"If this ranch were cursed, why would you work here for Ms. Susland?"

He smiled, slow and wide, drawing back well-formed lips from strong white teeth. It invited her in to the joke, made her a partner in it. It invited other things, too. Heat trickled an unsettling path down Rebecca's backbone.

"Because," he drawled, "I don't give a damn what people say."

"So I've heard. I've also heard this supposed curse certainly hasn't scared you off from Ms. Susland."

She regretted those rash words instantly.

She hadn't meant to imply anything about him and his employer, although she could see how it could be taken that way. She should have been more careful after having her ear bent with her landlady's gossipy speculation on that very subject.

So you're going out to Far Hills Ranch, are you? Helen Solsong had sniffed disapprovingly. *People say Marti Susland's been up to something lately, if you know what I mean. Why, he must be a good fifteen years younger than her, not to mention his wild ways. But I suppose it's the ranch he's after.*

Luke Chandler pushed off Rebecca's car, his eyes neither sleepy nor hidden now, but utterly cold.

"You heard right. I don't give a damn what people say—not about me. But anybody says things about people I respect, I don't take it so lightly."

"Mr. Chandler, I didn't—" Her hand on his arm stopped him as he was about to pivot away. He looked over his shoulder at her, his expression never softening. "I'm sorry. I truly didn't mean that the way I fear you might have taken it."

"Okay."

"Please, can't we talk? Maybe go somewhere and have a cold drink or—"

He stepped away from her hand and kept going. "Work to do."

He was halfway to the tractor when he turned back. Without preamble, he said, "A field's planted with a crop. A pasture's ground that's not worked, only grazed. Remember that."

Rebecca Dahlgren sat cross-legged—a position never allowed in Grandmother's presence—on the bed in her apartment and polished her shoes with a towel, saddle soap and a bit of soda water, the way Helmson had taught her years ago. She doubted, however, that the Dahlgren butler had ever had to scrape dried mud from a pasture—*field!*—off his shoes into the toilet.

She supposed *apartment* was rather a grand description for the combined living room and bedroom, compact bathroom and miniature kitchen carved out of the attic of Helen Solsong's house. As long as it provided the basics and a passable electrical system for her computer, she was satisfied. And this rental even boasted a private entrance via stairs that climbed from the double garage where she had the right to park her car.

It had taken a few days to accustom herself to the idiosyncrasies of the shower, the gurgle the refrigerator made at irregular intervals and the odd size of the bed that made single sheets too small and doubles too roomy. Now that all seemed oddly endearing because they were *hers*.

It was the first apartment she'd ever rented, and she'd felt triumphant the day she'd told Helen Solsong that she would take it, then handed over the first month's rent. It had seemed such a major step in her journey toward finally getting some answers. Almost as satisfying as the day four weeks earlier when the historical site commission had awarded her the computer consulting contract, giving her a reason to come to Far Hills.

Today had dimmed the triumph significantly, though. The only step she'd taken in her meeting with Luke Chandler had been backward.

Not only had she insulted the man, she'd gotten entirely too caught up in…other things. That was inappropriate with a man like that, whispered a voice in her head that sounded suspiciously like her grandmother's.

A man like what? With a great rear end and a broad chest and sleepy eyes that looked like they weren't interested in sleeping? probed a second voice with a taunt.

Over the years, Rebecca had grown adept at sidestepping the first voice, whether it came from inside her own head or from her grandmother's mouth. The second voice, however, was becoming unruly lately.

And this time, the first voice had a point. Not on the basis of snobbishness, but because Luke Chandler was a step toward something much more important than a great rear end.

She put her second shoe down to dry a bit before she buffed, and twisted around to open the drawer in the bedside table, withdrawing a leather portfolio. From an inside pocket she removed one of the copies she'd made of the old letter that had directed her quest here.

"...with a man like me, your mother accepting me is as likely as the Suslands giving me Far Hills Ranch. You know this is the only way..."

Rebecca stared at the words as if she didn't already have them memorized.

A man like me.

The man who was her father. Although *father* clearly was a title he had no interest in.

A man who'd created a life with a woman, then never showed the least interest in that life. That spoke of one kind of man. Yet the letter, with words that seemed to swing from affection to distance and hope to hopelessness, might have spoken of another kind of man.

There were too many unknowns. That's what had driven her, despite the risk.

A single mention, with no hint of this ranch's whereabouts or the relationship between the writer and these Suslands—except it didn't sound like he expected anything from them. A letter in hurried handwriting from some three decades ago, with a scrawled signature that might be Jack and had no last name. Found in one of four letters that had somehow evaded her grandmother's purge.

It had taken years of subtle, unobtrusive searching to find even this. And more than six months to turn the single clue into the reality of being in Far Hills, near the ranch owned by the Susland family. She hadn't gotten this far because she'd let lack of progress or even outright setbacks stop her.

So, Mr. Luke Chandler thought he was a big, bad immovable object? Hah! She'd been dealing with Antonia Folsom Dahlgren all her life, and she'd developed definite skills for dealing with immovable objects.

She'd simply adapt them and apply them to a Wyoming ranch foreman instead of a Delaware matriarch.

She needed to get onto Far Hills Ranch for considerably more than an afternoon of standing in a field watching a tractor go round and round, and Marti Susland had made it quite clear that the route onto Far Hills Ranch was through Luke Chandler.

Long after dark, Luke walked in the kitchen door of the Far Hills home ranch without knocking.

"Luke!" Five-year-old Emily squealed and launched herself at him, not letting her nightgown hinder her leap. He caught her with the ease of practice, swung her up in his arms and kissed her cheek. At the same time he directed a scowl at her mother.

"Marti, what the hell were you thinking sending that computer woman out to the Three Coyote Creek field while I was haying?"

"What do you mean, Luke? You can't be complaining about her interrupting your work, because I drove by when Emily and I came back from dinner at Kendra and Daniel's, and the haying was all done."

"No thanks to having some city woman standing there like a vulture while I finished."

"You made her wait? Oh, Luke, why didn't you—"

"Because I had work. Why'd you send her? Waste of time."

"I thought you'd enjoy talking to her. I thought she was charming—and very attractive. Didn't you think so?"

"How could anyone tell in that get-up?" he grumbled.

That was a lie. Sometimes the Wyoming wind could be a man's best friend. It could sweep back the sides of a jacket, then mold a blouse and skirt to a female form like loving hands. Didn't matter then that the blouse was buttoned up tight or the skirt was too long, because everything was there to see and be appreciated.

A hot pulse low in his body reminded him exactly what it had thought of long-legged, nicely curved Rebecca Dahlgren. Especially when her brown eyes had flared hot. Sure, it had been in anger. But it didn't take much imagining to shift that flare of heat to another source entirely, not with the wind tousling her straight, dark hair, and flushing her cheeks. Not when he'd watched her tongue sweep across wide, rich lips.

Considering the way she hadn't said what was on her mind even when her eyes did flare hot, she didn't match his usual taste for women who were as straightforward as he was. Although there was something a man could get to like about the feeling that there was a lot going on behind those brown eyes....

He caught Marti's speculative look, and clamped down on his thoughts. Narrowing his eyes at her, he demanded, "What are you up to, Marti?"

"Up to," repeated Emily, trying to imitate his intonation in her piping voice.

"Is that any way to talk to your employer?"

"Yes, when she's got a head full of foolish notions and schemes to match."

"I don't know what you mean."

"Thinking you have to make amends for what some legend says happened a century ago, Marti." She didn't meet his eyes, and he added with stronger emphasis, "Ever since you researched Far Hills history for that *Banner* supplement, you've been thinking only you alone could make things right."

"Not alone," she said softly.

He frowned. "You mean because of how things have worked out for Kendra and Ellyn?"

Marti had been in high clover the past year with her niece Kendra marrying Daniel Delligatti, then her nephew Grif returning home and making a family with Ellyn Sinclair and her two kids. Luke had his private suspicions that Marti had done a little pushing to get each of those couples over certain hurdles on the way to the altar, but she wasn't talking.

And he wasn't asking. She had a burr under her saddle about that crazy legend from a hundred years ago about a Susland doing people wrong. He was just grateful he didn't have a drop of Susland blood, so she wouldn't start meddling in his love life. Bad enough she was trying to give him a share of the ranch, as if he *were* a Susland. Actually being one would open a whole other can of worms.

As it was, Marti wouldn't listen when he said he liked being the foreman just fine. That he didn't want to be tied down to one place the way he'd be with an owner's share.

"Of course, that's what I mean." Marti's very eagerness made him suspicious. "Now Kendra and Daniel are looking out for each other, and Ellyn and Grif are so happy. No one could miss thinking that all is right with the world after seeing them work things out the way they have."

Yeah, someone could—him.

"That legend's damned nonsense, Marti." Rebecca Dahlgren had used a similar phrase this afternoon when he'd pulled out the curse to try to scare her off. Not that it had worked.

"Damned nonsense," echoed the little girl still in his arms.

"Emily, that's not nice language," Marti reminded automatically.

"Luke said—"

"I know, but Luke doesn't always use nice language.

Now, you go wash your face and brush your teeth before I tuck you into bed.''

Luke hugged Emily before setting her on her feet, and the little girl headed off with her usual bouncing step.

"Luke, I've told you, you've got to watch your language around Emily. She's like a sponge."

He grunted an acknowledgment of the old lecture. They both knew that was no promise to change his ways.

"Marti, what is this crock you fed that computer woman about me being the one to make the decisions?"

"Quit calling her *that computer woman*—you make her sound like she's made out of plastic and wires. Her name is Rebecca Dahlgren and she seemed very warm and human to me."

How warm and human would she feel pressed against—

"Fine. It's still a crock of—"

"It's not a crock. The right computer system could help ease the strain of paperwork. I know you do some tracking on that old machine, but there are sure to be faster, more efficient programs available now. You won't take the time to search them out, so it only makes sense to bring someone like Rebecca here."

"Why me?"

"I would think that would be obvious." Marti opened the dishwasher and started rearranging the glasses on the top rack as if it needed advanced engineering to fit in Emily's plastic cup when the thing was only half full. "You're the one who does that work. It's only logical that you be involved with selecting and implementing—"

He swore. "Now you sound like the computer lady. And I don't buy it. Is this part of that hare-brained scheme of yours to give me a share of Far Hills, Marti? I've told you, I don't want—" He broke off as his gaze rested on a name and phone number scrawled on the pad by the telephone.

When he looked at Marti, she was watching him. "You talked to that lawyer? Even after what I said last night?"

"Yes."

"Marti, dammit, if you won't listen to me, how about thinking about your family? How would they feel about someone who's not a Susland having a share?"

"They know it's the share for the person who's running Far Hills, and that's you. And they know you love the ranch."

"I told you, I don't want to be tied down—"

"Nonsense. You'll never leave."

Before he could respond to that flat contradiction of what he'd told her all along, she was continuing.

"Besides, Luke," she said with great dignity, "not everything I'd talk to a lawyer about would have to do with giving you a piece of Far Hills Ranch."

"No?" He didn't entirely believe it, since she was as hard-headed about some things as she was soft-hearted about others. "So what did you talk to him about?"

"*Her.* I keep telling you the lawyer is a woman. You know women can be lawyers or doctors or ranch foremen or computer consultants like—"

"Or ranch owners if they hold onto their shares." Before she could respond, he held up his hands in surrender. "All right, all right. Her—the lawyer's a her. What did she say?"

Marti pulled out a chair. "Sit down, Luke. I'll pour you a cup of coffee. Then I need to tuck in Emily and make a quick phone call. After that, we have to talk."

Chapter Two

If Rebecca had been able to move, she would definitely have made a note to herself to avoid this situation in the future. At all costs. Then again, if she could move, she wouldn't be rooted to the spot, staring at Luke Chandler's rear end.

And in one of those cycles of the vicious kind, that sight was what kept her motionless.

After receiving the phone call from Marti Susland last night, Rebecca had felt both relieved and fortified.

She'd gotten off to a bad start, letting her emotions lead her into saying things her head should have vetoed. *Do not indulge your emotions, Rebecca, or you will repeat your mother's failures.* Now she had a second chance. This time she wouldn't fail.

First thing this morning she'd put on sturdy woolen pants, layered two sweaters under her light jacket and laced up her hiking boots. She'd headed back to Far Hills Ranch, prepared to take on Luke Chandler once more.

There had been no response at the tidy frame building Marti Susland had described as the foreman's cottage.

Then she'd heard a sound from beyond the barn. She'd followed the mechanical clangs down a slope to a large metal shed with its double doors wide open, revealing a truck with its hood up, yawning toward her. Luke Chandler appeared out of the dimness of the shed beyond the truck, holding something dirty-looking in one hand and using the other hand to stuff a red rag partway into his back pocket.

He wore another pair of disreputable jeans—or perhaps the same pair—a faded shirt that might have started as green, a battered leather vest and the same hat as yesterday.

She opened her mouth to hail him, since he clearly had not spotted her, but never got the words out.

He stepped up on the front bumper with easy grace, spread his feet wide, apparently for balance, and bent from the waist to reach deep into the center back of the engine area.

Rebecca Dahlgren gawked.

The rag fluttered like an invitation to a bull that needed no encouragement. The old denim, faded to a color close to blue smoke except for a darker line at the seam that emphasized its path, stretched taut over his—her mind balked at its first word choice, and shifted to one less earthy. His *posterior.*

Outlined by the stretched-tight fabric, the muscles of his thighs worked to hold his position as he— Well, she didn't know what he was doing. It appeared to require tugging and straining that made him move in a way that one could almost think resembled…

Rebecca closed her mouth and swallowed.

Her palm and fingertips tingled, as if they felt the softness of the worn fabric over the firmness beneath it…except she'd never experienced anything like that, like this—like *him*—in her entire, proper Dahlgren life.

A curse erupted from under the hood, followed by a string of equally objectionable words, spoken in an almost crooning voice.

A new flexing and shifting of the muscles displayed before her riveted Rebecca's already elevated attention. Then came a grunt of satisfaction that warned her that this new movement was in preparation for straightening and, no doubt, turning around and drawing the conclusion that she'd been gaping at him. In other words, he'd catch her.

She dropped her head and shuffled a pair of minuscule steps forward as if she'd just arrived.

Raising her head, her gaze crashed into Luke Chandler's as he stepped down from the bumper, then turned to lean against the truck, one booted foot resting on the bumper, wiping his hands on the red rag. Was that suspicion in his eyes, or the reflection of her guilt?

"Oh!" she managed with a credible start. "Good morning, Mr. Chandler."

He frowned, but at least he didn't say anything.

"You might not remember—I'm Rebecca Dahlgren. We spoke yesterday and—"

"I remember."

"Yes, well, Ms. Susland called me last night and suggested I come back this morning. I'm not—I mean, I do have an invitation—I'm not trespassing."

Unhurried, he continued wiping his hands on the rag.

"I'd probably have given you a chance to explain before I shot you."

The slow deep drawl was dry as tinder. But she felt her face relax into a smile even before her mind registered the shift in the atmosphere between them.

"I wasn't so sure after last night. I'm sorry if I—"

"It's okay."

"I don't want you to think that I—"

"Why should you care what I think?"

Those words carried an edge that she could almost imagine was what she'd heard referred to as sexual challenge. She answered its broader question.

"I would hope that everyone I encounter would think well of me." Even to her ears that sounded priggish.

"Not possible."

"I disagree. If one behaves with courtesy and civility, it's entirely possible—"

"You come here this morning to argue with me?" He glanced up from where he'd wrapped the red rag around his left hand, apparently as a convenient place to store it. "You think that's going to make me think better of you?"

"Oh. No. I'm sorry, I didn't—"

"Actually, it might," he said with that same dry drawl. And then he grinned.

Rebecca would have liked to have denied her response to Luke Chandler. But there was no denying the fact that when he grinned, the tips of her breasts tightened into sensitized buds. Her breathing quickened. And so did her blood.

"I got my doubts you set out to argue with me. Not saying it wouldn't happen anyway, like some force of nature, but I don't see you planning it. So, if you're here to apologize, you've done that, and you and I can both be on our way."

She heard the words, understood them, but as if they came from far away.

"Ms. Dahlgren?"

"Wha— Oh." She blinked. Talk about indulging emotions! *Remember why you're here, Rebecca!* "I am sorry. I didn't—"

"Stop saying that." This time there was no drawl, no grin and she felt absolutely no inclination to smile.

"What?"

"Every other word's *you're sorry*. Stop it."

"I'm so—" She abruptly swallowed her automatic response.

Grandmother had always insisted Rebecca own up to failings, immediately and succinctly. She had a lot of failings by Antonia Dahlgren's standards, so she'd spent a lot of time owning up—at least to the ones she had any control over—with the all-purpose "I'm sorry." She hardly noticed the words anymore.

He had a point. Words were too powerful to become mere habit. Especially since she wasn't at all certain she'd meant the words half the time she'd used them this morning.

"I'll try," she promised, then clarified, "To quit."

For an instant she thought she detected an arrested expression in his eyes. Then he dipped his head in acceptance, cutting off her view. No doubt she'd imagined it, anyhow. Why would her promise to try to quit a verbal habit have any impact on him?

"So, why're you here?"

"For a tour."

"Tour?"

"Ms. Susland said on the phone last night that I really should see the ranch—*walk the land,* I believe she called it."

His brows slammed down in a frown. "She did, did she?"

She supposed most people would find him fierce. Neither his face nor body gave any hint of softness. Both his expression and stance declared there would be no budging this man. Those people, however, hadn't been raised by Antonia Dahlgren.

"She did. If you doubt my account, perhaps you should talk to her, and—"

"Don't get your feathers ruffled. I'm not calling you a bald-faced liar."

Rebecca found the latter reassurance scant praise and the admonition insulting, since she'd been practically dripping reasonable calm.

"I am not getting—"

"It's just what she would say. Don't know what's gotten into her lately, with this crazy idea about—" He snapped his jaw shut as if he'd just remembered he wasn't muttering to himself, then shot her an accusatory glance as if it were *her* fault. "No time today. Some other time."

Oh, no, he wasn't going to get off that vaguely. "When?"

"Hard to say. Ranching doesn't stick to schedules."

"Quit being such a pain, Luke."

Marti Susland's voice from the open doorway made them both turn in surprise. Another woman was with her, taller and grayer than Marti, with eyes equally intelligent.

The Far Hills Ranch owner aimed a glare at her foreman that appeared to have no effect on him at all. Her expression warmed to a smile as she turned to Rebecca.

"'Morning, Rebecca. I'd like you to meet my friend, Fran Sinclair." After the introductions, Marti took up the conversational reins again. "I'm glad to see you came back. I would stay to show you around myself, if I didn't have an appointment in Sheridan. But I'm sure—" another dire glare shot toward Luke "—Luke will show you around."

"Thank you, Ms. Susland, I'd—"

"Marti."

"Marti," Rebecca said with a smile. "I'd like to see as much of the ranch as I can, and hear all the details of the operation, so I can offer you the best setup for your needs."

She was looking at Marti, so she couldn't see any response from the foreman; maybe it was a guilty conscience that thought he seemed suspicious.

"I'm sure Luke can help you with everything you need. Tell you what, you get a look around Far Hills with Luke in the next few days, and then you come to lunch Friday, and we'll see where you're at by then. Okay, Luke?"

It wasn't an order, yet it carried expectations.

"Marti, this heap isn't running, and the boys have all the other vehicles."

Marti shrugged. "I'm confident you'll work something out." She gave Rebecca a look that might almost have been conspiratorial. "Luke's a wizard with engines. I'm sure he'll fix this. I've got to go now, but here's a supplement to the *Far Hills Banner* that might interest you. It's all about the history around here. Meant to give it to you when we talked yesterday. Kendra wrote it, and Ellyn did the design—they both live here on the ranch with their families, so it was a real family effort."

"Thank you. I look forward to looking at it." Rebecca's polite response almost faltered as Fran Sinclair sent a piercing gaze from Marti to Rebecca and back. What was that about?

"The research was fascinating," Marti said. "I found out a lot of things I'd never known, even though I've lived here my whole life. It gives an overview of the area's history plus how Far Hills Ranch was started. You might find that especially interesting—*personally* interesting."

The regional background could be useful for her work. Whatever personal interest she had in the Susland family ranch, however, was its more recent history. Regardless, she expressed suitable thanks.

"You're welcome. I'll see you Friday at noon, okay?"

"Yes, thank you, Marti. I'd like that."

As the two women left, Rebecca turned back to Luke. His easy posture hadn't changed, even though his mood seemed to have soured, and she heard him mutter something under his breath that sounded like a curse and the word *wizard*.

"If you don't think you can fix this old truck, then…" Rebecca looked over her shoulder to the large, shiny green pickup parked near the foreman's cabin in the distance.

"I'm *not* taking my new truck on the range for sightseeing." His tone left even less doubt than his words.

"I can drive my car—"

"That tin can wouldn't make it a hundred yards off the main roads."

She'd selected the car upon her arrival in Wyoming more for low price and high gas mileage than its off-road ability, but she wasn't ready to give up. "I can ride. If you have a pair of mounts—"

"*Mounts* would take too much time. I've got other things that need doing today. Like fixing this old rattletrap. You can wait to see if I can fix it," he allowed grudgingly.

She tugged on the inside of her bottom lip with her teeth. Although she'd brought papers to review to make full use of any spare moments, she hadn't planned on spending more than a portion of the morning here. "How long do you think that'll take?"

"Could take all day."

"All *day?*"

He nodded and she detected satisfaction in the gesture. She wished she could snatch back her words and wring every ounce of dismay out of them.

"When will you know?"

"I'll know better after I try to crank it up."

"Then, by all means, crank it up."

He pushed off from the bumper and sauntered to the driver's door. For a man who claimed to have such a full day of work, he certainly didn't hurry himself.

Prudently, she stepped to one side before he tried the ignition. It gave her a view of him in the driver's seat through the curved glass where the windshield turned from the front toward the side.

The engine coughed once, then roared to raucous life. The truck could probably be impounded for noise pollution, but it most definitely ran.

"I guess you *are* a wizard."

She grinned as she met his eyes through the windshield. He wasn't smiling.

Still, he got the last laugh. He leaned out the open window and announced, "If we're going to go, you'd best close the hood before you get in."

Rebecca Dahlgren of Delaware let out a most unladylike squawk as the top of her head connected with the roof of the old truck's cab again.

"Shock absorbers are shot," he called out over the rumble of the engine and the out-of-tune whistles of the wind through the gap between the body and door frame on his side.

"I'd surmised that," came back primly.

"Springs aren't much, either."

"That," she pronounced with dignity, "is a criminal understatement."

Luke bit back a grin as they jounced over the rutted road. Rebecca Dahlgren wasn't going to be as easy to dismiss as he'd initially hoped—*thought.*

Not that he'd given the stranger much real thought. Not after that talk with Marti last night.

He turned the truck sharply, and beside him, Rebecca braced one hand on the tattered seat, the other on the frame of the glove compartment that had long ago lost its door, and both feet against the floor.

This computer stuff was part and parcel of Marti trying to put Far Hills in his hands. But she wasn't pushing only the computer.

And Rebecca Dahlgren, of all the women in the world!

Straitlaced? Hell, she probably used a tape measure to keep her laces the proper distance apart. Her pants would have suited a nun. Or a coal miner. And above them, she had on enough layers to protect a linebacker for the Denver Broncos.

At least her shoes today were more practical than yesterday's. Though how she'd thought she could ride—*mounts,* he mentally snorted—with those clunkers on, he couldn't imagine. She'd have needed stirrups the size of a basketball hoop to fit those thickly treaded soles.

He wouldn't be a living breathing male if he didn't miss yesterday's skirt and nylon-clad legs.

Especially when he'd turned around and spotted her barely an arm's length away.

She'd worn a blush and a light in her eyes that he'd seen other women wear…although at the time those other women hadn't been wearing anything else.

And his body had reacted the same way. Except this hadn't been about a couple of adults knowing what they were about to do, and agreeing on what it meant and what it didn't mean. It had been a proper lady standing in front of him in clothes heavy enough to be armor and no such thoughts anywhere in her starched little soul.

Then, when he'd meant just to knock her off her MBA stride by pointing out she was apologizing all over the place, she took his words to heart. And that quiet, solemn pledge to try to stop saying *I'm sorry*. He should have laughed. Why hadn't he felt like laughing?

He steered across another rut just for the hell of it.

A faint *oof* came from beside him. It turned out to be a preamble.

"Tell me about Far Hills Ranch."

"What about it?"

"If I knew what to ask, I wouldn't need to ask."

He tasted the tartness behind her polite tone, and despite himself, he liked the flavor. He discovered a need to look out his side window.

"Pretend," she continued in that same tone, "that I'm a tourist and that you're a tour guide. Don't you think that's what Ms. Sus—Marti intended?"

They both knew it was.

"This is what's called a cow-calf operation. Calving season's in early spring. There's not much sleep then. Some of 'em need help, especially the heifers—they're the young cows.''

In as few words as possible he tried to boil down the cycle of the seasons to breeding, feeding, birth, seeding, fencing, moving, doctoring, irrigating, branding, haying, weaning, shipping, repairing machines, and more fencing, always fencing, while skipping most of the intricacies and variables that made every day different and unpredictable, frustrating and rewarding.

A section of fence that appeared to have dropped into Bender Creek caught his eye. They'd finished most of the fencing early this spring, but this section was late to grass up, so when the early branding and an outbreak of stomach flu among his crew had left more work than hours, this got pushed to the "later" list. Now, later had come, and the fence had to be upright before he put cattle out here this fall.

He flipped down the visor, took the pencil he kept jabbed into a tear in the fabric and made a notation on the piece of paper held by a' rubber band wrapped around the visor.

"So, a cow that produces strong calves year after year is more valuable than one that doesn't—how do you keep track of that?''

He turned enough to look at her from the corner of his eye. She'd processed all the information he'd given her and hit the bull's-eye, so to speak. "We mark them, get to know them. Remember from year to year."

"A computer program could certainly help track that. No matter how much you can remember, a computer can remember more. And it can cross-reference the data. A spreadsheet would…''

She was off onto an explanation of possibilities that sounded as intricate and frustrating as his job, though he had his doubts about the rewarding part.

As they crept across a section with ruts even rougher than usual, he found himself listening to her voice instead of the words. He also found himself glancing her way too often for his peace of mind or for this truck's remnants of a suspension system. He frowned and looked off to the left, and gratefully grabbed the first thing other than Rebecca Dahlgren to occupy his attention—a badly listing section of fence on the north border. Again he dropped the visor, and jotted on the paper.

She interrupted herself to ask, "What are you keeping track of?"

"Fences needing fixing."

She shifted closer to peer toward the paper. He watched the swing of her shining, dark hair just miss brushing his arm. Even without the touch, it raised the fine hairs there, like a sweet breeze.

"You have abbreviations for where the fence is?"

"What?" He'd heard her words, but he was a beat behind putting them together to make sense.

Still leaning across the seat to look at the paper on the visor, she turned her face toward him.

Her light brown eyes were alive with problems and solutions, probabilities and certainties. All he could think of, looking from the wide, warm eyes to her full lips, were the possibilities of pleasure there. The certainties of wanting more.

"Your handwriting's legible, but I still can't make sense of this, so I suspect you have a code."

"Yeah. Which field, which sides."

"How often do you have to repair each fence?"

"Hard to say."

"Try." That tartness was back. Along with a spark in her eyes that said she wasn't going to be put off so easily.

"Some winters are tougher than others on fence. Freezing, thawing, freezing again. In the mountains, we get wildlife coming through. That can be tough on fence. Some springs we get to all the repairs. Some we don't.''

"Surely it would help to have an estimate of how much material you're going to need for repairs each year. A computer system could offer you a projected range, if that would help.''

"It'd help more if the computer could repair fence, but, yeah, I suppose it would help.''

She didn't crack a smile. Much less give off the signs women did when they were interested in exploring those possibilities he'd spotted.

He'd pegged her from the start.

It wasn't just that she came from a different world—as a younger man he'd had a fling or two with wealthy easterners who'd wanted a taste of the Wild West. Not this one. It stood out all over her.

Everything serious and proper. Everything by the rules— and she had a million of them. Otherwise she wouldn't have to keep apologizing for breaking them.

"I can set up a computer program to track fence repairs, factoring in previous years' usage as well as weather variables. It would take a few years of data to fine-tune it to an acceptable projection. However, if you have back information, I could set it up to project a rough estimate of materials even before it had accumulated a pertinent data sample.''

Maybe a computer system wouldn't be all bad.

It would shake things up. Maybe that would be good for the operation. But the sort of shake-up Marti was pushing for was another matter entirely. What had gotten into that woman?

I don't want to be tied down—
Nonsense. You'll never leave.

Marti didn't understand him half as well as she thought if she believed that.

Far Hills Ranch foreman was a job for him—a good job,

but that's all. He didn't get tied down to places. Or people. That road wasn't for him.

He stopped the truck, putting it in reverse gear, because the ruts were so deep here that trying to turn could rip a few more vital parts loose from the undercarriage. He slung his right arm over the back of the seat, brushing Rebecca's shoulder on the way. And tried to ignore her startled expression.

"What's wrong? Why are you going backward?"

"I'm taking you back to the home ranch. We've done enough touring for today. I've got work to do. Real work. That's my job."

"Vince? Do you have a few minutes?"

"Sure, Rebecca, come on in."

Rebecca stepped into the commission director's office and sat in the metal chair that provided the only horizontal surface not covered with books, papers, folders or files. Vince Carling had enough paper packed into the tiny room to account for a small forest. Any piece of information she asked for, though, he retrieved in a flash.

"I was going to find you in a minute, anyhow," he was saying. "I talked to the folks up at Little Big Horn, and they said Friday morning would be good. That okay for you?"

"Yes, that will be fine."

Vince had suggested a trip to the Battle of the Little Big Horn monument to see how the National Park Service interpreted a site from approximately the same era as the historical site commission's. But that wasn't what she wanted to talk about now.

As she told him of her hopes of supplementing her contract at the historical site with one at Far Hills Ranch, his eyebrows ascended toward the glasses he customarily perched on a forehead tactfully termed "high."

Twice she found her words heading toward her less-than-successful meetings with the Far Hills foreman. Vince was not only easy to talk to, he seemed to have a rapport with the ranchers whose properties surrounded the 1860s site of Fort Big Horn. Maybe he could offer her some insights, some tips.

Both times she backed away.

Not because of her unruly body's response when Luke happened to be leaning into a truck engine. Or sitting beside her in the enclosed space of a truck cab. Or staring at her when she'd thoughtlessly moved too close then turned to face him.

She'd thought he was going to kiss her. For one, incendiary flash she'd been certain of it. That flash seemed to lodge inside her, burning in her throat as she tried to breathe, making each beat of her heart a pulse of heat, simmering low in her belly. It took all her Dahlgren control to not let him see her weakness.

But that had nothing to do with not bringing the topic up now. No, it boiled down to the roadblock named Luke Chandler not being Vince's worry. Besides, he might wonder at her determination to secure this job.

"I can assure you it will not interfere with my work here."

Vince's lips parted, but nothing came out.

"If you think it's going to be a problem, Vince…?"

"Problem? No, there's no problem. I was surprised, that's all. I didn't think you knew anyone around here. But as for working for Marti, that's no problem. She's a big supporter of Fort Big Horn. Backed us all the way on getting this computer system. Was on the search committee that found you, too."

"Ah, that explains how Marti came to contact me so quickly." Rebecca had wondered, but had not been about to question her good fortune.

"I suppose so. As for the work, your references all say

you can do any job you say you can do." He smiled, and Rebecca relaxed. "It makes sense. With a non-profit like this, it's not a huge contract and you'll have down time while we get approval for each phase."

"I'm so pleased you feel that way. If at any point—"

"Sure, sure, it'll be fine."

The rest of that Tuesday went smoothly and productively—a nice change from the start of the day.

Putting together a proposal for Far Hills Ranch meant starting nearly from scratch: she knew computers, but Luke was right that she knew nothing about ranching. That job, however, was pivotal to her search for the letter-writer. She simply had to get past her ignorance—and past Luke Chandler.

It didn't help that she hadn't gotten much sleep last night, what with working late over material from the library—none of it yielding any clues—then getting up early to be at the ranch. She'd have to get up even earlier to get there before Luke started work. She couldn't afford to waste time. She had a single needle to find in a limitless haystack, and only a few months to do it before her grandmother expected her to return to Delaware.

She had accepted long ago that most people thought her acquiescence to her grandmother was done with a greedy eye toward inheritance. Some, she suspected, thought her too weak to stand up to Antonia. Among the few who knew her well enough to know that neither was true, her friends from college still urged her to break away. Perhaps only two of the long-time Dahlgren servants, Helmson and Kit Dugan, recognized the truth: without Antonia, Rebecca would have no family, no history, no place.

"Good night, Evvie," Rebecca said as she headed out.

"Going back to Far Hills Ranch?" Evvie Richards asked from behind the reception counter, making no bones that she'd listened to Rebecca and Vince's earlier conversation.

Evvie didn't wait for an answer. "You're going to be working for the Suslands, huh? You know they say the place is cursed?"

"I don't—"

"Oh, me either," Evvie said a little too quickly. "A mighty interesting story, though. You heard how the first Susland 'round these parts had an Indian wife and three little kids he sent to the reservation so he could marry a rich white woman? The Indian wife came back and asked ol' Charles Susland to take care of their only child that hadn't died yet from illness at the reservation. When he said no, she cursed him and all his blood for turning away from his children, the tribe that had helped him, and her.

"Curse or no curse, that family's had its share of bad luck along with somebody else's. Marti's the last of the Susland name, ever since her half-sister died in a car accident, eight, ten years ago. The things I could tell you...."

Rebecca had been six years old when she'd learned how it felt to be the unwitting topic of gossip. It hadn't felt good. She tried to ease away. "Ah...well, I'd better—"

Evvie dropped that angle without a backward glance and tried another.

"You know Marti's got a little girl? Must be four or five now. Adopted her from an orphanage on some South American island a few years back. Guess Marti decided she wasn't gonna get married and have a baby the regular way— must've been near fifty when she adopted Emily." Evvie leaned forward on crossed forearms, bringing her impressive bosom even more to the forefront.

"That Luke Chandler sure caused a stir when he hired on six years back. Some folks remembered when his father was foreman, but it was the single women who sat up and took notice. There was a near parade to that foreman's house Marti had built, each one bringing brownies and cakes and such. Though 'parently the path to that man's heart bypassed his stomach. Not that he was a saint, if you know what I mean.''

Rebecca was afraid she did. She was even more afraid that she wanted to know more.

Grandmother often said small things give people away. *No matter how hard one might try to obscure the truth of one's origins, the small things give away that truth.* Now, it seemed to Rebecca, the small thing of her silence gave away her weakness.

''He made it clear right off,'' Evvie was continuing blithely, ''that he wasn't interested in a settlin'-down situation. Says no more than he means, that one. A few thought they could change his mind, and they got burned. None of 'em can say he wasn't clear as a cloudless sky about going his own way. Now, there's some saying it's because he and Marti found enough to keep 'em happy on the ranch, if you know what I mean.''

She hadn't wanted to hear this from her landlady before she first went to the ranch, she didn't want to hear it now. ''Evvie—''

''Me, I don't believe it. Why, she's known him all his life, practically raised him, same as she did that passel of kids who came summers. And now Kendra's back and married and a second little one on the way, and Grif and Ellyn happy as can be with those two kids of hers.''

Rebecca felt as if a wave of words, names and connections had broken over her head, leaving her sputtering and gasping.

''Not that I'd blame 'em if her and Luke did have some fun together,'' Evvie declared, skipping back to her earlier thread. ''Specially not Marti. He's a fine-looking man, and near twenty years younger than her. And that gives hope to all us past our first blush—or second. What I tell my Tom is, if I find out he's fooling around on me when he's on long hauls, I'll go look for one just like Luke Chandler—if Marti

Susland can do it, so can I. Tom hopes I'm joshing, but he's not positive, not clear down to his socks, and that's how I like it.''

While Evvie chuckled, Rebecca slipped away.

Chapter Three

With sunset melting into twilight, Luke spotted Marti heading toward his front door as he finished checking stocks of fencing, posts and staples for the morning. Marti had that look he'd seen on all the Suslands' faces now and then—a mountain-moving look. He mostly admired it…except when he suspected he was the mountain.

Sure as hell, Marti had found out from Ms. Rebecca Dahlgren, or some other source, that he'd dumped her protégé well short of a complete tour.

So he slipped out the shed's side door, got in the nearest ranch truck and headed out. In the rearview mirror, he saw Marti standing on his front porch, hands on hips. Yep, definitely a night for the Ranchers' Rest.

A few beers with folks who didn't ask a hundred questions and didn't prompt more inside his head. A generous burger, greasy fries. Songs on the jukebox. Maybe a couple games of poker without a lot of talk. Then home—after Marti gave up her watch.

His bubble of the envisioned peaceful night burst at the same time as Sally popped the top off his first bottle of beer.

"Hey, Luke, I hear this woman from back East who's living in Helen Solsong's attic apartment is quite a looker. And she's been out to Far Hills." Herb Tabben, who had a small place the other side of the county, watched Luke expectantly.

Luke grunted.

"You holding out on us, Chandler?" demanded Robby Greene. No amount of evidence to the contrary ever persuaded Robby he wasn't God's gift to women. "Afraid you'll lose the inside track?"

"Yep, that's what I'm afraid of," Luke drawled.

Everyone but Robby laughed.

Sally, who doubled as bartender and waitress, said, "The way I hear it, Robby, she's got enough money that if you could rope her instead of just swinging your loop 'round like usual, you could take your hand out of your Pa's pocket."

Robby clearly didn't like the digs included in that comment. But his interest overrode his pride. "How much money?"

Sally gave him a cool look. "I haven't been snooping in her bankbook. Find out for yourself."

"Ask Helen, she's snooped for sure," someone behind Luke suggested, drawing chuckles. Helen Solsong's tongue had hurt too many too often to be cut any slack.

"Hell, Helen probably made it up—you know how she's always trying to be so important," said Herb in disgust.

"I don't think so," ventured Frank Abserf. He was a nervous man, with a habit of pushing his hands through his lank hair that made those who bought insurance from him wonder if they'd made a mistake. As the next-to-youngest brother of Evvie Richards, however, he was the conduit for an impeccable source.

"What's Evvie say?" Sally asked.

Despite himself, Luke's eyes shifted to Frank's reflection in the mirrored surface behind the bar.

"Evvie says this Rebecca's from one of those real, real old families back East. Been here since the *Mayflower,* practically."

"That doesn't mean anything," Robby scoffed. "A lot of old families went through their money a long time ago."

"Not this one," Frank said simply. "There's some big estate in one of those states back East—"

Delaware, Luke's mind supplied unbidden.

"—lots of real estate, and even more money in businesses. Corporations," he elaborated importantly. "Evvie says it's not like the DuPonts or Vanderbilts, with their own business. The Dahlgrens invested in other folks' businesses."

"And a thousand Dahlgrens line up now for a piece of the pie." Robby seemed to hope he was conveying he didn't care to know Rebecca Dahlgren's net worth. Nobody was buying it.

Frank shook his head. "Evvie says there's just this Rebecca and her grandmother left."

"So little Miss Rebecca will inherit it all?"

"Uh-huh. That's what Evvie says. But she says you'd hardly know it. Rebecca's not flashy or snooty. Kind of quiet."

Luke wondered if there was a soul in this world that Evvie Richards wouldn't consider quiet compared to herself.

"And Evvie said something else."

"What?" asked several voices, including Robby's.

"She said that there's some big secret about this Rebecca. She's a Dahlgren, sure enough," he said staunchly, as if someone had questioned that. "But none of them other Dahlgrens got dark hair, dark eyes and golden skin."

*   *   *

Rebecca's spirits sank but her back straightened with Luke Chandler's first, dark glare toward her.

She'd arrived at Far Hills Ranch before he left his house this morning, even though it had produced a homicidal longing aimed at her alarm clock when it went off. As soon as Luke opened his door, she headed toward him. He didn't appear to be in a good mood, and his expression soured more when he saw her.

She produced a professional smile. "Good morning."

"You been here all night? Looks like you slept in your car, if you slept at all."

"I slept in my own bed."

"Glad to hear it," he muttered. Before she could untangle what that might mean, he added. "Looks like you could stand more time there. Go home, get rid of those half-shiners."

For a breath-held instant, she thought his extended fingers would brush against her cheek. Instead, they sketched a horizontal wave in the vicinity of her eyes.

"If you are thinking you will get rid of me by telling me I have circles under my eyes, you should know that I don't give up that easily." A flash of insight made her feel almost comradely toward him. "I'm sure you don't give up on a heifer if she doesn't have a calf the first year."

"Matter of fact," he drawled, "we do. Weed her out of the herd, ship her to market and sell her for what we can get."

"Oh."

Taking advantage of her surprise, he started that same maneuver of simply walking past her that he'd used the first day. This time she recovered quickly and countered it by turning on the heel of her hiking boot and taking three quick steps to catch up.

"Well, I will *not* be shipped off to market. I want this contract and—"

He stopped so abruptly she'd gone two steps past him before turning back.

"Why? Why are you so all-fired set on this job? Sure isn't because you need money, Ms. *Dahlgren.*"

"Ah. I see...." She extended the words with the sigh of a woman wise in the ways of the world and weary of them. "You've been investigating my connections, Mr. Chandler."

"No need to investigate. Around here, news comes to you whether you want it or not. And somebody new provides a fresh crop of news to talk about. It's not like where you come from, where people probably have a lot of entertainment, so they don't bother talking about each oth—"

"It's exactly like where I come from."

He stared at her. She wouldn't look away. Nor would she hurry into an explanation that would, by trying to cover up her unguarded words, point them out more sharply.

When he finally broke the silence, he took a new direction.

"I've got to get the boys started."

"Fine, then we'll continue our tour after that," she said breezily to his departing back.

Before following him to the new, large barn, she allowed herself a huff of expelled breath.

"Well, that went well," she muttered. At least he hadn't succeeded in shipping her off to market. Not yet.

Not *ever,* she vowed. She had one solid clue to her father's identity. She was going to follow it as far as it would take her. And that required access to the Far Hills records.

When she walked into the barn, Luke was perched on what looked like a section of wood fencing used as a door to a tack-room. Sitting atop it made Luke a casual, yet commanding presence over the eight men gathered nearby.

As if he needed any help handing out commands.

"...Ted, wrap up what you started yesterday, then take

the section north of Leaping Star's Overlook. Think you can finish it today? Walt, you go up there after you wrap up that bull pasture you thought you'd be done with yesterday. And I want it done this time, understand?"

"Yessir," said the young hand with the wide smile.

"All right, Ted?"

"Mph."

"What the hell have you got in your mouth, Ted?"

"Donuts," offered Walt, pinch-hitting for his friend whose puffed cheek and working jaw showed he was in no position to talk. Walt held up a donut, as if Luke needed a visual aid, then used it to gesture to the large bakery box now three-quarters empty, sitting atop a wooden crate. "Rebecca brought 'em."

Luke looked from the box to his men, all in various stages of chewing, to where she stood.

Before he could say anything, Ted swallowed, and said, "I'll finish that today, Luke. Barring disasters."

Luke slowly turned back to the men.

"Good. Okay, everybody got a two-way who might need it?" Heads nodded. "Get to work then."

With a detour to grab a donut or two, the men filed past her with nods, smiles and thanks. With the last one gone, she let her smile drop, and contemplated the man still sitting atop the door.

"Donuts, huh? You trying to bribe the boys?"

"I'm trying to get off on the right foot with them. *When* I get this job, I'm going to need a lot of data, some will come from them. And if I can't get preliminary information any other way—"

"If you get this information you say you need, give us a proposal and we say no, will you leave me alone to do my job?"

No. Not until she found out the connection between Far

Hills Ranch, the Suslands and the man who'd written her mother that long-ago letter.

She knew better than to tell him that truth.

"You have your job, I have mine. Mine is learning about this ranch, so that I can provide a useful and accurate proposal that will work well for Far Hills *when* you hire me to select and implement a computer system."

Hands propped so low on his hips they were nearly on his thighs, he muttered something, then hopped down with unerring grace.

"Get in the damned truck."

She stifled a grin when he snagged the last two donuts. The same rattletrap truck as yesterday started without a protest.

She took the offensive this time.

"I heard you ask the men if they had two-ways—radios?"

He made a sound of confirmation. His eyes never rested as he surveyed the unending rises and falls around them. To her it not only all looked alike, it all looked empty. She almost asked him what he saw. But she wasn't in this battered truck beside this shuttered man to learn about him. Another man was her quest. Luke Chandler was simply a means to her ends.

"Why the radios?"

"This is a big spread." He spoke absently. "Man alone can get hurt. Without the radio you might not start looking 'til sunset, might not find him for a couple days."

"So, you do think some technology's good?"

"Sure. I like VCRs, too."

She ignored the faint mockery. "That's a start. You don't have an aversion to computers in general? Or laptops in particular?" She slid her small model out of the leather envelope that fit in her large shoulder bag.

"Laptop?" The tilt of his head was decidedly skeptical.

"Actually, this is a notebook. You can read the screen at any angle. And even with strong or dim light, you can—"

"Never work."

"This might not be right for you, but there are extremely durable models available."

"A hundred degrees in summer, forty-below in winter?"

"I don't know," she admitted, making a note in a file. "I'll find out. Maybe you couldn't use it every day, just as some days your truck won't start." The flash of his eyes she suspected was amusement. "The army's experimenting with models for combat conditions, so—"

"What's the battery life? I'm out fourteen, sixteen hours, or more."

Without a word she uncoiled the accessory cord, plugged one end into the computer, the other into the truck cigarette lighter.

"That's fine as long as the truck's battery lasts. Besides, those keys are too damned small."

"It's a standard laptop keybo—"

He leaned over and stabbed a blunt-tipped forefinger down. What appeared was *eeewwsssss*.

"I will take all your specifications into account," she said stiffly.

He wasn't a means to an ends, he was an irritating, stubborn, male roadblock with eyes he kept hidden and a rear end that—

"Why don't you tell me to go to hell?"

Her head snapped up in surprise. "What?"

He was grinning. Oh, his mouth was straight and his eyes as masked as ever, yet she knew—*knew*—he was grinning.

"Tell me to go to hell. It's what you want to do."

Damn right, she wanted to. She swallowed hard. *Letting one's emotions rule was a sign of weakness.*

"That would hardly be professional." Did he notice she

hadn't come out and denied she wanted to? "And it would hardly be the way of securing Far Hills Ranch as a client."

"Maybe, maybe not. Might ease that starch in your backbone."

"Starch! I—"

If you can't curb that temper, you'll end up like your mother. She has a sentimental disposition that considered love the excuse for every shortcoming. Temper or sentiment, it's all the same— Indulge in emotions, and you will come to the same end.

Rebecca blinked, and the tanned, tough, unshaved face of Luke Chandler snapped into focus in front of her. The misalignment a third of the way down his nose and the scar on his chin testified he had followed his own advice—and likely more than once—to tell someone to go to hell.

She couldn't afford that luxury.

"Posture was emphasized when I was growing up," she said blandly. "Now, about the history of the ranch…. Marti said your father was foreman here and you grew up on Far Hills."

"What's this got to do with a computer?"

"Knowing the history helps give me a complete picture of the enterprise and its workers." More important, it edged her closer to discovering if his time overlapped with the most likely period for her father to have been working here. And it changed the subject. "So you lived here all your life?"

"Except eleven years."

"Those eleven years were spent…?"

They'd reached a wide creek. Before she could do more than wonder where the bridge was, he downshifted and eased the truck down the bank and into the water. They were across and climbing the opposite low bank before he spoke.

"Denver. College. Three ranches in Montana."

She ventured an interpretation. "Your family moved to

Denver after your father quit as foreman, then you went off to college—studying something to do with ranching, no doubt.'' His grunt acknowledged she had that right. ''You tested out your learning at apprenticeship jobs, before coming home to Far Hills.'' *Home.* ''It must be wonderful to have somewhere you belong.''

He turned toward her; she didn't meet his look. If she didn't look at him, maybe her words—she couldn't believe she'd spoken them aloud—would die in the air.

''I'm just passing through. Besides, I thought you'd lived all your life in Delaware?''

''Yes. Now, getting back to the potential for a laptop—''

''You don't belong there?'' Twinned with the dryly amused skepticism of his words, she heard true interest.

''No.''

He braked the truck to a stop, yanked a hand brake, switched off the ignition and turned in his seat to face her. She felt the weight of his unspoken questions, but that wouldn't have bothered her. No, what tempted her to stumble into an explanation was the seductive belief that he would listen without judging. Might care. Might even understand.

That last thought was what brought her back to reality. How could he understand what she didn't?

''That's all off the point. As you've said repeatedly, you have a good deal of work to do, so you had better start this truck, and get on with it.''

''So happens, I stopped the truck in order to get on with my work.'' He reached into the well behind the seat and drew out a pair of stained, dirt-stiffened work gloves.

Before she could respond, he'd swung around and was out of the truck, the door slammed firmly behind him.

Chapter Four

She gathered her wits and her bag before she exited her side.

At the back of the truck, Luke was sitting on the lowered tailgate, trading his cowboy boots for knee-high rubber boots.

"What are you going to do?"

"Clean ditches."

"Ditches?" She looked around. She saw only scrubby grass, clumps of sagebrush and dirt. "Why do you clean them?"

"We clean 'em so water can get through. To see one—" he hoisted tools to his shoulder "—you'll have to follow me."

They climbed a dusty rock-strewn incline, then pushed through a thicket of scratchy bushes that snatched at her shoulder bag when they weren't snagging her jacket, before clambering down descending terrain. He seemed to cut through the bushes like a snake, and deal with the rise and fall of the land like a mountain goat. Still, she followed him.

"Stay here," Luke ordered abruptly. He took his denim jacket off and hung it on a dead branch. "It might look dry, but there's water underneath and you'll get those things soaked." His dismissive nod made it clear *those things* applied to her hiking boots.

With that he headed off to her left, disappearing from sight.

"When am I going to see a ditch?" she called after him.

"You're looking at one." His voice sounded eerily close, since she couldn't see him. "Two feet ahead, then look down."

And there, partially masked by the tall, tough grass and the short, tough bushes, was a cut through the earth that could be called a ditch. On the far side, she saw a field with new growth shooting up amid the stubble of cut hay.

"Is this for drainage?" she called out, talking over the dull sound of tool contacting vegetation.

"Irrigation. We rested this field last year, and had rain pretty regular all spring, so we didn't need to irrigate until now."

She shrugged out of her jacket, laid it down and sat there, with the notebook teetering on first one then the other of her cross-legged knees.

She fired questions at him: where they irrigated and when and how often and how much and what methods. He answered in short bursts as he steadily worked into her line of sight, then disappeared to the right.

He returned with the tools propped over his shoulder. "C'mon. This one's done."

"Now what are you going to do?" If his next task yielded as much new information, she would make real progress in no time.

Before plunging back into the bushes that separated them from the truck, he answered, "Clean another one."

The second ditch followed a similar pattern, although they reached this one from the field side, where the vegetation wasn't nearly as thick as that they'd fought through at the first ditch. Could Luke have taken the most difficult route to that first ditch in an effort to shake her off? Definitely.

The other difference was that Rebecca's system sustained a jolt of something like adrenaline when Luke worked into her line of vision this time with his shirt gone, leaving only a damp and skin-clinging undershirt as covering.

She kept her head down, rapidly typing notes about potential methods of planning and tracking irrigation when he came over to where she was seated to hang his shirt on a branch near his jacket.

She'd seen male chests, of course. From her earliest years of swimming lessons at the club, through teen forays to the beach, and her grand total of two lovers. And his wasn't even bare.

Why did that seem worse? No, not *worse*. But the layer of white cotton somehow showed more than no covering would have. Or was it because there was more to show? Broader shoulders, a fuller chest, ropey muscles whose outlines showed clearly through the thin fabric with each twist and extension. Muscles molded by necessity. Utility and grace combined.

A gap between his back and the jeans' waistband formed as he bent to dislodge a branch. The white material of his undershirt disappeared into that gaping V, inviting a hand to follow its softness, down to the hard curve inside that pressed as tightly against the faded denim as it had yesterday morning....

The sound of a sigh—*her* sigh, for heaven's sake!—when he disappeared from view to her right, caught her up short.

She redoubled her questions, sometimes not giving him a chance to answer before she fired the next.

At their third stop, when she grabbed the notebook computer, he groaned. "You couldn't have any more questions."

She could—she did—but probably not about ditches or irrigation. And if she got him to tell her anything about what she really wanted to know, she wouldn't need notes to remember.

She slid the computer back into her bag.

He hadn't bothered to button his shirt after retrieving it when he'd finished the second ditch. Now he slid it off with a shrug.

This ditch was less congested. Luke was making quick progress, and his shirtless form stayed in sight only a brief time. He had already disappeared to her right when Rebecca felt something against her cheek and pushed it away. Then something hit her shoulder.

She looked up, and got a raindrop square on the chin.

"Oh! It's raining." She scrambled up, shaking out the jacket she'd been sitting on.

The change in her position brought him into sight. He didn't look up, forking another mass of debris out of the ditch.

"Yeah? Afraid you'll melt? I don't think you've got enough sugar in you to worry about it."

For no reason that comment made her want to grin.

"Not sugar, bits and bytes," she said with mock sternness. "And they're not supposed to get wet."

"Told you a computer wouldn't last out here. You get wet, you get hot, you get cold, you get grit in your eyes, you get tired. And you keep working. Until the work's done."

She stood without moving, watching his efficient, confident motions. The rain came down harder. Weighted by the water, her hair dropped all at once from the pins that held it. It would be streaming in a moment. Her jacket was already soaked through.

He finished the last few forkfuls. "And when it's done," he said with a grunt of satisfaction, "*then* you get dry. Let's go."

With no wasted movements, he took his tools, jacket and shirt, and strode across the stubbled field toward the truck.

The rain roused a spicy scent from the land. The heavy drops made small craters in the dirt at her feet. She slowed her steps, falling behind him.

From beside the truck, he looked back. "Are you coming?"

She spread her arms shoulder high, palms up to cup the moisture. "Thought you didn't mind getting wet, Luke."

"I work through it. That doesn't mean I like it."

She tilted her head back, closing her eyes and opening her mouth. "Maybe you should—like it, I mean."

"If you're not worrying about sugar, what if you melt all that starch of yours?" His voice had dropped, and picked up a timbre that rasped across her nerve-endings like a bow low on a viola.

A huge raindrop hit the base of her exposed throat, exploded like a single-serving water balloon and slid down her breastbone and into the valley between her breasts. She shivered with the sensation, and a pleasure she refused to examine.

"The starch goes much too deep to melt."

She turned around once, then twice.

"I don't doubt it goes right to the backbone." He cleared his throat. "Minute ago you couldn't wait to get out of the rain. Now, you want to dance in it? Make up your mind."

She laughed, finally raising her head and opening her eyes. Moisture dripped from her eyelashes onto her cheeks, adding a more intimate curtain of rain.

Rain had always meant staying inside, to avoid any chance of getting wet or dirty. Rain had meant playing with a decorum that granted Dahlgren House the respect due it. Rain had meant no chance to escape into the woods beyond the formal garden.

"This is so different. It's like a gift. A brief, passing gift, to enjoy while it's here. Not like in Delaware. When I was a girl and I'd wake up and see that thick dismal blanket over the sky that meant rain was there to stay for days, my heart fell to the ground. It seemed so— What?"

"Nothing. Get in the truck. It's going to open up."

He brushed off water beading on the heavy denim of his jacket, then, from inside the truck, he turned and tipped his head forward to drain his hat of the water it had collected. He placed the hat carefully on the dashboard ledge.

He was right about the rain. The drops blended into a sheet. She jumped into the passenger side of the truck and yanked the door closed against a sudden gust of wind.

He barely showed any effects from the rain. But then he hadn't danced in it like he was celebrating the end of a drought.

She felt like someone coming out of hypnosis, who, despite all the assurances, really had clucked like a chicken on command.

What was he thinking?—other than that she had absolutely lost her mind.

Nothing, he'd said? No, that look he'd given her hadn't been nothing.

She squirmed out of her dripping jacket while he turned the ignition key.

"Hey! Don't go slinging that thing around." Luke took her jacket off the seat, and dropped it to the floor by her feet. She'd already discovered that her hiking boots were not entirely waterproof, and the waterfall that came off the jacket didn't help.

"Do you have a towel I could use on my hair?"

He fed the hesitant engine more gas and the truck jumped forward. "Not one that you'd want to use."

She looked up at the challenge of that. Then, remembering what she'd seen on his gloves, decided that was one bit of bait she wasn't going to rise to.

She leaned forward, caught her hair in both hands and twisted it gently, squeezing out water in a stream. She let it fall, then twisted in the opposite direction, a trick she'd learned when she'd finally grown her hair long in college after all the years of chin-length cuts.

Her top sweater was rapidly soaking through to the one below. She grasped the hem and pulled it over her head, tugging it free carefully after bumping her elbow against the side window.

Damn. The other sweater was damp, too. She crossed her arms and took hold of each side of that hem, and started to tug.

A sound from beside her froze her.

"It's wet," she said defensively.

"How many damn layers do you have on?"

His gaze was on the strip exposed by her rising sweater. A strip covered by a cotton shirt and a silky camisole. Without the hat shielding his eyes, what she saw in his gaze brought heat to every portion of her body, covered or uncovered.

She saw disappointment that there were more layers. And she saw unsatisfied lust.

She couldn't remember any male ever looking at her like that. Not the few hormone-driven high-schoolers who'd met Antonia's approval; not the equally hormone-driven college guys who most definitely would not have met her approval. Not even the two men Rebecca had slept with.

A jolt nearly knocked her off the seat.

The first instant she thought it was the outward manifestation of what she was feeling. The second, she knew it was the truck.

Luke jerked his head around toward the front of the truck, swearing prodigiously under his breath. The engine had stopped. And through the waves of rain, she could see that the truck had its nose in the creek and the back slanted up toward the northwest, where the sky was already clearing.

Luke Chandler had driven right into a creek.

Unexpected laughter came before she could stop it. She still held her sweater's hem in a cross-armed grip, though her arms had dropped to her waist. Not even that position helped hold in the laughter bubbling up.

"Laugh one more time, and you'll be back out in the rain, lady." Beneath his would-be growl she heard the humor, and she made no effort to stop.

The failure of his repeated efforts to restart the engine sobered her up some. "What's wrong with it?"

"What's wrong with it is it's a rattletrap, and I'm not a damn wizard no matter what Marti says," he grumbled.

He jammed his hat on and opened his door, stretching partway out. She turned away from the wind-driven rain, relieved when he pulled back in, slamming the door and removing his hat.

He dug in the deep pocket of his jacket and brought out a two-way radio. He stared down at the radio two long beats before adding to his previous comments, "And a nose full of water didn't help."

He looked out his window, although the rain streaming down the glass had turned it as opaque as a curtain, while he pressed the radio's button and spoke into it. "Luke to all Far Hills. Who's closest to Tumbleweed Creek?"

After a pause long enough to make Rebecca remember his words about the size of the ranch and the dangers that made two-way radios a necessity, a voice crackled to life.

"That'd likely be me—Walt. I'm still fencing that bull pasture."

"Good. C'mon up here with the gray truck. We need a pull."

"Uh, now? It'll be a half-hour before I finish."

The hesitation was clear in the younger man's voice. He apparently carried the sting of Luke's words from this morning about finishing up, and didn't want to leave the job now.

"Finish, then get up here."

"Okay."

Luke signed off the radio, then cursed under his breath. This time, she thought, he meant it. Was he lamenting the time away from work, or the time with her?

Too bad, either way, she thought defiantly. It didn't have to be a waste of time for her. So, they were alone in these few square feet of space. Isolated by the rain, the moisture bringing his scent of wet cotton, disrupted soil and vegetation, hard work and a tang of leather too strongly to her. Or was she breathing it in too deeply?

"We could talk."

Her words came out so choppy and abrupt that she didn't blame him for looking at her like she was speaking a foreign language.

"What?"

"You can give me more information about the ranch."

He flicked the ignition key part way, then turned on the radio. Obviously, answering questions wasn't high on his wish list.

She lifted one brow. "That's fine as long as the truck battery lasts."

He acknowledged the return of his own words with a twist of his lips and a slight nod.

Determined to be reasonable, even though he was mule-headed, she pointed out, "We can't go anywhere. We can't even get out of the truck. We might as well—"

"I could get out. But I won't."

Now that response was a two-edged sword. He took a slice at her that she'd be unfit to try to climb out, yet let it be known in his backhand way that his particular brand of chivalry didn't allow him to leave a woman alone in a truck stuck in a creek in the middle of a rainstorm.

By her count, he'd circled the dial twice, finding six stations of complete static and one with just enough sound getting through to recognize a farm report.

While he leaned forward to fiddle with the radio with his right hand, his left hand rested atop the steering wheel. At first, she thought that what she saw were reflections of the rain's tracks on the windshield. After a moment, though, she realized the marks across his knuckles, fingers and onto the back of his hand were the silvery threads of scars.

The urge to question parted her lips. The memory of gloves worn longer than necessary and that red rag wrapped around his hand closed them.

He switched the dial once more and brought in a distant, unidentified classical station with crystal, mournful clarity.

"Oh, it's Chopin."

He grunted, but didn't move the dial.

The music flowed into the truck's cab. Any deficiencies from the radio or the transmission were masked—even enhanced—by the syncopation of rain on the truck roof. It was like every heartache any human had ever suffered, transformed into music.

And then it was gone.

Static followed after a short silence, and Luke switched off the radio.

"My heart fell to the ground." Rebecca hardly realized she'd spoken aloud until Luke turned to her.

"What was that you said?"

There was no reason not to tell him. "My heart fell to

the ground. It's a phrase I think of when I hear music like that.''

"You said that before. Where'd you learn it? It's unusual.''

With the power of the music still washing over her, she considered that. "I suppose it is. My mother used it when—'' she stopped, knowing she'd gone too far to let it drop. She breathed in, then out before finishing ''—when I asked about my father.''

He didn't say a word, but she felt the drag of his will.

"I've never met my father.'' She'd given that answer often enough, to questions that ranged from innocently friendly to purposely barbed. "I don't even know his name. When I was little and would ask my mother about him, she'd cry, and say *My heart fell to the ground.*''

She reached into her bag, and pulled out a foil-wrapped bar.

"Hungry? I suppose it's only fair to split it with you.''

"Candy?''

For the first time, his eyes flicked away from her. Heck, if it kept him from looking at her, she'd give him the whole thing no matter how cavernous her stomach felt.

"Granola.''

He grimaced like a little boy offered castor oil. "No thanks.''

"It's good for you. Lots of energy.''

"Don't need energy to sit and wait. Why'd your mother say that?''

She chewed slowly. He couldn't expect her to answer with her mouth full, and maybe Walt was a faster fencer than he'd predicted. Maybe—

Luke's eyes narrowed, and he repeated, "Why'd she say that about your father—*My heart fell to the ground?*''

"I suppose it was her way of saying he broke her heart. She was pregnant, and he deserted her, so she returned to

Delaware.'' She kept it matter of fact. "Not that she told me that. She didn't tell me much of anything. I barely remember her. She died when I was six.''

"Six is plenty old enough. You must remember things."

"Not much. We didn't have a great deal of contact. Grandmother had charge of my upbringing. Mother drank. She'd stay in her rooms most of the time. What little I remember… It's mostly her sleeping a lot, and the smell and…''

"And?"

"Waking up some nights to find her sitting on my bed, stroking my hair, and crying without a sound. I'd want to put my arms around her, but if I moved, she left, so, I'd lie there, feeling—''

She shook herself, then gave great attention to wrapping the rest of the granola bar. How had she let herself stray so far from facts? "I'm sorry. My, all this from hearing a bit of Chopin.'' She forced a smile as she looked up. "Think what Beethoven would have done.''

He was staring at her, his eyes intent, searching her face the way he had searched the land yesterday, reading the tiniest signs. The urge to look away and protect whatever he might be seeing clashed with the pride that wouldn't let her.

It was the same pride that held her marble-statue still even when she realized he was reaching one hand toward her.

His fingers brushed the side of her jaw before his thumb touched just beyond the corner of her mouth.

"Crumb.''

She watched his lips form the word, but it took an extra beat for the sound to make sense. And that coalesced a segment of the sensations bombarding her nerves into the reality that he had flicked an errant seed from the granola bar from the corner of her mouth. But there were still all those other unexplained sensations. And he was moving his thumb again, his gaze following its path.

Slowly, the side of his thumb brushed across her lips, from the depths of one corner, to the rise at the center, down to the far corner, then back to the center, where it lingered.

She wanted to lick her lips. She wanted it desperately. To slide her tongue across the same terrain he'd just touched, to even touch his thumb, to taste his skin and— No. A shudder rose up in her, whether from fighting against the longing or from the longing itself she didn't know, but she straightened away from his touch before the shudder could betray her.

His hand dropped away and his gaze came back to her eyes. Why couldn't he be wearing that darned cowboy hat now, when she would have paid good money to have her view of his face obscured?

Forcing a bright smile, she asked, "Do you know classical music, Luke?"

"No."

"Oh, you seemed…"

"No."

"I'm sorry, I shouldn't—"

"There you go again." He finally looked away from her. Relief had never felt so much like disappointment before. Although it also opened the door to other reactions, like curiosity.

"Don't you ever say or do anything you're sorry for, Luke?"

He slashed a look her way. "No."

He was telling the flat-out truth. That was what flummoxed her. "Never?"

"I don't care if someone else doesn't like what I said, so there's no sense saying sorry."

"People will think you're—"

"Don't care."

"Aren't there times you say or do something that you're

sorry about not because of the other person, but because it's not what you thought you should say or do?''

''If I do, there's no sense saying I'm sorry to myself.''

''Perhaps,'' she conceded. ''But I can't believe you never care what other people think of what you say or do.''

She caught the twitch at the corner of his mouth, so she was partly prepared when he said, ''I don't care what you believe.''

''People do form opinions of you, whether you care or not. Of course, one cannot please everyone, that would be unreasonable. Still, one has an obligation to maintain a certain level that has come to be expected of one's name. And if one lowered that level for whatever reason, one has an even greater obligation to make up that deficit. It's a debt owed to all the others of that name and—''

''Are you still talking about me, Rebecca?''

She jolted.

His right eyebrow lifted. ''*One* doesn't like to stop a flow like that, but *one* gets to wondering.''

It was too biting to be humorous, but held too much humor to be offensive.

''My comments were inappropriate. In a business context such as this to step into the personal—'' he tilted one eyebrow, and they both knew they hadn't *stepped* into the personal, they'd waded in ''—is uncalled for. I know you don't like people saying they're sorry. But I do apologize.''

''That's—'' He broke off, listening. ''Truck.''

''Stay here,'' he ordered without looking at her as he put his hat on. Only when Luke opened his door did she realize the rain had let up to a drizzle.

He swung himself up to stand on the door frame, his torso angled out, then carefully turned around. With a grunt of exertion, he jumped toward the solid earth where the back wheels of the truck still rested. Through the small, partly fogged-up back window she saw Luke coming to his feet as Walt came up.

From their overheard conversation she realized some of the creek bank had given way under the front wheels of the truck. The crumbling earth left the truck sharply angled, though in no imminent danger of being swept away. But it meant it would take more equipment than the lightweight truck Walt was driving to get it out.

Luke and Walt's discussion faded as her mind wrestled with other matters.

She hadn't given the possibility of their being in danger a thought. Not one thought. She'd sat in the cab feeling perfectly secure. Had she believed so strongly that Luke would take care of things that she'd abdicated all her brains? So caught up in the sense of the two of them, alone in the world, that she'd forgotten everything else? What on earth was wrong with her?

She slung the strap of the bag carrying her laptop around her body and had opened the door by the time Luke came around to her side of the truck. He scowled when he saw her starting to back out of her door, her feet searching for the bottom of the door frame.

"I told you to stay put."

"I'm capable of getting out of a truck."

"Yeah? If you're wrong, you'll slide right into the creek. How'll your computer like that?" He didn't wait for an answer. Holding on to the side of the truck bed, he stretched out his right leg and propped his foot on the extension by the wheel well that vaguely resembled a running board. "Put your foot on my thigh, then swing around me and catch hold of Walt."

"I don't—"

"We don't have time for you getting prissy on us."

"Prissy!"

She clamped her teeth down and stretched that first long

step to his angled thigh. If her heavy hiking boot's grid dug into his flesh, she was only following orders. And she couldn't help it that her heavy bag slipped around and clipped his shoulder before bouncing off his face.

A string of curses accompanied her as she swung her free leg to gain momentum, and clasped Walt's outstretched arm to reach solid ground.

"You did that real well, Rebecca," said Walt. "You're real graceful."

A grunt from Luke seemed to contradict that compliment.

"Thank you, Walt," she said with a smile. "And thank you so much for coming to rescue us. I don't know what we would have done if you hadn't been here."

Walt sent a rather alarmed look toward Luke, who as far as Rebecca could tell, showed no reaction.

"Uh, glad to be of help." Walt swallowed. "Uh, you want to drive, Luke?"

"No, you go ahead." As Walt trotted toward the other side of the gray truck, Luke ordered her, with a jerk of his head toward her bag, "Give me that thing. Damned near a lethal weapon."

She handed over the bag with no sympathy. "Only to people who go around giving orders all the time."

He ignored that, sliding the bag into a gap behind the seat, then nodding for her to climb up.

As Walt clambered in the other side and Luke swung in behind her, the sight of a gearshift lever in the space where her legs and feet should have gone stopped her momentarily. The men bracketed her, so she had no choice but to seat herself with as little fuss as possible. That left her shoulders and torso between the two men, but to give Walt access to the gearshift lever, she had to swing her legs to her right, toward Luke.

With her hands folded in her lap, she nearly echoed one of the postures approved of in Miss Meacham's deportment class. The image of wearing this outfit in front of that formidable woman brought a totally unexpected giggle.

Luke slanted a questioning look toward her.

Which reminded her of how his left thigh pressed against her right one. How his longer legs bridged hers from the knee down. So the back of his calf now and then brushed against the front of her shin with the rocking, jolting motion of the truck.

She tried to eliminate the contact by drawing her feet as far to the left as the gearshift would allow, at the same time tilting herself away from him.

So she was entirely off balance when Walt called out, "Hold on! We're going off road!" a split second before jerking the wheel to the left. The truck lurched in the same direction, and Rebecca threatened to tumble into the driver's lap.

In the instant before that could happen, Rebecca felt a strong grip on her right thigh, clamping her against an even stronger solidity.

The truck righted for an instant, and she sorted out the sensations bombarding her as Luke's large right hand hooked around her thigh, above her knee, holding it tight against his own leg. Even with his arm angled across his body, his hold was strong enough to counterbalance the slide of her center of gravity toward Walt.

Fighting the truck's motion, she shifted her posterior, and brought her left leg back into place. Which left Luke's hard, hot hand pressed between her legs.

"You can let go now, I'm—"

"Hold on," came Luke's terse order in her right ear.

When the truck jolted as hard to the right as it had to the left, Rebecca did exactly that, grabbing with both hands to the only stability within reach—Luke's right arm. As the pitch and roll of the truck flung her against Luke, the force of her hold on his arm drew his hand higher and higher between her tightly clamped thighs.

The truck shimmied, and the friction was incredible. A shudder passed through her tensing muscles, clamping her hands even tighter around Luke's arm, until the side of his hand was tight against the juncture of her thighs, his thumb nestled in the crease between her torso and thigh. With no direction from her mind, her hands flexed around his arm, and his hand seemed to stroke and rock against her.

She heard a sound—part squeak, part moan. Oh, no, that was *her*.

She dropped her hands from his arm, and the pressure of his hand immediately eased. He removed it only by slow degrees as the truck's rocking gradually subsided into a more familiar jouncing.

Walt whistled. "Whoo-hee!"

Luke drew back, and she resumed her original position. The brushing of leg to leg was not only still here, but now served as a reminder of what had just happened.

"Sorry 'bout that." Walt eased his grip on the steering wheel. He flexed his fingers, one hand at a time. "Stupid cow, lying smack dab in the middle of the road. Didn't see her in time coming 'round that curve to stop. Had to go around or hit her."

"You were going too fast, Walt," Luke said evenly.

Rebecca forced herself to glance toward Luke. Her downcast eyes reached only his lap. That was more than enough to tell her that their adventure had affected him strongly— very strongly.

She felt the heat of a blush flowing up her neck and spilling into her cheeks. She could do as little about that as she could about what she feared was triumphant pleasure fluttering in the pit of her stomach.

"I know, Luke. It was stupid."

"We almost flipped."

"I know, I know. I'm *real* sorry, Luke, Rebecca." Walt's crestfallen face broke into a smile then. "Hell of a ride, though, wasn't it?"

Rebecca had pushed thoughts of the morning to the deepest corner of her mind, walling them there with a full day at the historical site. After a quick meal, she drove to Sheridan to continue her time-consuming search of old newspapers for any shred that might explain the letter's reference to Far Hills.

At her apartment, she read her notes from the historical site, jotting questions for the next morning. When she'd almost nodded off with her cheek resting on the eraser of her pencil, she decided she could safely go to bed without those barricaded thoughts escaping.

Wrong.

She shouldn't have talked so much.

And of all things, about her personal history. She certainly shouldn't have told Luke about her mother. She rarely told anyone about her family, except two college friends, now scattered, one to London, the other to Florida.

Emotions. She'd let them lead her into these revelations, and then she'd let them slop all over as if she had no restraint at all. And why, of all the people she'd encountered in Wyoming or anywhere else, had she said all that to Luke Chandler?

She replayed everything she'd said. At some point, the tape finally ran out and she slept.

But when she woke with a start in the pearlized gray of earliest morning, with the covers twisted around her, her breathing erratic, and the memory of the dream real enough to make her ache, she knew it had not been conversation she'd dreamt of.

* * *

Emily was in bed and Luke finally had Marti's attention Thursday night to talk about grazing the North Uplands section. Then the kitchen phone rang.

"If you think we can do it without overgrazing up there," Marti was saying as she headed for the phone. "That's my concern. Hello? Oh, hello, Rebecca." She turned and looked at him significantly as she identified the caller. "How are you?"

He kept his face blank. That took some doing when an image surged into his head—an image of a woman with her arms stretched wide, her head tipped back, her dark hair hanging loose and a trickle of water sliding down her long, smooth neck, beneath layers of clothes, down to where a man's mouth could bring another kind of moisture. Bad enough Rebecca had interrupted his thoughts too many times to count—at least more times than he *wanted* to count—now she was interrupting ranch business.

"Uh-huh…. Oh, yes, Vince is right. You should see it." A couple more neutral uh-huhs confirmed Marti was listening.

"Oh, that doesn't mean you have to miss lunch," Marti said at last. "I have just the solution. Luke's heading up that way himself tomorrow morning. He has to pick up truck parts in Billings. So, he'll drop you off on his way, do his business and pick you up on his way back. You can get Emily at the baby-sitting co-op, and we'll have lunch when you get here."

Marti's mouth twitched as if she was fighting a grin, and her voice was breezy enough to skitter tumbleweed.

"I can't imagine why it would be a problem. But I'll check. He's right here." She clamped a hand over the mouthpiece, and addressed him. "Rebecca's got an appointment at the Little Big Horn site in the morning. She's worried she might hold us up for lunch. Since you're going up—"

"You said to wait for the courier to deliver the parts."

"The way you grumbled, I knew you'd never be that patient," she retorted. "Admit it, you were planning on going up."

He'd been thinking of sending Walt. That didn't appeal anymore.

"You heard what I told Rebecca—that okay with you?"

He'd have been dead set against the idea if he hadn't gathered that Rebecca was trying to backpedal her polite rear end out of spending time with him. However, even the prospect of making prim Rebecca squirm didn't wipe out another cause for caution.

"Marti, are you—?"

"You want me to tell her you said no?"

He swore then muttered, "Fine."

Marti uncovered the mouthpiece and looked away. "Luke says that will be fine. He's looking forward to it. He'll pick you up at eight. That should get you up there in plenty of time. And we'll see you at lunch! Good-bye." She hung up.

"Pick her up at eight," Marti said. "She's staying in that attic apartment of Helen Solsong's. Now, tell me about the North Uplands."

He gave her a long, warning look before he let himself be drawn back into ranch business. "With the dryness lately, we need to keep the cattle up top longer. We'll have to move them more to avoid overgrazing, and that'll keep me and the boys—"

"Ellyn and Grif will help. Meg and Ben, too. Kendra's out, but Daniel can sit a horse, and I can still do a thing or two."

"Yeah, you can do a thing or two."

On horseback, and meddling in a man's life—if he let her.

Chapter Five

Breathing hard from the steep climb, Rebecca reached the big monument, then turned to look down the hill at the scattering of white markers for men who'd also made a last stand on this hillside, but whose names were seldom remembered.

She'd taken advantage of her Park Service contact being tied up with an unexpected conference call and of an imposing iron gate being open to walk the land.

She smiled slightly at her mental use of that phrase—Marti's influence, obviously.

To the south and slightly west she could see the rising line of mountains that she supposed were the Big Horns. Down their spine, farther south yet, was Far Hills Ranch.

In the wide space between that distant landmark and where she stood, the land rolled and bucked, now placid and fertile judging by huge rectangles of crop-green, then ragged and folded in on itself like a quiche someone had poked a finger into. One finger-poked area beyond the iron fence created a gap that gave her a view of water, curling around a cut bank, lined by cottonwood trees.

Did the fields prosper thanks to irrigation ditches kept open by a man who might strip his shirt and bend and—

No. She would concentrate on what she'd come here for. Putting thoughts of the starkly silent and uncomfortable ride here out of her mind. Giving not another thought to the man who'd sat beside her.

Focusing on the markers, she noted their simplicity, and their dignity. The markers, white marble rectangles with slightly rounded tops, were set amid a feathery bed of tall grasses, probably the same sort that had grown on this hillside more than a century ago, maybe a thousand years ago, now turning from summer green toward the straw color of the tall grass Luke had been cutting that first day....

Luke Chandler. He could never be anything except an enigma to her—and an obstacle if she let him. Just as she would never be anything to him.

She knew what sort of man he was. She'd heard it from Helen before she'd even met him. That her own and Evvie's observations absolved him of being the worst kind of womanizer didn't clear him completely. And she was not the sort of woman to interest that sort of man.

As long as she remembered that, she'd be okay. She wouldn't let her emotions lead her into folly. She didn't need to concern herself about his emotions, because it was blindingly clear that a man like that didn't fall—

"That's where some say he fell."

Rebecca jolted at the voice from behind her.

A woman about her own age, dressed in the gray shirt, green slacks and straw ranger hat of the National Park Service stood beside her. Her name tag said Lorraine Talking Bear. She nodded to Rebecca.

"Down there, by the river. And without their leader, the

blue soldiers didn't know what to do. They tried to get back up here. Some did. Not enough.''

Custer. She was referring to George Armstrong Custer. Glory hound or hero, Custer was probably the primary attraction for many park visitors. And the fall that this ranger was talking about was of the last-stand kind.

''Why is the monument here if he fell there?'' Rebecca asked.

''Maybe they didn't think tourists would be willing to climb down there and then all the way back up,'' she said with a smile. ''It's sure a good view up here. Besides, it would upset all those images of the gallant officer fighting to the end amid his devoted men—songs and paintings and stories. And that's still the official version.''

''With all those things saying he fought to the last, what makes you think he fell down there?''

''Oh, that's *always* been the account from our people.''

''Our people?''

''I thought— I assumed— You're not Indian?''

''No, I'm from Delaware,'' Rebecca said inanely.

''I'm sorry.''

''No, no, nothing to be sorry for. It was a—''

Natural mistake.

The words never came out of her mouth. She didn't know if it *was* a mistake. Her hair was barely a shade lighter than the other woman's. Her eyes and skin had a lighter tint, but that didn't mean they didn't witness Native American blood.

Native American made as much sense as Hispanic, Middle Eastern, Pakistani, Indian and Asian—all of which she'd wondered about. More sense, since the letter's clue had brought her to an area criss-crossed by the history of many tribes.

She made herself smile. ''It's fascinating to hear the Native American accounts.''

''Indian's fine with me.''

Rebecca listened attentively to the ranger's accounts passed down by the handful of survivor Crow scouts who had fought with Custer, and by the Cheyenne and Lakota who had defeated him and his troops that day.

She immersed herself in the information, as well as the knowledge gained from the staff. That left only a corner of her mind to face a new recognition.

She'd been so focused on the individual identity of the man who had helped conceive her that she had given little thought to where he might fit in a broader picture.

Oh, she'd realized he might well have a family, other children. A whole different life that wouldn't include an unexpected daughter. She'd been very clear-eyed about that—at least she had since outgrowing her childhood fantasies of a large, warm family that would welcome her with open arms.

Since she'd searched in earnest as an adult, she'd been so focused on her personal history she hadn't given thought to the possibility of having a heritage, an ethnic history that she knew little or nothing about.

"Did you get what you needed?" She made her polite inquiry as the truck Luke drove with such competent non-chalance merged onto I-25, heading south.

"Got what I ordered. Can't tell yet if it's what I need. You?"

She certainly hadn't ordered any of her conversation with Ranger Talking Bear. Had it given her what she needed?

"Something happen?"

He'd shifted his scarred left hand to the top of the steering wheel, allowing him to turn more toward her. A bug under a microscope couldn't have felt as closely scrutinized as she did.

"No. Nothing. I mean, nothing out of the ordinary. I got good information from the rangers."

She launched into an explanation of what she'd seen and been told—as it pertained to her work for Fort Big Horn. Her immersion in the familiar details ended abruptly with the sound of a yawn.

"I'm so sorry I've bored you." She didn't care if he did object to her using *sorry* when she clearly didn't mean it.

"It was more your topic than you."

Irked at him as she was, she couldn't deny a sliver of amusement. Talk about damning with faint praise.

"History shouldn't bore you. The study of the past can be fascinating—with the right teacher."

"No matter the teacher, there's nothing going to budge the past an inch one way or the other. Nothing you can do to make it worse or better or different."

Were they still talking about the academic study of history, or had he shifted the topic? Or was she reading too much into it?

"Without knowing history," she protested, "you make the same mistakes over and over again."

"Not if you're smart."

Grim and terse, the words flashed a huge Stay Out sign.

Her mouth opened to push right past that sign before her mind caught up. It was exactly the sort of impulse she'd fought all her life. The sort that made her foolishly wade into the mess and swirl of emotions.

She opened her leather notebook. There was no further conversation until they reached town.

"Oh, Luke, would you mind dropping me at the Far Hills Market while you get Emily? I would have picked up something to bring to Marti earlier, but…"

But she'd thought she wouldn't be going to this lunch, until Marti outmaneuvered her on the phone last night.

"There'll be plenty to eat."

"That's not the point."

"Always thought the point of lunch was to eat."

"Bringing something is simply a polite gesture."

"Marti doesn't set much store in gestures." Clearly neither did he.

"However *you* might feel about such things, a hostess thinks better of a guest who brings a token of appreciation for the invitation."

"You're going to the wrong places if you're only welcome because you bring something."

"Just because you don't give a...a *darn* what people think of you," she said, slewing around in the seat to glare at him, "doesn't mean the rest of us have to forget our manners."

"Okay." He'd stopped the truck, and now he shifted toward her, his arm along the back of the seat; his hand could have grasped her shoulder if he'd wanted to.

"Okay?"

"Okay, go get your *token*—not that the Market's got a big stock of tokens—and I'll come by after I've picked up Emily."

Giving in to her temper was not the thing to do. Especially since they'd stopped by the post office, almost directly across the street from the Market. Both the post office and Market had a steady stream of customers, many of whom nodded at Luke.

As a fallback position, she adopted chilly dignity. "Very well. Thank you."

"Welcome."

She gave him a quick look as she closed the truck door, and wished she hadn't. He was laughing. At her. Again.

With tension lengthening her back and tightening her shoulders, she crossed the wide street—aware of him watching every step—and was nearly at the Market when a voice brought her up short.

"Oh, Rebecca! How delightful to run into you," gushed her landlady, Helen Solsong. "I have so wanted to introduce you to my dear, dear friend Barb Sandy. Barb, this is dear Rebecca Dahlgren. Of the Delaware Dahlgrens.''

Rebecca nearly groaned. "How do you do, Ms. Sandy."

"Oh, please, do call me Barb."

Her smile twisted at the sound of a powerful truck engine being given more gas than necessary. Rebecca refused to look, but the other women's heads spun around fast, and they growled disapproval.

"That *man*." Helen's tone shifted from acid to sugar in a breath. "Rebecca, dear, I've been meaning—"

"Excuse me." A weathered woman with two preschool kids trailing her was unable to push her loaded shopping cart clear of the doorway because Helen and Barb Sandy blocked her way.

Rebecca automatically stepped back. The two older women hesitated, then followed. As the shopper pushed the cart down the slight ramp, then struggled to turn it to the right, Barb said, "I'm surprised she has any money to spend on food with all the cash that Herb of hers spends at the Ranchers' Rest."

Helen nodded sagely. "You wouldn't think she'd have so many children with him spending all that time there, and I hear she's expecting again."

Neither had made any effort to lower her voice, and Rebecca saw red creeping up the woman's neck as she began loading groceries into the back of a dirt- and rust-streaked pickup. Rebecca looked away, an old queasiness kicking up.

Grandmother, why do the ladies at the pool whisper about me?

She'd come back from a swimming lesson at the country club. She was six, and for the first time, an uneasiness she'd never given voice to had crystallized. Those looks, those whispers among the mothers of the other children truly *were* directed at her.

Her grandmother had looked at her over the top of her

half-glasses without putting down three engraved invitations she held.

Don't be hysterical, Rebecca.

I'm not. I'm… She blinked her eyes to a furious dryness. *Is it because…because I don't have a father?*

It's because your mother is a fool. And you are her daughter. They'll whisper about that forever. It's all the more reason you must never—never—give them cause to whisper more. You have a responsibility to the Dahlgren name to see that you add no more disgrace.

Only much later did she understand the significance of having no father—that she was a permanent badge of her mother's foolishness.

"The seventh!"

Barb's disapproving voice snapped Rebecca back to the present.

"It's been a pleasure to meet you, Barb," she started in the polite formula, "but I really must—"

"Oh, no, you can't go," objected Helen, wrapping both hands around Rebecca's arm. "I hardly get to see you."

"Work keeps me busy." She smiled stiffly.

"I would hope you wouldn't be working so much that you would be prevented from spending time with congenial company."

She couldn't conceive of company much less congenial than these two women. But she couldn't let them guess that.

Why not? It was another voice. One that sounded suspiciously like Luke Chandler's.

Because they would think I was rude.

You're worried what they'd *think?*

"I worry about you working so much," Helen was saying. "And now I hear you're taking on a job for the Suslands at Far Hills Ranch."

"I hope to, yes. I enjoy my work tremendously," she said brightly. "And I'm learning a great deal about ranching."

Barb satisfied herself with a disparaging sniff. Helen said, "You might learn more than your upbringing has prepared you for out at that ranch, Rebecca."

"Marti Susland has been wonderful," she heard herself saying. Whatever the letter-writer had felt or experienced from the Suslands, Marti had been absolutely pleasant and helpful.

Helen pursed her mouth. "Looks can be deceiving."

"True. So true," concurred Barb.

"What I say is that's a strange group at Far Hills Ranch. Live and let live's all very well for some who don't care what kind they associate with—I've got higher standards."

"I'm sure you do, but I really should be going—"

"And I consider it my duty to warn a young woman like you—someone from a *good* family—"

"I'm sure there's no cause to warn me—"

"You know Kendra had that son of hers a good two years before she got around to marrying the father? Came back here pregnant, not married, and expected everyone to bow down to her just because her mother had been a Susland and she'd been on TV. Not an anchor, even, just a reporter." Helen's tone indicated that that might have been the worst sin of all.

"And this husband of hers—this Daniel Delligatti—I don't care what they say about what a great pilot he is and what he's doing with that search and rescue—I say he's not really an American, and no one can tell me different."

"Ellyn," took up Barb, not to be outdone, "who used to be such a nice girl, always so smartly dressed by her mother, started living out there after she came back, and became, well, I hate to say it—" the relish in her tone belied her words "—*hard*. Even Colonel Griffin ended up being a disappointment, falling back in with that group and marrying Ellyn, who'd already been married once and had two children."

Rebecca felt as if her head were spinning one way and her stomach another. They faulted Kendra and Daniel for marrying after they had a child, and now they were faulting this colonel from marrying someone named Ellyn because she'd been married before?

"And Luke Chandler…at least Daniel Delligatti has manners, even if he is a foreigner. You'd think someone who'd spent his early years here in Far Hills would know to answer a few civil questions about his family, and what his plans are. Why, all I asked was when he was going to settle down, and he said *When hell freezes over* and walked away."

"So rude," murmured Barb.

"And the women he's taken up with!" With dizzying details of who was related to whom and what their family scandals were, Rebecca heard a full accounting of Luke's romantic relationships since he'd returned to Far Hills. She tried to excuse herself twice. Both times Helen simply tightened her hold.

"And I just say," continued Helen, "it's awfully funny how much time he spends with Marti Susland. Course she's worth a good bit of money. Besides, it's always been said Luke Chandler loved that ranch better than any human being."

Rebecca didn't think her situation could get any more uncomfortable…until the green truck rolled past, now with the top of Emily's head visible in the child's seat in back.

"Speak of the devil," Helen said, glaring toward the truck.

"And there's another one…that Emily. Treats her like a princess, Marti does, but if you ask me, Matthew Delligatti isn't the only child on that ranch who's not legitimate."

Over a renewed queasiness, Rebecca protested, "She was an orphan. From that hurricane on Santa Estalla."

In the middle of the next block, the green truck made a

lazy U-turn amid light traffic, and headed back, now on the near side of the street.

"That's what they *say*." Helen put her hands on her hips. "You've got to wonder why they would have let a single woman over forty adopt a child if everything was…proper."

Rebecca edged away. Not even the habits of a lifetime could make her smile. "I really need to run now. Good day."

She ducked into the Market, heading down an aisle unseeingly. At the back of the store, she drew in air, then exhaled long and slow. She looked around for an appropriate token to take to Marti. In all Antonia's lectures on such matters, she'd never covered the niceties of going to lunch at a working cattle ranch where you thought your hostess might have been a long-ago enemy of the man you suspected was your father.

Rebecca settled on macadamia nuts in an interesting jar and a bunch of carnations from a bucket by the registers.

Back outside, she blinked against the brightness, looking left, then right, before spotting the green truck practically straight ahead.

As she climbed in, she smiled at the dark-haired preschooler in the child's seat in the back of the four-door pickup.

"Hi. You must be Emily. I'm Rebecca."

She received a shy smile in return. "Mama said you're coming to lunch."

"Yes, I am. Your mother invited me."

Rebecca was pulling her seat belt across her body when Luke spoke. "If you're looking for your friends, they left."

"They're not my friends," she said sharply. "I was looking for the truck when I came out of the store."

"Could have fooled me. Three of you looked downright cozy."

"I was simply being polite. Helen is my landlady and it's reasonable to want to remain on good terms with her."

"If you say so," he said evenly. "What I wonder about is if that dash into the Market was meant to keep me from seeing you with them, or to keep them from knowing you were with me?"

"Don't be ridiculous." Cold and precise, her words were meant to end the conversation. She asked over her shoulder, "Emily, did you have fun at day care?"

"Babysitting co-op," Luke corrected.

Rebecca gritted her teeth, but gave the child another smile as she amended, "At the baby-sitting co-op?"

She'd *needed* the macadamia nuts, she told herself while listening to Emily's happy account of her morning. It was the reason she'd asked Luke to drop her off.

Or was Luke right? Was part of the reason she'd ducked away so that Helen and Barb wouldn't know he was picking her up? So she wouldn't be tarred by the same brushes they wielded with such abandon?

She had reason not to trust the people at Far Hills Ranch with her real reasons for being here. Still, she felt suddenly smaller.

Chapter Six

"Those clothes will work fine."

Marti had come out the kitchen door to greet them when the truck pulled up between a new four-wheel-drive and a bright blue pickup. Marti freed Emily from her seat, and the girl dashed into the house. Then Marti gave Rebecca a quick survey and made her pronouncement.

"Uh, good," Rebecca said, feeling rather lost. She glanced down at her cotton shirt, cabled sweater, sturdy khaki slacks, and heavy-duty black boots. "I needed to be able to walk around the grounds."

Marti patted her arm absently. "I'm sure you had a good time."

"Fine for what, Marti?" Luke demanded.

"To ride out after lunch. We're going to help you move that herd to the North Uplands this afternoon."

"Marti—"

"With all of us, we can move them without pulling the

rest of the boys off their other work. And Rebecca'll want to join us, won't you? To see more of how the ranch works? Of course, you will. C'mon in now and meet everyone and get something to eat."

With that, Marti headed in.

"Guess you're going to get your wish to ride, Ms. Dahlgren." Luke said. He made it sound like this was all her doing. "If I can find you a proper *mount* after lunch."

The word *generous* hardly did justice to the spread Marti had on an oval table set by a large kitchen window that looked out over Far Hills land. The macadamia nuts, placed in a glass dish, looked like a single apple in an orchard. Wheat, white and rye bread, two kinds of rolls, thick roast beef, sliced meatloaf, chicken by the piece or the slice, tomatoes, lettuce, mustard, mayo, butter, homemade pickles, potato salad, bean casserole, fruit salad, chips and dessert...oh, dessert.

"I've never had chocolate cake like this before," she said.

"Secret ingredient's coffee," said Kendra Jenner Delligatti. "If you can get Marti to give you the recipe, you'll know you've arrived."

Kendra was one of the reasons the lunch had been chaotic. One of many reasons, as the various branches of the family had gathered at the main house from their homes elsewhere on Far Hills Ranch.

By the time they'd had that conversation about dessert, Rebecca thought she had the outlines of the relationships clear. Kendra and Grif were cousins, and Marti's niece and nephew. Grif was the only son of Marti's oldest sister, who had died when Grif was a boy. Kendra was the only daughter of the middle sister, who had died a few years ago.

Grif, now a colonel in the army and the commander at nearby Fort Piney, had recently married Ellyn, a widow with two children, Meg and Ben.

Fran Sinclair, as well as being Marti's friend, was Ellyn's step-mother-in-law from her first marriage, and clearly a great favorite of everyone.

Kendra wrote part-time for the local newspaper and was married to Daniel Delligatti, a pilot who ran the region's search and rescue operation. Their four-year-old son, Matthew, was going to have a sibling around New Year's.

Kendra, Grif, Ellyn and Luke had spent childhood summers together on the ranch, along with a couple of other youngsters.

That was as far as Rebecca had gotten. Except to see that the easy camaraderie and teasing seemed built on a bedrock of respect and affection. Maybe that only came when you'd known someone since childhood.

"The number of occupations you all have is fascinating," Rebecca said. She was seated beside Ellyn, with Luke straddling a chair next to Kendra, whose husband sat next to her. Grif was on the phone with his office in the other room, the two younger kids were playing and the two older kids were assisting Marti and Fran in putting away the voluminous leftovers—she'd refused other offers of help, but Ben and Meg had begged to do it in order to cut the time before they could start riding.

"A lot of people away from ranching country don't realize how many ranchers have other jobs—not always by choice," Kendra said. "Farmers, too. I didn't realize it myself, until I started working for the *Far Hills Banner.*"

"She's got a big paper back East interested in an essay on the subject," said her husband.

"Daniel," she scolded mildly, "we said we weren't going to say anything unless it was certain."

"Aw, this is family. Besides, it'll happen. They'd be fools not to buy that piece."

"Plenty of fools back East," said Luke.

"Luke," protested Ellyn and Kendra simultaneously.

"Of course," Rebecca said brightly. "There are fools everywhere. Just as there are one-dimensional people everywhere."

"You mean Luke?" Daniel asked, with pure deviltry in his eyes.

Now the rebuke was, "Daniel!"

Rebecca felt her cheeks heat at having her dig brought out in the open. What on earth would they think of her? Trading barbs with Luke Chandler in private was bad enough.

"I'm sorry, I shouldn't have—"

Luke was talking at the same time, and his deeper tones covered her words like a bass drum over a violin. "That's me. Ranching's what I know, and it's what I do."

She made another effort to make amends. "Many people are never lucky enough to know what they want to do, much less do it."

He tipped his head and raised one brow, which she translated as a "suppose so."

"This one?" Fran scoffed, tapping Luke on the shoulder. "This one was meant to square off with Mother Nature from the get-go. And stubborn? He could have been so sick he was dying and he wouldn't have admitted it."

"Dyin' would've been better than that stuff you made us take."

Groans and grimaces from the other Far Hills Ranch summer veterans confirmed Luke's opinion.

"Tell us the truth, Fran," said Kendra. "Was it really horse liniment? That's what we all thought."

"Oh, you bunch of babies," Fran said as she headed off.

"Don't let him fool you, Rebecca," said Ellyn. "Luke's a man of unsuspected depths. Take his recognizing that Daniel was playing Chopin, for instance."

Luke glared at Ellyn, clearly letting her know he didn't appreciate her revelation.

"Sometimes having people around who've known you since you were a kid is a pain in the butt," he muttered.

"Language, Luke," came the mild scold from Marti as she passed by.

"Wait a minute," Rebecca objected, "you said you didn't know classical music."

"Can't say I know it. More a passing acquaintance." He shrugged.

Kendra hooted. "Typical Luke. He always was the most close-mouthed individual you'd ever hope to meet," she said to Rebecca.

"Man's gotta have some secrets."

"I think you've got several other men's share of secrets, Luke," Kendra retorted.

"Why would you make a secret of knowing classical mus—ouch!" Rebecca's turn toward Luke had been brought up short by a painful and unexplained tug at her scalp.

"Oh, Emily, honey, what are you doing?" Ellyn asked. "You know you don't pull hair."

Rebecca pivoted in the opposite direction, and discovered Emily Susland standing behind her, holding a length of Rebecca's hair that had swung over the chair back. Beside her was Matthew Delligatti.

"Not pulling," Emily said.

"Good point," Luke contributed. "Rebecca's the one who moved."

Ellyn shot him a stern-mother look that appeared to have no effect. "But it hurts Rebecca," she explained to Emily.

Without releasing the hair, Emily said to Rebecca. "Sorry." Then she held up her fist as if she'd captured a prize and pointed at Matthew. "See. Just like mine."

"Let go of Rebecca's hair, Emily," instructed Marti calmly as she came up behind her daughter.

Emily complied as she presented her grievance to her

mother. "Matthew said I didn't have hair like anybody else."

"Mine hair like Daddy's," Matthew said, beaming around at the adults as he parroted something he'd clearly heard.

And with that innocent comment of the little boy, proud of his thick, dark curls because they were so like those of the father he'd come to know recently, Rebecca understood so much. Too much. She understood his joy at the connection, at finding at least the beginnings of an answer to *where did I come from?* She understood his pointing it out to other children. And she most deeply understood how Emily felt the need for her own connections.

Even simply another female with straight, dark hair.

Marti scooched beside her daughter, her brown and gray waves in marked contrast to Emily's smooth fall of hair. "Our hair doesn't look much alike, does it? Yours is so beautiful."

"This," said Daniel with a smile that drew responding smiles from the other adults, "is beginning to sound like a shampoo commercial. C'mon, Matthew." He hoisted his son on his hip. "Let's go round up some dogies."

Luke swung out of his chair. "How many times I gotta tell you, Delligatti? Cattle, head, cows, critters—not dogies."

The awkward moment was passed amid chuckles and the bustle of getting a group all headed in the same direction.

But Rebecca found herself wondering a short time later as she led her assigned horse to the trailer, what Marti was saying to Emily, as they sat on the steps by the kitchen door, the little girl's hand resting so trustingly in the woman's. And she felt an inexplicable stab of longing.

Helen Solsong was right about one thing. Nothing in Rebecca's upbringing had prepared her for an afternoon like this.

They rode in pickups because, Marti told her, that was the fastest way to get riders and horses to where they needed them. They loaded the horses into a large trailer and the humans into the trucks, and headed out in a surprisingly short time.

She was relieved to be assigned a seat beside Ellyn Griffin in the pickup driven by her husband, with the two kids riding in the back of the slow-moving vehicle. She'd had enough of being in pickups with Luke. Ellyn passed the time by telling stories about childhood summers at Far Hills Ranch, with occasional additions from Grif. After thirty minutes of driving, Rebecca had to ask, "Are we still on Far Hills land?"

"Oh, yes." said Ellyn. "The section where the main ranch and our houses are is just the original home ranch. Whenever land became available, the Suslands bought up whatever they could. The only area where the Suslands always had luck was business."

"Are you talking about the curse?"

Ellyn glanced toward her husband. "Legend might be more accurate. But, yes, that's what I mean."

"Did bad things really happen to the Suslands?"

"Get Marti to show you the genealogy chart. It's amazing—a little eerie, even—the number of unnatural deaths. Although Marti seems to think there's been a sort of corner turned when it comes to the legend," Ellyn said. "But you should talk to her about that. She's the expert on the family."

"Here we are." Grif pulled up behind the trailer.

Luke, already astride a black-maned buckskin, was assigning positions as the rest of them mounted up. Fran and Kendra, with Emily and Matthew, would drive a pickup to meet them at the gates to these North Uplands where the cattle would spend their next couple of weeks.

Rebecca swung her right leg wide to be sure she cleared the unfamiliarly bulky saddle and came to rest in its deep sway more emphatically than she would have liked, only to look up into Luke's assessing gaze.

All he said was, "You and Daniel head to where the south and east legs of the fence join then turn around and move the critters ahead of you. Slow and steady. Don't run any pounds off them."

That, Rebecca found, was sometimes easier said than done.

Many of the cows, with their calves alongside, moved placidly ahead of the horses, especially when those horses' riders hollered, waved their hats and swung their ropes now and then. She picked up those tricks by watching Daniel, a hundred yards or so to her left, and at a much greater distance, Ben on her right. She caught glimpses of the others farther ahead.

But as they moved over a hill into a wide valley, then up a higher hill, a few cows pivoted and lunged and whirled away like lumbering, four-footed basketball players trying to get around a defender. Her horse responded like a star defender without any coaching from her. In most of the catch-and-retrieve maneuvers, she was simply along for the ride, doing her best not to hinder Chester.

"Hey, why'd they put you on the drags?" Daniel asked once when they were within hailing distance. Rebecca had heard the others teasing him about being a much better pilot than a horseman. That had to be true—or he'd have crashed any plane he took up. "You're good."

She laughed. "Chester's good. I'm just hanging on."

"You sure look a lot better doing it than I do," he said ruefully. "If this thing had a rudder. I'd know what to do."

A white-faced cow broke from the pack on Rebecca's right, heading back toward a creek that ran roughly parallel with their path, and Chester dashed after. They circled around and Rebecca used the end of the rope to flick at the cow to urge it toward the herd.

Rebecca came to know that white-faced cow well over the next hour. It seemed every time she turned around it had made another dash for the creek. She had shepherded it back to the fold again—a growing herd of cattle as the others brought cows in from the sides—when she noticed Luke watching from the far side of the creek. She hadn't hindered her horse in getting White-Face back into line. At least he'd have to give her that.

He was moving toward her when White-Face made yet another break. Chester spun to give chase. Luke shouted, "Hold your horse!"

She automatically obeyed, fighting both Chester's instinct and her own.

Luke and his horse angled slowly toward the creek. White-Face kept a watch on him but didn't shy away. Instead she made a direct line for a spot about a quarter-mile back down the creek. Mirroring Luke's moves, Rebecca brought her horse in an easy loop farther back on the creek. . White-Face let out one low bellow, then a second. A higher, thinner sound answered. In another second, a calf broke out of the brush on Rebecca's side of the creek and ran with that funny rocking motion of cows toward White-Face. She nosed the calf once, then immediately began grazing.

In that second, Luke started his horse across the creek with noisy splashes, calling out and waving his free arm.

White-Face jolted away, found her old nemesis—Chester and Rebecca—there and took the only direction free of annoyances, toward the main herd. Her calf followed along.

Mud sprays decorated Luke's chaps and his horse's hindquarters, as they trotted parallel to Rebecca and Chester, all of them trailing after White-Face.

"You'd never have won that battle. She was trying to mother up with her calf."

Rebecca asked the question that had been on her mind the longest. "What are drags?"

He angled a look at her, and maybe he suppressed a grin. "Back of a herd, slow-goers."

"And who herds the drags?"

The grin won out. "Greenhorns."

"Tell this greenhorn one more thing, how did you know White-Face was looking for her calf?"

He shrugged. "She was going someplace particular. Her calf had probably been trailing for a while. Mama's instinct's strong. She's not going to leave her calf behind."

He wheeled his horse and headed off. And she could only be grateful. He might have believed the well of tears in her eyes was from the sting of dust. She knew better.

Mama's instinct's strong. She's not going to leave her calf behind.

Rebecca's mother's instinct hadn't been strong enough to offset her weakness. And her father had never wanted her at all.

Rebecca scrubbed her sleeve against her eyes. What was she doing crying?—being jealous of a cow, for heaven's sake. The absurdity almost made her laugh. Chester twitched a shoulder as if he'd sensed her mood. She patted him.

"C'mon, Chester. Let's go herd some cows."

The pace slowed as the swollen herd fed uphill through an open double-wide gate. Rebecca didn't realize that was what was causing the slowdown until she and Daniel, now with Ben and Ellyn close enough to call back and forth as they drew the herd closer and closer, crested another of the higher-reaching hills.

The pickup Fran and Kendra had been driving with Emily

and Matthew was parked there with all four in the back, watching the proceedings.

The cows, like passengers getting on a subway train, became restless with the delay. Some tried to push ahead. Others peeled away like they had run out of all patience. That's when riders and horses went into action.

"Don't crowd 'em," Luke called out to Ben at one point. "You just get 'em mad. And then you can't do anything with 'em."

They all did some retrieval missions, but without a word being said, the most difficult ones were left to Marti, Ellyn and Grif. The ones that seemed hopeless went to Luke.

Rebecca watched as he took on a particularly recalcitrant cow that had reached the gate, then refused to go through, clogging the opening. The cow feinted. Luke and his horse cut off its path. The cow tried another way. Cut off again. A third way. Another roadblock courtesy of Luke Chandler.

An unexpected chord of familiarity sounded in Rebecca.

The action-reaction dance. The man not overtly trying to force the cow in the direction he wanted, yet methodically, relentlessly cutting off every avenue of escape. Until there was only one. The one the man had wanted the cow to take all along, through that gate. The cow might think it had finally found a route to freedom, away from the interference of man and horse, but it had been outmaneuvered. Herded.

She knew just how the cow felt as it rambled off to distant hills, and the other riders congratulated Luke on a job well done.

Because that's what Luke had been doing to her.

Perhaps on a slightly more sophisticated level—but not much.

He had ignored her, delayed her, distracted her, misled her, goaded her—anything to postpone or prevent her from pulling together the contract proposal which she needed in order to have access to the records that might—*had* to lead her to her father.

And she'd let this ranch foreman, this *cowboy,* manipulate her into wasting so much time that at this rate, the contract with Fort Big Horn would be over before she got one look at the Far Hills records.

"You want to quit?" Her tormentor's voice came unexpectedly from beside her.

"Quit! No way."

"You're going to be sore." A dip of his hat brim indicated her position on the saddle. "Your, uh, legs."

Heat bloomed in the part of her body he'd referred to obliquely, while a deeper heat seemed to feel the imprint of his hand there once more. Her muscles screamed out for her to shift in the saddle—to relieve the tension or drive it deeper?

Damn the man!

He was trying to maneuver her—once again—the way he had that cow. Distracting her, goading her until she lost sight of her direction and took whichever one he left open.

She raised her chin, narrowed her eyes and spoke with cool disdain.

"I have been riding since I was five years old. I have never had sore legs. Not once. Ever."

She reined Chester away, then stopped, twisting in the saddle to look back at him.

"And I don't quit, Luke Chandler, so you might as well get that into your head."

Not waiting for an answer, she urged her horse to a fast trot and came up to Marti.

"Marti, may I talk to you?"

"Sure. Why don't you drive back with me to the home ranch?"

"That would be perfect. I think it's time I tell you what I have outlined for Far Hills Ranch."

* * *

Luke had known Rebecca and Marti together would be trouble. Knew it even before they got into the same pickup. He didn't need the triumphant look Rebecca shot him as they unloaded at the home ranch to tell him so.

Hell, it was exactly why he'd been stonewalling her.

He might not know every twist and turn of the path Marti had in mind, but he saw the general direction. And this computer project had something to do with Marti's plans to tie him to Far Hills Ranch with a share of ownership. Or *was* it the computer project?

He yanked the saddle off Apollo less smoothly than usual, and the buckskin gave him a what-got-into-you? look.

Luke added an extra handful of oats to his ration, then gave him a quick rub.

''All set?'' he called out to Ben and Meg, who'd helped him finish with the horses. They turned the horses into a big back corral that stretched northeast. Then the three of them headed for the main house, the two kids chattering about their horsemanship.

If Marti had something brewing that had to do with Rebecca directly, it could only be that bee she had in her bonnet about Leaping Star's legend and the Susland Curse. But he was damned if he could see what it was.

''Whose car is that?''

Luke followed Meg's pointing finger. A dark blue, middle-of-the-line sedan had joined the pickups and four-wheel-drives parked by the main house.

The kitchen door swung open in front of them, and Matthew, one hand still stretched up to the doorknob, beamed at them

''Ben! Meg! Unca Robert here. My Unca Robert.''

They stepped into the kitchen to find a mild-looking man with thinning dark hair and thick dark-framed glasses. He'd removed his suit jacket, leaving a vest, crisp white shirt, dark tie and suit pants.

Robert Delligatti, Junior, had been in college when his diplomat parents had adopted Daniel as a child in South America. That much Luke had gathered. He'd also gathered the adopted brothers hadn't been particularly close. There must have been a breakthrough, though, because Robert had been showing up more often.

Having just introduced Rebecca, Marti was saying, "…and you remember Luke, who runs Far Hills, don't you, Robert?"

"Foreman," Luke corrected, shaking the other man's hand. "Good to see you, Robert."

"It's a pleasure to see you again, Luke."

"Robert had an unexpected opportunity to stop over here on the way from Washington to San Francisco," Marti said.

No airline Luke had ever heard of made stopovers in Wyoming between Washington and San Francisco. He looked from Marti's pink cheeks and sparkling eyes to the raised eyebrows, speculative looks and grins from the other Far Hills adults.

"That was lucky," Luke said.

Robert met his gaze, a hint of amusement deep in his dark eyes. "So often a man has to make his own luck, don't you find?"

Maybe Marti wasn't such an unattached Susland after all. Robert Delligatti, Junior, better treat her right, or he'd find out the boys in Washington weren't the toughest he'd met.

"A man who makes his own luck should know to appreciate it."

"Indeed." Robert concurred.

"Now, c'mon, everybody, I've got so many leftovers from lunch you're all going to stay to supper," Marti said hurriedly.

While the others murmured agreement, Rebecca objected, "Thank you, Marti, but really, I should go—"

"Nonsense. You can't leave me here with all this food. And I can't let you go hungry after putting you to work all afternoon."

Marti turned away as if that was all settled, and Luke grinned at Rebecca's expression. It was nice to see somebody else steamrolled by Marti's good intentions.

"Let's eat outside. It's going to be a beautiful sunset. Luke and Grif, make sure the table's sitting solid. Ellyn and Kendra, you get plates. Fran and I'll start unloading the fridge...."

They made a bigger dent in the provisions this time. The mood was decidedly mellow as the sun slid behind the Big Horn Mountains, burnishing the clouds to streamers of gold. With seats on the benches limited, Luke had perched on the fence next to the table. Ellyn sat nearest to him, with Rebecca the next one in.

"After everything I had at lunch, I thought I'd never eat again," Rebecca was telling Ellyn as they each swung their legs over the bench to face the glowing sunset. "But when we sat down, I was starving. I've eaten as much as I did at lunch—maybe more."

Her tone sounded divided between horror and awe. Ellyn laughed. "All that work you did and all that fresh air you swallowed this afternoon builds up an appetite."

"How about all the dust I swallowed?"

The two women laughed. Ellyn got up, and Luke found himself looking directly into Rebecca's eyes, still glowing with amusement.

She wanted to look away. He saw that. He also saw that she wasn't going to.

"You did a good job this afternoon."

Her mouth formed a soft O with no sound. The gold from the sunset intensified the honey tone of her skin, made her eyes gleam like a precious gem, added glints to the rich darkness of her hair.

"Thank you."

The kitchen screen door slapped closed, and he welcomed the excuse to look away.

Marti and Robert had just come out together. Marti held papers, and wore a big smile. Robert remained a step behind her, while she came to the end of the table.

"Listen up, everybody," Marti said to the adults. The four kids were busy at the swingset in the fenced-in play yard. "I have some wonderful news."

Luke stared at the papers as if he might be able to read them from this distance.

"Robert's been helping me—" she turned and beamed at him "—and he's brought me the okay, so I can tell you all." She drew in a deep breath. "I've been hoping to adopt another child almost since Emily came into my life. And now I'm going to have that opportunity—a baby girl from China."

Sounds of surprise rose from around the table.

"China's made it harder for foreigners to adopt, so Robert's help has been invaluable. Now I've got the okay, and it's really going to happen. I'll be going to China soon, and I'll come home with a sister for Emily. Don't say anything to her yet. I haven't wanted to tell her until I was sure, but tonight I will."

A tide of congratulations and exclamations rose. He wasn't as surprised as the rest, since Marti had told him a while back that she had the lawyer working on it.

"Wait, wait, there's one more piece of good news. Far Hills Ranch is coming into the computer age, and Rebecca is going to pull off that miracle. She's outlined a proposal for me, and I've accepted it. So starting right now she's officially part of the Far Hills crew. And I know—" Luke caught the warning look Marti shot at him "—everyone will cooperate. Completely."

Daniel, sitting on Rebecca's other side, told her that was great news, adding that maybe once she finished, he'd talk to her about a set-up for the search and rescue program. Then he joined the group around Marti, offering hugs and encouragement.

As if Rebecca felt Luke's eyes on her, she turned to him, her gaze questioning and defiant.

"I suppose congratulations are in order."

"Yes, they are." She used that cool tone.

"It wasn't you, Rebecca," he surprised himself by saying.

His gaze slid to where Marti was hugging Ellyn, happy as could be, thinking she had everybody lined up. He saw Rebecca had followed the direction of his gaze. He had the uncomfortable feeling she had followed his thoughts, too. He turned toward the waning light.

"Guess a computer can't hurt," he offered before he went to offer Marti congratulations on the adoption.

Chapter Seven

Luke drove her home.

It only made sense, since Fran was staying overnight at Far Hills, and everyone else had kids to put to bed. It should have been awkward. It wasn't.

She was tired, sated, mellow. Her muscles ached, while her spirit hummed with accomplishment and peace.

For no reason she could think of, a fragment of her conversation while driving back to the home ranch with Marti surfaced. She'd been presenting her proposal—off the cuff and informally, marveling that she rather enjoyed it. Determined to be open and fair, she'd also presented the downside.

"Without the full cooperation and acceptance of the primary user, in this case the foreman, the system won't be anywhere near as effective for you as it should be—"

"Oh, Luke will accept it. And he'll use it."

She'd tried again. *"Marti, he's made it clear he doesn't care to have me—"*

"Now, that's where you're wrong. Luke does care." Marti had slanted her a look of mischief that had called up Rebecca's final words *to have me,* and made Marti's answer that Luke did care to *have* Rebecca Dahlgren.

No, no that was her own misguided response entering into it, Rebecca decided as she reviewed the conversation now. Marti couldn't have meant that. Although her next words were ambiguous enough.

"With some folks, it takes reading the signs to know they care and who they care about. Some people leave nice clear road-signs, like an interstate. Other folks, you have to learn to read signs like the Indians taught the trappers to do."

Before Rebecca could respond. Marti patted her arm, adding, *"Don't fret. It'll all work out fine. Luke's a good man."*

The truck swayed into a turn, and Rebecca blinked back to the present to realize they'd driven into Helen's driveway.

Luke pulled behind her car, near the steps leading to her apartment. She gathered energy to perform the monumental task of opening the door.

He turned off the headlights and switched off the ignition. With his hand still on the key, he glanced at her. Reflected light from somewhere cast harsh shadows under the bones of his face, but didn't mask his eyes. Or maybe she'd become better at reading him.

Her heartbeat jumped from an unnoticed background rhythm to something hard and fast and commanding.

He released the key and turned away from her to get out. With his face no longer visible, he paused, then tossed his hat inside and closed the door.

Opening her door, she pivoted in the seat and put her legs out first, the movement so familiar she didn't even look. What wasn't familiar was the height of her seat from the ground.

She started to stumble. Luke thrust out his hip and arm to brace her. She grabbed onto him with both hands and held on as three quick almost dance-like movements brought them safely to rest with her back against the frame of the door, one hand clutching his left arm and the other his right shoulder, while his hands held her securely at the waist.

"Guess there's a first time for everything, isn't there, Rebecca?"

"What?" His words barely registered. The rhythm of her heartbeat should have been shaking the ground.

"You've got sore legs. After—" one side of his mouth lifted in a slight grin, drawing her focus "—riding."

She lost all interest in explaining about pickup seats being high or her legs not being sore. Besides, right at the moment, she did feel noodle-legged.

He was going to kiss her.

He lowered his head, his mouth inches away.

"Scared?"

"No." She said it too quickly. Not even she believed it.

She couldn't stand to see his recognition of her lie, so she looked away. And caught a motion from the corner of her eye.

Something moved beyond his right shoulder.

There it was again—a twitch of the light-colored drapes in Helen's otherwise dark dining room.

Luke twisted around to follow her gaze over his shoulder. He held that pose an instant before turning to her.

"Worried what Helen Solsong will think of you."

It held no rise of a question as *Scared?* had. He wasn't asking; he was stating. But it carried a miasma of other elements. Fatalism, amusement, disappointment, regret, they blended together like the dust behind the herd this afternoon—each bit kicked up by an individual animal, but the whole blended so tightly no one cause could be separated from another.

"I'm a stranger here," she said, stepping back. "And the good opinion of people is vital to my ability to do my job."

"Your job?" It stopped just short of mockery. His hands dropped from her waist. "Get in the habit of makin' choices to be accepted, and when it comes time to do something that won't get you accepted, you won't have the muscles to pull it off."

"So your answer is to go off on your solitary way?"

"Yup."

"What if you need people's help?"

He shrugged. "Swap help for help, service for service. Straight up. No good opinion involved."

"What if people have nothing to swap? If they need you?"

"They shouldn't. Nobody should rely on me." Before she could do more than note the sharpness in that, he was going on. "What you need, Ms. Dahlgren, is to start telling people to take a flying leap."

"You enjoy thumbing your nose at the world, Luke, but I'm in no position to do that."

"Why?"

"Because I'm—because I—" She stood straight, her chin level, her mouth firm. "I have a responsibility to reflect well on the family name."

"Family name."

There was enough venom in that for her to stare at him. Other than tension in his shoulders, she saw no change.

"It's a very old and respected name. The family name is important to my grandmother, whose mother was also a Dahlgren. My mother…my mother made mistakes, and that was very hard on Grandmother. Respecting the family name is the least I can do to repay her."

"Sounds like you should tell Grandma to take a flying leap, too."

"I would never do that. My grandmother is all I have."

*   *   *

Still aching from wanting and not having, Luke braked to a stop with the truck's headlights glaring at the figure of Marti Susland sitting on his front steps.

"Shouldn't you be keeping an eye on Emily?"

Her only reaction to his irritable greeting was to hold up the powerful baby monitor she used. "I'm keeping an ear on her. But I want to talk to you. If you'd been more available, I'd have talked out this computer thing with you before giving Rebecca the okay. If you've got real reservations—serious, logical reservations—then this is the time to spit them out."

"What I've got reservations about is—" Luke swallowed the words, burying them down where so many of his words were kept. "What are you up to, Marti?"

"I don't know what you mean. A computer should be—"

"Hell, yes, but this isn't about a computer." She didn't say anything, and that was a kind of answer. "Dammit, Marti, I know you. You think I don't know you had a hand in getting Grif back here after all those years? You think I haven't figured that you pulled a few strings in getting Daniel settled here?"

"And look how those have turned out—They've answered two parts of the curse. *You turn away from your children, so your blood will be alone. You turn away from my people, so your blood will have no home,*" she quoted. "There's only one part left. *You turn away from me, so your blood will be lost. Only when someone loves enough to undo your wrongs will the laughter of children live beyond its echo in Far Hills.*"

He'd been afraid of this. "Marti, it's a story you told us as kids. That's all. It doesn't—"

She was shaking her head. "Daniel came for his child, changed his life for his child and Kendra. Grif refused to turn his back on Ellyn, the kids, or the people of Far Hills, staying here to turn the closing of Fort Piney into something good. There's one part left. *Only when someone loves enough to undo your wrongs will the laughter of children live beyond its echo in Far Hills.*''

Her eyes dropped to the baby monitor.

''One part left,'' she repeated. She raised her head. ''Then the curse will be gone.''

''Putting aside it's all nonsense, what could you think would solve that last part?''

''A Susland who loves enough not to turn away from love.''

''You?'' He jerked his hat off in frustration. ''Because you're the only one over the age of five, Marti.'' He pushed his fingers through his hair, massaging the ache at the back of his skull. *Women!* If they weren't making one part of you ache, they found another to torment. ''But I keep feeling this squeezing in my gut that says it's not your own life you're trying to meddle in.''

''Don't count me out, Luke Chandler. Having gray hair isn't the end of life—or love—you know. Besides I already told you, there are going to be changes in my life with going to China to adopt another baby. That's bringing more love here, not turning away from it. That could answer the curse.''

He'd like to think she thought so. But as they said good-night, he had his doubts.

Rebecca unlocked her apartment after another evening at the Sheridan Library. The session's one moment of excitement and hope had left her even more drained than all the moments of futility.

Listed among old birth announcements from Billings, over the border in Montana, she'd found a child named Rebecca. The announcement referred to the birth as ''last month,'' which made it the same month as Rebecca's birth. The parents were listed as Mr. and Mrs. Pryor, though, so it had to be a false lead. Still, she'd checked the name in current phone books.

When the last one had turned up as empty as all the others, she'd forced herself to return to the newspapers until the library closed. All she wanted now was to go to sleep. And not to dream.

Because she'd dream about him again, and it would be another night without rest.

"I should have kissed him and got it over with."

Automatically, she started to put a hand over her mouth. But no one could hear her. Alone. In private. Not responsible for what anyone else might think if they heard her, because nobody could hear her.

The light on the answering machine blinked insistently.

Her heart took a strange skip, and she pressed the button fast, before she had to examine that too carefully.

Rebecca. The voice on her answering machine began, not identifying herself because there was no need. *Your correspondence has become unsatisfactory in detail and frequency. I shall expect a phone call, although that will not eliminate your obligation to write complete and intelligible letters.*

She'd found letters increasingly difficult. There were too many things she couldn't write. Certainly not why she'd sought out the contract at Far Hills Ranch. Also not about the easy friendship offered by members of the Susland family. Not even about the feel of the wind, the smell of the cattle, the sight of the birds wheeling over them. Not about Luke Chandler.

She could just imagine Antonia Folsom Dahlgren's response to the foreman of Far Hills Ranch. She'd probably make Helen and Barb seem like leaders of his fan club.

No, no, Grandmother wasn't like them. She had strong opinions, but she was fair. And she surely was too smart to entertain any notion as misguided as Helen's small-minded suspicions about Luke and Marti.

It was laughable. Luke's kindness, protectiveness, loyalty and affection for the Suslands were clear to anyone who looked with honest eyes. And impossible not to admire. But as for anything romantic between him and Marti…. She almost wished Helen were right. It certainly would make dealing with Luke easier. Less…tempting.

If he were involved with Marti—or any woman—surely she wouldn't have thoughts about kissing him. Or dreams about a lot more.

Yes, tempted was what she was.

Maddening, stubborn, difficult, generous…eyes that gleamed, a slow, deliberate smile that made her ribs suddenly too small for her heart's pulse, and a big, roughened hand that held her secure and safe while the world turned her sideways.

Saying wild things out loud in private was one thing, but she hadn't lost all sense. Temptation was meant to be withstood—that's what made it temptation.

More important, Luke and everything he did formed an obstacle to her goal. An obstacle to be overcome. Just like temptation.

She had the job. Not that it was doing her much good.

Marti had taken Emily and gone with Robert Delligatti for a three-day program in Denver for prospective parents of Chinese orphans. With getting ready and the drive down and back, she was unavailable for a week.

Walt, Ted and the other hands gave Rebecca as much information as they could in the few moments they had available, but their knowledge was limited to the current running of the ranch. Which was helpful, without aiding her real quest.

Any time she asked about people who might have worked

at Far Hills around the time of the letter, she invariably received, "Don't know nothin' 'bout that. You'd best ask Luke."

And Luke Chandler was as elusive as the mythical unicorn.

The hands reported he'd taken to giving them their next day's instructions the evening before. As far as she could tell, he was never at home, never answered his phone, never showed up in town. After two and a half days it was time for a new approach.

The opportunity to put that new approach into action presented itself even sooner than she'd hoped. She was backing her car out of Helen's driveway, when she spotted Kendra Delligatti across the street, going into the church where the baby-sitting and after-school-care co-op was housed.

Rebecca parked and followed the noise into a large basement room with padded flooring, five play areas, a piano, and nearly a dozen preschoolers. The noise level held her rooted to the spot inside the door. The noise and the joy.

The kids played—drawing with colored pens, building orange and green castles with blocks, creating sculptures out of clay—with an intensity, an abandon that robbed Rebecca of breath. And not a single adult was telling them to be quiet or not to make a mess.

Kendra was putting her purse away in a cabinet. A man Rebecca recognized from the gas station was sitting on the floor assisting the castle-building of two little girls. A young blond woman was overseeing the sculpture by picking up globs of clay that occasionally went astray. Two other women scanned the room while they kept a conversation going.

"Amazing, isn't it?" Kendra said from beside her.

"Amazing," Rebecca repeated, certain Kendra had no idea *how* amazing to an only child raised by Antonia Folsom Dahlgren.

"Please tell me you didn't come to volunteer, because you're such a nice person, I'd hate to see you have to be committed."

Rebecca laughed. "I didn't come to volunteer. I caught sight of you coming in, and hoped I might have a word."

"Sure, as long as it's a loud word. Let's go sit." She gestured to chairs along the wall near the piano.

"With Marti gone," Rebecca started, "I was hoping you might help fill in gaps in my information on Far Hills Ranch. In order to provide a foundation for current information, I'm looking at the history. That will, uh, let me get a start on my work."

"You're not talking about that legend, are you? Because I'm the skeptic in the group. Marti's the true believer. Ellyn leans that way, and so does Daniel." She tipped her head. "I'm not sure about Grif or—" she pinned her gaze on Rebecca's face "—Luke."

Rebecca ignored the implications swimming in Kendra's eyes. "It's more recent history I'm talking about. Personnel records. The workers hired, say twenty-five, thirty years ago, in order to compare with current hires. I thought since you spent childhood summers here..."

"Sorry, other than a couple of the old favorites—Pete used to cook and there was a Sven for several summers who carved us little toys—I'm no help. I doubt Ellyn would know much more. Grif might, because he was a little older, but really, with Marti gone, Luke would be the one to ask."

"So I keep hearing."

Kendra's head came up, her eyes bright with interest. "He won't make time to talk to you?"

"All he's made as far as I'm concerned is himself scarce."

Rebecca pulled her lower lip between her teeth as if that would stop the words retroactively. Some of her discomfort faded as Kendra's attention shifted to her son Matthew's loop-the-loops around the play area with a toy airplane in hand.

"Ahhh, Luke's never been much for talking. No, Matthew—no dive-bombing. Even when we were kids, Luke tended to go off by himself. And since we've come back as adults, he's talked very little about himself. He's just Luke— there when we need him, good with the kids, great with the ranch, and such a part of Far Hills, it's like he never left. But he did, just like the rest of us. Only…"

Kendra continued slowly, seeming to consider the accuracy of each word. "I'd never thought about it before—Luke never talks about his life between the time his family left Far Hills and when he came back as a hand."

They lapsed into silence, both watching the kids' antics.

All Luke allowed to the outside world were odd fragments that slipped loose from the tight cocoon he kept around himself. Short ends hard to grasp, but perhaps leading somewhere for someone with the patience to follow them.

"Kendra? Ellyn mentioned something about one time when Daniel was playing music, and Luke recognized Chopin."

Kendra's eyes darkened immediately with old pain.

"I'm sorry. I shouldn't have asked—"

"No, it's okay."

Kendra's hand on her arm kept Rebecca from standing. Slowly, she sank back to the chair as Kendra spoke.

"It was a tough time for Daniel and me. Especially for Daniel. We'd been apart and he…he'd been involved in something and felt he hadn't done enough, when he'd already done more than should have been asked of any person."

Rebecca suspected there was a great deal more to this story, but it was Kendra's story to tell, not hers to ask.

"Daniel's playing…well, it was his way of expressing this. Luke heard him, and called me. Until then, I hadn't realized what Daniel was holding inside.'' She let out a deep breath and straightened. ''That's all there is to it, except Luke recognized what Daniel was playing as Chopin.''

And, Rebecca thought, Luke had recognized enough of the emotion behind Daniel's music to call Kendra.

''Thank you.'' She caught a speculative gleam in the other woman's eyes. ''It helps to know as many facets as possible of a client—or a potential user—to maximize the customization of the system.''

''Uh-huh. And whether Luke knew classical music would be something you'd need to know to set up the computer system,'' Kendra said in deadpan agreement.

''Yes, well—'' Rebecca stood ''—everything helps. Thank you.''

''Wait, Rebecca. There was something else he said…I was so preoccupied with Daniel, but *something*…. Got it! Luke said Chopin wanted people to hear pain in the beautiful music. Something like that—no, wait. He said someone once told him that—that the someone believed that about Chopin's music. *She* believed that.''

''She?''

''Yes, the someone was a she. I'm sure of it. You get a reporter's ear, and I'd bet next year's raise that Luke said *she* told him that she thought Chopin wanted to hear the pain in the beautiful music. You probably didn't want to hear that—''

''Oh, no, it's nothing like—''

''—but believe me it's better in the long run to know. I finally learned the lesson that you have to know what the past truly was before you can let go of it.''

The other woman's obvious sincerity quieted Rebecca's protests. ''Thank you, Kendra. I appreciate your help.''

''Afraid I wasn't much help.'' The gray eyes surveyed her. ''At least not about the hands who used to work at the ranch.''

Rebecca simply smiled and said goodbye. She had the door open when she heard her name being called once more.

"Rebecca! Wait a minute!"

Kendra gestured for her to stay put, while she retrieved a canvas tote and hurried back, making an abrupt stop to avoid a collision with an apparent stagecoach hold-up reenactment, and tip-toeing around a precariously balanced block castle.

"Rebecca, I do have one thought—about the hands who worked at the ranch years ago. Records are kept in the home ranch office. There's an entrance off Marti's office in the house and one from outside." She slid her hand into her tote, and pulled out a set of keys. She set to work detaching one. "Take the path toward the kitchen, and keep going around to the back. You'll see it. The records are in a small room off the office. You should find what you want there."

"I don't know...with Marti not there..."

Kendra put a key in her hand. "It'll be fine. Absolutely fine."

Chapter Eight

Luke did not need another chore. He had enough to do keeping up with work while twisting his schedule like a pretzel to keep out of range of Rebecca.

He'd almost made a really bad mistake. But he'd been saved.

It rankled that he'd been saved by Helen Solsong, but you couldn't pick and choose your salvation. She'd saved him partly by her bull-in-a-china-shop nosiness, mostly by being the lesson that reminded him of what made Rebecca Dahlgren bad news.

You enjoy thumbing your nose at the world, Luke, but I'm in no position to do that…. I have a responsibility to reflect well on the family name.

Hard to believe he'd needed to be told that not twelve hours after how Rebecca acted at Far Hills Market. Even a jackass that had been kicked in the head a few times could've figured that one out. By the time he'd driven her home, it had slid right out of his jackass head—replaced by the image of how she'd looked astride a western saddle, wearing jeans and a simple shirt, dust on her cheeks, her eyes spitting fire when he asked if she was ready to quit.... She didn't much resemble the woman who'd tiptoed across the field toward him that first day.

Ever since then it seemed like any time he turned around, she was there. What nearly got him into big trouble was letting himself enjoy that.

The way she'd start off each time they met with that chin of hers stuck out and her mouth firm, practically setting off neon signs saying Strictly Business, was a red flag to any bull. Teasing her across those silly "that's not appropriate" lines she kept harping about was almost too easy.

Maybe that was his first mistake. Because beyond those lines was a Rebecca a darn sight more tempting than "strictly business." It didn't help that her increasing tendency to wear ranch clothes showed off her feminine curves even better than her proper suits—hell, was it his imagination or was she even moving differently?

He had enough on his mind. He didn't need Kendra insisting she had to have the figures from last year's payout to the Susland descendants for some legal thing for Matthew. You'd think she'd have kept it with her own records. Kendra usually didn't let details slip. And that business about it would take him so much less time to find because he knew where to look—

Someone was in the office.

Through the window, he could see the open door to the file room, and a shadow moving beyond it. Without moving, he watched.

A slender shadow. A dark-haired slender shadow.

Tension ebbed out of him, but the adrenaline that had flooded his system took a new turn and concentrated in a dangerous area. If he hadn't been so damned curious, he'd have walked away.

Instead, he silently reached the outside door, tested the knob and found it unlocked. He eased the door open slowly so the motion wouldn't attract attention.

He shouldn't have bothered to be so careful. Rebecca was too engrossed to notice a little thing like a man sneaking up on her. Before he closed the door behind him, a lick of breeze skittered into the file room and ruffled the papers in a folder she held open. Did that alert her? Oh, no. She simply held the top of the folder open with her chin, smoothed the papers with her hand and kept reading.

Now he was not only curious, but irked. What right did she have coming on to his ranch, where he was responsible, and not have the sense the Good Lord gave a grasshopper?

He was all the way to the door of the file room, leaning the middle of his back against the jamb, one bracing leg extended and the other leg crossed over it, and it still wasn't until he spoke that she knew he was there.

"What do you think you're doing?"

"Oh!" She spun around, juggling the folder. He had to give her credit, she collected herself in record time. "You startled me, Luke."

"I meant to."

She blinked. "Why?"

"The door was open."

Looking past him, her dark brows dropped in a frown of memory. "No, it was locked. Kendra gave me the key. So I could start my work without waiting for Marti to return— since you haven't been available."

He ignored the needle in that. "It might have been locked when you got here, not when I got here."

"If you have a problem with my having a key, I suggest you take it up with Kendra. She *is* a part-owner."

So much for subtlety.

"You should have locked the door behind you," he said bluntly. "Especially when you're so deep in what you're doing that a lightning bolt wouldn't catch your attention. And you haven't answered what I asked to start—what are you doing?''

''Oh, just looking at old personnel records.''

Did she think that sounded casual? Or truthful?

''As a matter of fact,'' she started in a tone she probably called breezy and he found suspicious as hell, ''I see a notation here that the records from before 1975 are in a storage facility. If you'll give me the key, I'll go out there and check them and return the key when I'm—''

''Why?''

''—done. Why? Because I wouldn't want to inconvenience you any more than I absolutely have to.''

He kept to his point. ''Why do you want to see them?''

''Seeing what information earlier documents included will help determine if the software format needs to be expanded.''

The woman couldn't lie worth spit.

He, on the other hand, was a better than middlin' liar, as the guys at the Ranchers' Rest knew from their poker games.

''Good idea.''

He shifted against the door frame, putting more of his weight forward. She watched him, and she still didn't have a clue what was coming—or how to avoid it. He rocked forward onto his front foot, snatched the folders, and was back leaning comfortably against the door frame before she drew in a single, audible breath.

Give her her due, though—she might not anticipate, but she recovered quickly. No gaping or gasping or sputtering. Just a chilly, ''Please give those back.''

Instead, he flipped through the folders once, then twice.

''Funny thing. Looks like you're only including old timers with Indian names in your research.''

He handed over the folders—he'd seen what he wanted to see—though he placed them far enough out on her flattened hand that she had to reach forward with the other one to save them from falling. That made her take two quick, balancing steps toward him so he could see the other thing he wanted to see—that quick, undeniable flare of light that gave her brown eyes the warmth of a blaze.

She clutched the folders to her chest, and made a move as if to get by him to the main room. She stopped short. She didn't have much choice, unless she was willing to climb over him. And he wasn't in any condition to make a quick change of position, not without letting her see what that flash in her eyes had done to him.

She turned back into the store room.

"Fine. You want to know why I was looking at these folders?"

"I'd admit to some curiosity."

"I was wondering if any of these would have been my name—if my father had bothered to marry my mother."

Now, *that* was some of the truth. Not all of it, but a sizable chunk.

She was continuing. "I guess...I guess being out here has made me think about the possibility that this—" Her gesture was probably meant to take in her hair, eyes and skin. It also called his attention to the length of her neck, the swell of her breasts, the curve into her waist and out to her hips, "—could be a sign of Indian heritage."

"What if it is?"

"What do you mean?"

"What are you expecting from him when you find him— your father?"

"I'm not expecting anything." She'd gone east-coast stiff again.

When a cow planted its feet and got the look now on Rebecca's face, there was only one thing to do—take a different approach "Okay, what are you planning to do when you find him?"

"Do?"

"Throw yourself in his arms, crying *Daddy?* Spit in his eye?"

"I'm simply curious. I believe that's natural."

Even after she finished that answer, he could see her mind working over his question. But it wasn't her mind that was tormenting him. At this rate, he wouldn't be moving for a week.

"I suppose," she said, "I would ask why he left my mother pregnant and unmarried."

"For somebody all worked up about what people think, you talk enough about your father not being married to your mother."

"Not to most people." Recognition of what she'd revealed widened her eyes and rounded her mouth, but again, she recovered quickly. "I mean, it hasn't ever been a secret. It wouldn't have made sense trying to keep it a secret when Mother returned to Delaware with me and no husband, would it? Not among so many people who knew the Dahlgrens. Grandmother said—and I'm old enough now to understand—that it was better to have it out in the open than to try to pretend it didn't exist and have everybody whispering behind your back."

She winced slightly, as if remembering something or someone. Or maybe *not* remembering someone—a father she'd never known.

As a kid, he'd followed his Dad's every move like it answered the biggest riddle in life. Maybe it had in a way, because that's how he'd learned to ride and rope and ranch. No matter what had followed, he had that, and he had it from his father.

"Now, if you'll excuse me, Luke, I have work to do in the other room."

She came close, as if she thought crowding him would get him to move out of her way. With her drawn up straight and him propped against the doorjamb, they were eye to eye. Close enough to see the tiny flecks of gold and black and green that gave her eyes a special glitter. Close enough to smell a clean warmth that seemed to go directly from her skin to his groin.

"If you don't mind, Luke…"

She sounded sterner now. Or was that worry? She should be worried. There was no Helen Solsong to save her—or him—this time.

"I mind."

He hooked one hand around the back of her neck, drawing her in to meet him halfway as he leaned forward.

She sucked in a breath just before their lips met—surprise maybe, or something else. Either way, it drew his breath in to her, and it left her lips slightly parted. He played his over hers, feeling the full curve of her bottom lip from outside to inside, first with his mouth and then with his tongue.

She swayed into him, brushing the side of her breast against the inside of the arm he'd extended to put a hand over the back of her shoulder blade. He pressed that arm tighter against her, feeling a change in her flesh. She felt it, too, and started to draw back.

He went with her, turning her withdrawal inside out, by letting it carry him to her side of the door frame, so their legs tangled, his pelvis fit against hers and his whole chest could brush against the tightening tips of her breasts.

She tasted of the tartness he'd heard on her tongue more than once. And of the sweetness he'd seen in her eyes. And of the warmth he'd felt on her skin. All that, rolled together. Every taste a man needed to sustain his soul.

He took it all in. He delved for more. He feasted. Felt it filling him, and yet the craving only deepened. He wanted more…more…needed more…

A soft, moaning sound came from her, sending urgent blood to his groin. Her fingers curled into the hair at the back of his neck. Her tongue slid against his, flitted into his mouth.

What tastes did she gain? What did she draw from him? *Needed more…*

Was she needing more from him, too? Another surge in his groin and the chill of reason in his brain came simultaneously.

He lifted his mouth from hers. They were too close to look each other in the eye. He focused on the corner of her mouth, reddened, moist, slightly puffy, and listened to their harsh breathing, unsynchronized but somehow creating a rhythm.

She stepped back, half a step. She should have been running.

She wasn't.

He would have been running.

He couldn't.

Her dark lashes lifted slowly. Caution created a sheer curtain over her eyes, but in the depths, down where the green and gold and black glinted, he read passion.

"I'll leave you to your work." His throat felt like sandpaper; he refused to clear it.

"Okay." She said it slowly, like it was a foreign language.

"Okay." He swallowed. He moved cautiously, his alternative being making an adjustment that she was sure to recognize. At the outside door, he turned back.

"Now lock the damned door."

It was near sunset two days later, and he'd almost reached the path that led to the front door of the Ranchers' Rest when he heard her voice behind him.

"Luke—I want to talk to you."

He'd known Rebecca had spotted him when her little car going one way passed his truck going the opposite one on

Kaycee Road. In a single flash of her face as they came abreast, he'd seen the recognition, the memory, the embarrassment, the heat and then the determination. He hadn't considered that the determination might overcome all the rest and bring her to the Ranchers' Rest.

Still, there she was, steaming toward him. She was wearing jeans. Not as tight as some wore them, but cut close enough to remind a man who didn't need any reminders of what the curve of her thigh felt like under his hand. His body surged in abrupt awareness. He cursed under his breath.

This was nothing but trouble. She might not believe it, but he had a few rules himself. One was not getting involved with a female who was headed in a whole different direction from him. No matter what happened when he kissed her and she kissed back.

"I've been trying to get in touch with you, and you've been avoiding me."

Hell, yes, he'd been avoiding her.

The kissing they'd done in the file room had proved the desire crackling between them, like the whip-cracks of lightning between a pair of opposite-charged clouds. So Luke had done the only thing a sensible man could do—he'd kept as much distance as possible so there wouldn't be any more discharges of lightning.

"Avoidin'?" he drawled.

"Yes," she snapped. "Just like you were doing before Kendra gave me the key to the office and we—"

She stopped so abruptly he should have heard brakes squeal. Too late, though, at least for him. He was seeing and smelling and feeling their kisses all over again.

"We'll talk later." His voice sounded a little husky.

"Now."

He could see her digging in. He tried another tack. "You shouldn't be here."

"Why not?" She looked around as she asked, and the widening of her eyes when she spotted the name over the door said he didn't need to answer. He did anyway.

"Not the place for someone worried about her reputation."

"You're going in," she accused.

"I don't have a reputation, least not one to guard."

"You could change that with some effort." He saw the honesty in her rise up and force the next words. "Maybe more than *some* effort. I'm afraid some people think—" she flashed a wary look at him "—some people, uh, speculate about the…relationship between you and Marti."

He was half tempted to make her spell that out.

"I know."

"You *know!*"

"Been saying it for years."

"Then why did you get so angry when I—?"

"Everybody 'round here knows the ones who've been saying it are fools. Seemed you might be a fool, too. But people 'round here wouldn't know that yet, so you might be dangerous."

"If you know, why don't you do someth—"

"Because I don't care."

He might have more than an ordinary itch for this woman, but he was not going to start caring what people thought just because she got herself tied up in knots about it. That's one line he'd never cross. He'd seen what came of that, and he'd be damned before he let that happen in his life again.

"*I* care—" Her own vehemence seemed to startle her. She pulled in a quick breath. "I, uh, I don't want to see you—or any fellow human being, I mean—especially someone like Marti, or even the ranch—hurt or thought poorly of, especially when it's based on misinformation. It's not right that people talk that way…."

"Won't hurt me." He cleared his throat. "Or maybe

you're worrying that people will start thinking something of you for having anything to do with me? Just tell 'em it's business.''

She glared at him. Then, instead of making it easy on him, she gave him a level look and said in a voice that came too damned close to breaking for his comfort, ''I'm trying to make you see how you could make it easier on yourself. You know, it's not like I'm defending people like Helen.''

''That's the hell of it, Rebecca Dahlgren. If you did, it would all be easy.''

He walked away then. When he couldn't keep his mouth shut, it was time to get away. He went into the familiar dark of the Ranchers' Rest, and closed the door behind him.

That was so like Luke Chandler. To turn it around on her. Like she was messing up his life by trying to find a middle ground between him and the people talking about him. Why the man insisted on not only letting the world think the worst of him, but almost invited it, was beyond her.

How he could then turn it around to make it look as if she were the one with the problem, was hard to excuse. *If you did, it would all be easy.*

Easy to dismiss her? Easy to keep her out of his life?

Was she letting what she wanted his words to mean mislead her? Should she even be wanting the words to have had that meaning? Wasn't that asking for trouble? Wasn't that letting her emotions rule her?

The way they had when he'd...

She didn't form the rest of the thought. It didn't matter. Her body didn't need a complete thought to respond.

Okay, so there were emotions going on—hot and potent emotions. Okay, so she wasn't accustomed to this. Okay, she'd even admit she found it all...*startling.* Even a little frightening,

Was this how my mother felt?

She'd always thought her mother must have been an out-of-control emotional type. Surely that fit with a woman who would let herself be taken in by a man. But what if Suzanne Dahlgren had been reasonable all her life? In a way that made more sense, since she had been Antonia's daughter, her only child. So if she'd once been sensible, then fell apart over a man...

The completion of that thought was frightening.

And all the more reason for Rebecca to keep her mind on the business of tracking down the missing link to her personal history.

She had made some progress. Sorting through the records that were available, she'd determined that none of the ranch's post-1975 employees with Indian-sounding names had been old enough at the time of her birth to have been a likely candidate as her father.

A list of names from the five years before had been in one of the folders, and it had possibilities. Until she saw the complete files with age and other information, however, she couldn't know for sure. And to see the file she needed the storage area key from Luke.

Who had just walked away from her again.

"Damn him."

She looked around. No one was there to hear her. That meant no one was there to see what she did, either.

He was not going to distract her. He was not going to stand in her way—more accurately, he was not going to walk away when she needed his cooperation.

She took in a deep breath, then headed for the battered door. The metal handle felt suspiciously sticky. She gave it a quick turn, and released it as soon as possible.

From the dazzle of the setting sun, she entered a cave. A black hole where she knew life existed only because she could smell the yeastiness of spilled beer and the staleness of old cigarettes, hear the thump of glass against wood and

feel the warmth of a number of bodies packed into a con-
fined area. She couldn't see a thing for those first few seconds.

She couldn't hear much, either, as she became aware of
a decided hush. Only the jukebox speakers wailed on un-
fettered about someone drinking alone under the light of a
neon moon.

"You need help, honey?"

A woman's voice, a little raspy, not unfriendly, came to
her out of the darkness.

Rebecca blinked and a face to go with the voice separated
itself from the shadows. Uncompromisingly red lipstick on
a small mouth, robin's-egg-blue eye shadow over tired-
looking eyes.

"Uh, no, thank you. I think I'll just…"

The rest of the room, which stretched one narrow arm to
her left and one to the right was coming into focus, and with
it, the unabashed stares of the half dozen or so men scattered
along the bar and at a few tables. To the far left, two stood
beside a pool table, cue sticks in hand, game temporarily
suspended while they gawked at her.

She felt like the proverbial fish out of water. She could
only hope her flopping around wasn't too visible. Doggedly,
she looked into face after face. A few were vaguely familiar,
none was the uncompromising visage of Luke Chandler.

"Did your car break down? You need to call somebody?"

"No, thank you. Someone I need to speak with came in
here, so I followed—" which no longer seemed such a good
idea "—and…"

"Someone you need to talk to, in here?" the woman repeated, as if the two halves of that thought wouldn't fit together.

"Yes, I—" She swallowed, gathered her wits and her
aplomb to turn back to the woman with a gracious smile.
"Thank you. I see my party in the corner."

Luke was facing the door. His were the only eyes not pinned on her as she made her way to his table. He had his right elbow hooked around the back of the chair and his left hand curled around a bottle of beer. With one knee bent and the other leg extended into the aisle, he presented a picture of relaxed male arrogance.

"Luke, we got, uh, sidetracked, I still need to talk to you—about business."

He raised his chin. He said nothing.

"May I sit down?" That had a bit of an edge to it.

"Suit yourself."

"Thank you."

The chair leg scraped against the uneven wooden floor with a goose-bump-raising squeal. Instinctively, Rebecca looked around. Every face was turned to her. "Sorry."

No one said anything. No one looked away.

As she sat, Luke took a swig of beer.

"Nothin' to be sorry for. They don't mind the noise, and they were looking at you anyway."

"I know you don't like my manners—"

"Can I get you something, honey?" The waitress had materialized at her side.

"Oh, I…"

"They don't have white wine," Luke said flatly.

Rebecca couldn't decide if he'd said that to spare her the embarrassment of asking for it, or to emphasize that she didn't belong here.

"How 'bout a beer?" the waitress asked.

Her nametag said Sally. Rebecca smiled at her. "Thank you, Sally. I don't care much for beer—"

"No mai-tais or pink ladies, either."

Luke's second contribution left little doubt of his motivation. "I'd like an ice water—" without looking at him, she knew Luke's mouth was slipping toward a smirk "—and a Scotch on the rocks, please, Sally."

Sally blinked at her, then nodded and headed off to fill the order. Luke said nothing, and neither did she. When Sally returned, she brought the water, the Scotch and another bottle of beer for Luke, though he hadn't finished the first.

"I'll get this round," Rebecca said with a bit of a flourish. She looked at the figure scrawled at the bottom of the standard restaurant form. "Sally, I think you missed my drink. This only covers the beer."

The waitress leaned over, bringing a wave of perfume with her. Rebecca steeled herself to keep from drawing back.

"Nah, that's right. Scotch and the beer."

Rebecca paid the amount and added a more than generous tip.

"Say, thanks!"

When she saw Luke leaning back with one eyebrow cocked up, she said defensively, "I believe in tipping."

"That wasn't a tip, it was a bribe. You planning on doing something you don't want Sally to talk about?"

Defiant, she looked directly in his eyes, which glinted with amusement and something else. "Like what?"

"Like," he drawled, "drink that Scotch, maybe?"

She picked up the glass and did something she'd never done before in her life—she didn't sip, she didn't take a mere swallow. She put back a slug.

Chapter Nine

"What I want to know is how come you got all that education and now you're puttin' all your time and heart into fussin' about dead men instead of live ones you got right in front of you."

The tilt of his head took in the other denizens of this bar and somehow excluded himself, even though he was the live man *most* right in front of her. Luke slanted her another of those looks from under the shadow of his cowboy hat that made her want to snatch it off or pull it hard down on his nose.

"Because," she snapped, "the dead men are more interesting."

When he'd ordered a burger and fries, she'd declined to get anything to eat, hoping her restraint would convey that she was here strictly on business. She'd steered clear of family issues, but he'd pulled a good deal of information out of her about her education and professional background.

"Well now," he drawled, "I'd never have figured you for kinky. Not—"

"Kinky?" she sputtered.

"—with that prim kind of look, and those careful clothes."

She opened her mouth to dispute those assessments, then stopped herself. She wouldn't give him the satisfaction.

"Thank you," she said, making a show of folding her hands precisely on the table. "I strive to give an impression of professionalism and decorum."

"Always said you couldn't judge a book by its cover," he murmured. "And you've proved my point."

Anyone who spoke in such a low tone deserved to have their words ignored.

"In the interest of broadening your mind, I will say that I am interested in what you call dead men and others call history because the choices people made even three hundred years ago affect what our lives are like now. Look at Far Hills Ranch." She leaned forward. "Imagine how different things might be if Charles Susland had stayed with Leaping Star instead of pushing her aside and marrying a rich white wife. There probably wouldn't be a Far Hills Ranch today, or a town. I'm not saying he was right—not at all—but his actions, his personality have an effect, even now. Or what if he had listened to Leaping Star? If he'd taken care of their child and that child had survived, what might have happened then? Would his marriage to Annalee have endured? Maybe the Susland line would have died out a hundred years ago."

The corners of his mouth tucked in like he might be fighting a grin. "You sure there's nothing kinky about this? You get awfully worked up about it."

She became aware that she was leaning so far forward that her breasts nearly brushed against where her hands were still crossed atop the table. She straightened with assumed ease.

"People make a mistake when they look at history. They see it as a straight line. They see what *did* happen and they think that's what *had* to happen. But each step was filled with choices. And the people living then—just as we do now—had to make choices."

"What difference does it make knowing what their choices were? Those old choices were decided and it's done. Can't be undone. It's called history because it's not happening now. And we live now."

"You've thought more about this than you've let on."

Something flickered across his face that she suspected was irritation—at her or himself?

"Hard not to with Marti going on about the old fort and the ranch's history."

"History teaches us the mistakes not to repeat, and sometimes it teaches us the things we *should* repeat. Besides, it affects what's happening now, every day in your life and mine."

"You mean that stuff about Far Hills Ranch not existing? If it didn't, I'd be at another ranch. I'd still be the same."

No, you wouldn't.

The thought hit her even more powerfully than the Scotch. He was part of Far Hills Ranch, and it was part of him. She couldn't explain it any better than that.

"Other things, too," she said lamely.

He tipped the beer bottle nearly upside down as he drained it. Then he challenged, "Like what?"

Like what? Her mind went blank. She could think of nothing. She took a quick gulp of the Scotch, feeling the burn of it down her throat and into her chest.

"Take your name, for instance," she offered, her relief making her sound incredibly pleased with herself. Or was that the Scotch?

"What about my name?"

"Chandler's something you use every day, and it's a piece

of history. It's what they called the craftsman who made candles. Somewhere in your ancestry, you must have had a candlemaker.''

''Horse thief more likely.'' Still, he sounded not quite as unyielding. ''Even if it's so, I'm just using that string of letters, not caring where they came from.''

''Okay, well, I'll tell you one with practical use.'' She lifted the glass of Scotch, which had only a quarter of its golden liquid left. ''I use the six wives of Henry the Eighth any time I have something to drink.''

''How's that?''

His voice was ripe with skeptical amusement, but she answered solemnly, ''If I can say the names of the six wives of Henry the Eighth, in order, then I know I have not had too much to drink.''

''How often you have to use that?'' he asked wryly. ''Can't imagine a lot of partying at Grandma Dahlgren's, unless—''

He stopped abruptly, and she knew he'd remembered what she'd said about her mother's drinking. It didn't bother her. She felt oddly insulated. Besides, *partying* was not what her mother had been doing.

''It got me safely through college.''

''Okay, let's hear it.''

Supporting his crossed forearms on the table he leaned far across it, until his face was only about twelve inches from hers. ''Let's hear those six wives. Right now.''

''You think…? Are you intimating that I have had too much to drink?''

''I am not *intimating* anything—'' The sound of that word, or maybe the way he said it, seemed to reverberate through her. ''I'm saying I want to hear those six names— in order—right now.''

Chin up, eyes level, she recited: ''Catherine of Aragon, Anne Boleyn, Jane Seymour, Anne of Cleves, Catherine

Howard and—'' she couldn't keep the triumph from her tone ''—Catherine Pair.''

That should show him.

''That last one—was that Pear like the fruit? Catherine Pear?''

She frowned. ''Henry never married anyone named Pear. Why're you trying to confuse me?''

''Not me, Ms. Dahlgren. You're doing it all by yourself.''

She had a very odd feeling—a simultaneous certainty that his statement had significance, and an inability to puzzle it out.

Why would he say Henry the Eighth had been married to a piece of fruit? Pear? Where could he have…?

''Parr,'' she enunciated clearly. ''Catherine Parr. She was the only one to outlive him.''

She sat back, waiting for him to look impressed. He didn't.

''Oh. Maybe Anne of Cleves…they lived apart from the start, and I don't remember when she died. It might have been after him. I used to know.''

But she couldn't remember the details now to save her life—or her dignity. And she'd said Pear instead of Parr. That could only mean—

She stood abruptly.

''If you'll excuse me, I'll be leaving now.''

''Rebecca—''

''Good night, Luke. I know we didn't finish our business, but I feel it's time for me to go home. I will contact you—'' she spoke with care ''—at your earliest convenience.''

He sat for a moment, watching her walk precisely between the tables and barstools. Very precisely. *Damn.*

He dropped some bills on the table for his meal and headed after her.

"Oh, hell, no, Chandler's not interested in some rich broad," Robby Greene said with loud derision as he passed.

Luke pushed out the door without pausing.

A quick glance showed him she was crossing the parking lot—away from her car, parked precisely amid the welter of casually angled pickups. The overhead light was bright enough that he could see the crease down the back of her jeans, the belt where her blouse neatly slid inside the waistband and the shift of her hips as she walked.

He stretched his stride so he'd catch up with her faster, and trim his observing time.

"Where're you goin', Rebecca?"

She turned her head, without stopping. He matched his pace to hers.

"To my apartment."

"Walking?"

She looked at him, eyes serious. "I am not precisely drunk, but I believe it would be wiser to walk than drive."

He muttered a curse, sighed, and snagged her elbow, drawing her to a stop. "I can drive you."

"Thank you, but I don't think—"

"I can't name the six wives of Henry the Eighth, but I never could, so you'll have to take my word on it."

"I believe you. You ate a full meal with those two bottles of beer." He was torn between amusement and surprise that she'd kept an eye on his intake of alcohol and food. "My concern is, if you drive me home, how would I get my car in the morning?"

He refrained from pointing out that she would have faced the same problem if she'd walked home. "I'll drive your car."

"Oh. Okay. Thank you."

She turned and started back toward her car. Her movements were remarkably steady for someone who'd missed the detail that if he drove her car, he'd have to find a way back here to his truck.

She handed over her keys without fumbling and settled into the passenger seat, hands cupped in her lap, staring straight ahead while he adjusted seat, mirrors and steering wheel for his larger frame.

"You don't drink much, do you, Rebecca?"

"No."

Her mother's legacy, he suspected. He'd already stepped into that one once tonight, he wasn't going to do it again.

"Why'd you do it tonight?"

"I was nervous."

He didn't know what to say to that, and she added nothing. They drove in silence until they stopped for a red light at otherwise deserted Main Street.

"I live on Canyon Street, off Seventh," she said.

As if he hadn't picked her up there. As if he hadn't taken her back there. As if he hadn't almost kissed her in that driveway more than two weeks ago.

"I've been there, remember?"

"Oh. Of course. I wasn't…thinking." She'd faced him to say those words, now she turned straight ahead. "I don't want to go home yet. Can't we go someplace else?"

"I don't think you should—"

"Oh, no. Not anywhere to drink. Just someplace…else."

He frowned, but turned short of Canyon. "Where to?"

"I don't know. We could drive around awhile."

That had a hint of a plea to it. Maybe he'd take her directly home after all. He didn't want Rebecca sounding small and vulnerable. It wasn't safe.

Then she spoke again and it had enough snap to it to ease his mind. "After all, it's my gas we're using."

"Where is this?" she asked as soon as he stopped her car.

"It's as close as we can get in a car to Leaping Star's overlook."

"Oh."

The syllable packed a lot into it. Before he could sort out the elements or remind himself of the reasons not to try, she was on the move.

"Hey! Whaddya think you're doing?"

"Walking," she called back over her shoulder as she did just that.

"Rebecca—" He loped to catch up. Admittedly the moon and stars lit the sky, but she was heading over rough ground on a path that ran near the edge of a sheer drop. "That's not a good idea."

"You haven't liked any of my ideas—not computers or donuts or talking or...or anything. But I like my ideas. And I want to see Leaping Star's overlook."

He hooked a hand around her upper arm. "Rebecca—"

She spun on him "Quit! Just quit scolding me and ordering me around like I'm a child with no sense and you're my...my grandmother!"

He looked at her, preparing hot, sharp words of his own. Instead, he said, "I'm going first. Hold onto my belt."

He moved ahead of her on the path. When she didn't take hold as he'd instructed, he pulled her hand to the back waist of his jeans, waiting until he felt her fingers wrap around the sturdy leather.

Oh, yeah, this was a great idea.

Somehow they made it to the overlook. It must have been luck and instinct, because his mind was definitely not all on the task.

As the path opened into the clearing at the back of the overlook, he reached around and took her hand to remove it from his belt. Somehow he ended up not releasing it as he guided her to the fallen log that served as a rough seat.

"Oh, look..." she whispered as she sank to the log. "Tell me what I'm seeing, Luke."

"Far Hills," he said gruffly. There was a reverence in her tone that touched him despite himself.

"What parts? Is that the home ranch?"

"No, that's Ridge House. Main house is over there—see?"

"This must be what it looked like those nights Leaping Star stayed up here, hoping Charles Susland would change his heart and take care of their child."

"Darker then. It was darker even when I was a kid."

"You came here when you were a child? Alone?"

"Sure."

"But your parents, they let you?"

"Had other things on their minds." She'd turned to him; he knew that even though he was looking out over the land. "Came up once when the power was out to see what it must have looked like in the old days, but the backup generators had already cut on." He squinted as if he could filter out the man-made light. "Even with that, even with the lights and fences and irrigation ditches and planted fields, the land doesn't change, not really. Not the land, and not the seasons, and not nature. They don't change."

"No, they don't," she agreed softly. "They're here, no matter what. And you fit right in with them. Part of them. Part of this place. Part of these people. Part of this land."

"It's a job. Don't go reciting poetry about it."

"It *is* a kind of poetry, knowing where you belong, and being there. Having friends around you that you trust, who accept you and trust you back. Having a place you love. Having a job that suits you. A home."

The thread of wistfulness woven into otherwise simple words kept him from shaking off her description. Even though he'd just come back temporarily. Passing through. No obligation. No responsibility, other than to do a good job. He could walk away any time. Move on, free and clear.

"I can't imagine you anywhere but here, Luke," came

Rebecca's soft voice, as if to refute his thoughts.

He shifted, ready to say it was time to go.

And felt the touch of her lips against the right side of his mouth. Maybe she'd intended to kiss him on the cheek, and his movement had provided a different landing spot. Maybe not.

She didn't jolt away.

She seemed to float there next to him, breathing in and out, with that faint motion brushing her lips against the side of his mouth. Slowly, he brought his head around toward her.

Her eyes were on his mouth. The lashes dark and long, not quite hiding the soft, warm brown of her eyes.

The look jolted heat into his groin.

She drew a particularly deep breath, held for an instant, then kissed him again. Lips to lips.

He tasted a blend of Scotch and her, and that was enough to short-circuit any noble commands his head might have issued. He didn't grab her—that was as noble as he could hope for right now. Holding still, and waiting.

If he touched her—if he thrust his tongue into the warmth of her mouth…

She hadn't been sure a week ago in the office. Not sure at all. Despite how her body reacted. Was she now? Or was this the Scotch? Was this the moonlight and night and the mountain?

Damn, he wanted her.

She jerked away with a gasp. Instinct had his hands reaching for her, discipline stopped them before they took hold.

She didn't even see it. She had her head down.

"I'm sorry, Luke. I shouldn't— That was… After I made it clear… I keep making…" Her hands fluttered with no more sense than her words.

"Let's go."

Her head came up though she didn't meet his eyes.
"Luke, I—"

"Forget it. Let's go."

He pulled all the way to the back of the drive, and went
around the front of the car. She was negotiating the stairs
fine. When he followed, she gave him a quizzical look over
her left shoulder, only faintly wary. Apparently she hadn't
yet recognized the problem she would have faced at the top
of the stairs if he hadn't followed.

"Here're your keys," he offered when she hesitated.

She accepted them without touching him, opened the
door. He took a single step inside for a precautionary look
around. A woman who left the door unlocked the way she
had at the ranch office wasn't as careful as she should be,
so he scanned the room. He was also curious. Nothing
wrong with that.

He surveyed Rebecca's classy touches against the fading
mediocrity of the apartment. Her leather bag, a scarf he suspected was silk draped over the back of a small sofa, books
and folders neatly stacked where a desk met the wall, a pen
that might be gold on a pad next to an answering machine
that kept company with her laptop. His gaze slowed at the
bedside table. More books and papers, a lamp, a huddle of
photographs each in a polished wood frame.

An older woman, sleek and certain, with softly graying
hair and a hard mouth—had to be Grandmother. Another
photo with three generations—a somewhat younger version
of the grandmother, with a dark-haired girl who had to be
Rebecca at about Emily's age, and a young woman, who
looked like the grandmother with the personality leached out
of her, probably Rebecca's mother. A less formal photograph of Rebecca and two other attractive young women all
wearing college sweatshirts. A slightly fuzzy snapshot of a

man nearing retirement age dressed in a suit beside a rounded woman with a smear of something white on her cheek.

His eyes went back to the picture of the three generations. Rebecca, vibrant and open with her little-girl smile, sat between the two women, yet seemed apart from them. No wonder she'd felt she didn't belong. She *didn't* belong with those two. At least she hadn't then. But she'd learned, oh, yes, she'd learned.

She would dismiss him now, thank him with the cool politeness of her pedigree. Pretend nothing had happened. Or try.

But she didn't. She was looking beyond him, through the open door, down toward her car in the driveway.

"How stupid of me. How will you get home?"

"I'll manage."

"But you'll have to walk...."

"I'll manage," he repeated.

"I can give you a ride in the morning. You can sleep on the couch—"

"No."

"I'll give you a pillow and blanket."

"I don't want a pillow and blanket."

She looked up at him then, eyes slightly hazy, but guileless. "Don't you?"

They were standing too close. She leaned against the wall next to the door, head tipped back. He was angled to face her, one shoulder still propping open the screen door. He saw her hand moving, saw the touch coming, and did nothing to avoid it. Stood there and let her fingertips float over the stubble at the turn of his jaw, tracing his old scar. Stood there and let her voice seep into his blood.

"What do you want, Luke?" she asked, not meaning it the way his body took it. Not meaning it that way at all.

And then he wasn't just standing there any more. The door was banging shut because he'd jerked his shoulder away, because he was surrounding her where she stood against the wall. He dropped his mouth onto hers and answered a question she hadn't meant.

Her lips were hell on discipline. Her softness pressing against him blasted pride to kingdom come.

She lit up like the northern lights. Shimmery and mysterious. Ever-changing, and with a faint, stirring sound that seemed to come from all of her, not just her throat.

He touched his palm to her throat to feel that sound as well as hear it. Traced it down, the vibration stronger at the notched hollow at its base.

And lower. Slipping beneath the soft fabric of her blouse to the indefinable softness of her skin. The first, easy swell of her breast, the thin barrier of her bra. Sweeping his hand down, his fingers stretched, brushing across a tip he could feel tightening. He shifted, so that point pressed hotly against his palm.

Her tongue met his, more than accepting the thrusts, greeting them, meeting *him*. His left leg rocked high between her thighs. It would be soft there, too. Where his hand had held her when the truck nearly flipped. Soft and firm. Just like her mouth. Just like her breast.

Stroking, his fingers slipped under the looseness of her bra strap and found the sweet, sweet softness of her. Pushing away the material, brushing her nipple with his thumb, cupping her and drawing her free. He circled the hardening flesh with his thumb, felt her hands clutch, one against his back, the other at his shoulder. That wasn't enough.

He left her mouth with regret, then wiped away the regret with the sweetness of the pebbled nub. Circling now with his tongue. Feeling the pleasure jab at his groin, as they rocked against each other, increasing the ache they longed to ease. Until the pleasure was too fierce, too close.

He brought his mouth back to hers, thrusting his tongue deep into the warmth, accompanying it with a strong, slow rock of the hardness at the juncture of his legs against the softness at hers. Feeling the dampness of her nipple pushing against his bare chest—his shirt was open, and he didn't even remember it happening—and hearing her groan.

If he took her now…laid her on the bed, himself beside her, over her, inside her…

And then?

And then.

She'd still be who she was, and he'd still be who he was.

He yanked away from her, hands holding her shoulders against the wall, elbows locked to keep himself from falling back against her or dragging her to him. You didn't take advantage of a woman who'd had too much to drink.

He got himself out to the top of the stairway, closing the doors firmly behind him, without another word. Because that was another rule—you didn't give women like Rebecca Dahlgren the soft words that might mislead them into thinking you were a man that you weren't.

Rebecca woke with a throbbing headache centered between her eyes and an unsettled queasiness low in her stomach.

A hangover. She wished with all her heart it was a hangover from alcohol. How easy that would be. How clear to treat. How quick to overcome.

Instead, she had a hangover from Luke Chandler. Not from having too much of him, but from wanting too much.

Wanting so much that she let herself forget her dignity, her reputation, her real reason for being here, even her self-preservation, and threw herself at the man.

She groaned. Following him into the Ranchers' Rest was forgivable. Even the conversation and the drinks there were understandable. But postponing the moment he would leave her by asking him to drive around, then *kissing* him...

She couldn't even claim she was drunk at that point. Unless it was drunk on him. He'd seemed so much a part of the sweet night breeze, the pine tang around them, the mysterious mountain behind them and the immutable land spread before them. Or maybe they had all seemed so much a part of him.

And she'd seen him so clearly in that moment. Seen that somehow he'd been deeply disappointed by his family. Seen that his attempts to deny his connections to Far Hills—the land and the people—were somehow connected to that disappointment.

She'd kissed him.

And when his movement had brought their lips together she had practically begged for more. He'd stopped, not her.

It was even worse at her apartment.

Lying in bed last night for long hours, tossing from one unsatisfying position to another, she'd replayed each word, and she'd felt mortification flush up from her toes to her forehead at how her words must have sounded to him.

I'll give you a pillow and blanket.

I don't want a pillow and blanket.

What do you want, Luke?

She squeezed her eyes shut now against the memory. She would swear her conscious mind hadn't ordered those words, hadn't meant them the way he must have taken them. But her subconscious...?

If he hadn't stopped, she might have woken up with entirely different aches this morning.

No, face facts. If he hadn't stopped, there was no *might* about it. She would have made love with him.

Was this what it felt like when your emotions got out of control?

Her gaze went to the photograph of her mother. It looked as if that part of the photo had been exposed to too much light or had faded away over the years. But it had been the original that had been fading away. Already a ghost before she died.

Rebecca would never become her mother.

And if that meant keeping her distance from Luke, then she would. She would write a note to express her appreciation of his gallantry—not using that word, of course, because Luke would scoff at the notion—and then she would do her best not to allow herself into any situation where her subconscious might start wanting Luke Chandler to make her feel.

Chapter Ten

Luke eased his new pickup into the left lane of the inter-state to pass a lumbering flatbed truck. Well clear of that vehicle, he eased the pickup back to the right lane.

That's when his gaze caught on the tops of two heads close together in the backseat.

He hadn't been particularly surprised when Marti'd said that instead of flying from Sheridan, she wanted him to drive her to Denver to catch a plane to Los Angeles, where she would then connect for the long flight to China. And taking Emily along made sense, so mother and daughter could spend time together before she left.

What made no sense was the other passenger. The one seated on the far side of the front seat—Rebecca.

Only as they turned out of Far Hills Ranch onto the high-way had Marti made the announcement—in the blandest of tones—that they needed to pick up Rebecca. She'd rolled right along with the explanation that she'd figured he might need a hand with Emily on the long drive back, not to mention some company.

He'd snorted at that, since Rebecca had done her level best the past week to be as far from his company as possible.

Oh, he'd received a note, no doubt written with that golden pen he'd seen

> Luke,
> I know you find apologies unacceptable, even when they are warranted, but I hope you will accept my sincere thanks for your consideration.
>   Rebecca L. Dahlgren

Consideration? For not putting her down on that bed and himself between her legs? She sent a damn thank-you note for that? He didn't think so.

She was letting him know that she recognized she'd had a narrow escape, and it wasn't going to happen again.

Hell, that's how he'd wanted things from the start. He wanted nothing to do with her rules and responsibilities and fussing about the good opinion of others. He might wish she'd seen it earlier, before he knew the taste and the feel of her, but it was still a good thing she'd finally realized it, too. A damned good thing.

Of course, she could have been a little more subtle. It wasn't that he wanted more than a polite *How're you doing, today,* now and then. Instead, she'd skedaddled like a prairie dog spotting a coyote the couple times he'd caught sight of her.

So the idea of her being good company for the drive back from Denver was laughable.

All he'd said was, "Why not Ellyn or Kendra?"

"They have their own families to tend to."

"Does she know I'm driving?" he'd asked, as if it were his ability behind the wheel Rebecca might object to.

"Oh, yes, she knows," Marti had said breezily.

Marti had continued to be annoyingly breezy as they'd loaded Rebecca's small bag into the storage box and Rebecca herself into the front seat. She'd balked, then Marti'd said she wanted to sit by Emily in back, and that was that.

Marti's voice broke into his ruminations.

"Luke, we'd better find a place to stop to take a break."

He met Marti's eyes in the rearview mirror and she tipped her head slightly to indicate Emily.

"Marti, we're not even to Casper. If we stop this often along the way, we won't be there till midnight."

"That's why we're driving down a day ahead."

"Don't know why you couldn't have flown, anyhow," he grumbled.

"We've been through that—I want to spend this time with Emily. It's important."

He muttered a curse; Marti either didn't hear it or decided to let it go this time. The next opportunity, he exited from the interstate and pulled into a service station.

"Might as well fill up as long as we're here," he grumbled, as Marti unhooked Emily and headed off to the ladies' room.

As Luke took the printed receipt from the machine, Rebecca popped out of the passenger door, and glared at him across the width of the truck bed.

"You can just quit blaming me for this awkward situation, Luke Chandler."

"Didn't say a word."

"As if you needed to! Everybody talks about how you don't say much, but you get your point across just fine." It didn't sound like a compliment. "I want it real clear that this wasn't my idea. It wasn't my idea to come."

"Didn't say it was."

"You didn't have to say it. You *never* have to say. I can

see it, even with that wretched hat on. Anybody with two eyes and half a brain can see it.''

The woman didn't know dangerous from a donut. She might be thinking now that she'd dodged a bullet when he'd walked away from her bed and her willingness that early morning last week, but she was walking a hell of a lot closer to the edge now. No woman from back East with enough rules to measure from here to China and back, was going to start talking about his hat.

''What,'' he said in a tone that could stop stampeding cattle, ''about my hat?''

It didn't stop her.

''It hides your eyes—as if you didn't know it. As if that wasn't why you wore it all the time, like a shield. Leaving—''

''It's no damned—''

''—it on—''

''*Shield!*''

''—in the car and—''

''Truck—it's a truck.''

Her face intent, she waved away both his protests with one distracted hand. ''But you've been coming through loud and clear, Luke, never fear. You don't need words and I don't need to see your face to know you didn't want me along on this trip. And all I'm saying is, I didn't want to come, either.''

He could believe that. But believing it and conceding it had a good stretch of country between them.

''You're here.''

She pulled her bottom lip in, her top teeth just visible. How would it feel if those teeth tugged at *his* lip. Or maybe his ear. Nibbled across his—

''I'm here because Marti asked me to come along.''

Jerked away from his other thoughts, he was testy. ''You ever heard of *no?*''

She flushed, quick and painful to watch. She'd clearly thought he'd been referring to last week.

"Marti's a client." Any inclination to clear up Rebecca's misunderstanding, to erase her embarrassment, vanished at her words, stiff with being spoken through firm lips over a raised chin. "I know you think it beneath you to consider how other people view you, I prefer to remain on good terms with my clients. So when Marti said she hoped I would be free to take this trip, I didn't feel I was in a position to say no, especially since—"

That bottom lip disappeared again. This time, his libido unloaded both barrels at him—the image of her teeth on his flesh combined with the memory of the taste and feel of her bottom lip when he'd toyed with it, kissing and sucking, and—

"Especially since what?" He cleared his throat.

She shot him a snooty look. She didn't want to answer. But she didn't back down. At least not with him.

"Especially since she'd already ascertained from Vince that I didn't have pressing obligations for the period of time encompassed by this trip."

He rested one forearm on the roof of the truck and his opposite foot on the frame of the door. "She ascertained that, did she?"

"Yes."

"Guess the only thing to do is make the best of a bad situation, then."

"Yes." The angle of her chin upped another degree.

For some reason, his mood took a definite turn for the better. "Just remember…"

She took the bait he dangled. "What?"

"I'll stop for Emily, I'm not stopping for you—since I know you wouldn't want Marti to think poorly of you by holding us up."

"How considerate."

"Yeah, it is." He patted his open palm on the truck roof. Waiting until she'd started to head the direction Marti and Emily had taken to add, "And one more thing."

"Yes?"

"Don't crowd me."

Just before he ducked his head into the truck, he had the satisfaction of seeing her coolness crack into a glare.

"Well, this has been a real pleasant way to start this trip to China."

Rebecca searched Marti's face for a sign of sarcasm. There'd been none in her voice.

The best Rebecca could say for the past twenty-four hours of driving to Denver, a restaurant dinner for the four of them (with only two talking), a night in a motel not far from the airport (Marti and Emily in one room, her and Luke each in separate rooms), this morning's breakfast (a repeat of dinner) and the trip to the airport was that there had been no more harsh words. There had been few words of any description between her and Luke.

"Now, Emily, how'd you like to go for a walk with Luke? Mama wants to talk to Rebecca, okay?"

"Okay," the girl agreed readily, smiling up at the man propped against the waiting-room wall near their seats. "C'mon, Luke."

His eyes narrowed—in suspicion at Marti?—before he put out his hand, and Emily took it immediately.

Rebecca felt as if that strong grasp squeezed her heart, and not nearly as gently as he treated Emily's hand. It had nothing to do with the reality of the man. It was simply a conditioned, emotional response to the image of a rough male being tender to a small child. It was exactly like tearing up at a greeting-card commercial.

Beside her, Marti sighed.

"She's going to have some real adjusting to do when I bring the baby home."

It was the first worry of any sort Rebecca had heard Marti express. "I'm sure everyone has doubts..."

"Oh, this isn't doubt. It's reality. Emily's used to being the center of my universe, and close to that with Luke. She's going to have some adjusting to do, that's all. It's natural." She chuckled. "'Course, natural isn't always easy."

The memory of the little girl's hand holding up Rebecca's hair to show that someone else had hair like her own flashed into Rebecca's mind. Just as Rebecca had when she was a child, Emily faced the growing recognition that she looked different from her family, and that definitely wasn't easy.

Marti turned and placed a hand on Rebecca's arm.

"That's why I wanted to talk to you."

"Me?" About looking different from those around her, and how that felt when the realization spread across a child's mind? No. Those had been her own thoughts, not Marti's meaning.

"Yes, I'm hoping you'll help Luke while I'm gone. He'd never admit it but he's worried about taking care of Emily on his own. It'll be good for him, but he's going to need help."

Rebecca stiffened. Did Marti have some reason to think Rebecca would be spending time with Luke on any basis other than professional? Had she heard something? Had he—?

"Kendra and Ellyn will be there for him and Emily, but with you on the scene, so to speak, starting on the computer system, I thought I'd mention it to you, too."

Well, that should teach her to read something personal into Marti's comments. Here she had the opening she'd been waiting for. The moment to bring up her need for access to the records while Marti was gone. Instead, she was getting all tied up in knots about what Marti knew, or what she thought she knew.

"I'd be happy to do what I can. Although I suspect that will be very little. Emily's such a sweet girl and I see…" *some of myself in her.* No, she wasn't going to reveal that bit of personal history. She should get back to the topic of her work.

She opened her mouth to do just that, but what came out was, "What do you tell Emily?"

"About what?"

"I'm sorry. I shouldn't have asked."

"How 'bout letting me decide after I hear the question." Marti smiled. "Tell Emily about just having a mom and not a dad? About being adopted? About her biological parents? There're a lot of things I could be telling Emily about that might interest you, give me a clue, Rebecca."

Rebecca couldn't stop an answering smile, though it faded quickly. "I guess all of those, but mostly I was thinking about what you tell her about…what she sees in the mirror…dark hair, dark eyes, different features."

"I tell her they're beautiful. But that she has a responsibility to fuel that beauty from inside."

"That won't be what people see when they look at her. They'll see that she's different." Bitterness—her words were flavored with it, tasted of it. Where had all this come from?

"I hope I've been teaching her—and keep teaching her that it doesn't matter what people see."

"That's a wonderful ideal, and within the protective cocoon of Far Hills Ranch, that's probably true. The outside world isn't that easy. Once she's grown…"

Marti shook her head. "It's still not what other people see or even what she sees in the mirror that matters. None of that is what makes her the person she is. That depends

PATRICIA McLINN 153

on what she sees when she looks *out* at the world, not what the world sees when it looks in.''

It was a nice philosophy, and maybe it even worked for someone living in Wyoming, where there weren't all that many people looking in in the first place. Especially for a woman who knew who she was and where she came from. But in the world Rebecca had lived in before falling down the rabbit hole that had brought her to be sitting in the Denver airport talking to Marti this way, what people thought of you defined you. And changing that definition took constant, careful attention to what you said and what you did. That was something her grandmother had made clear from her earliest days.

"Mama! Mama, Luke said he'd get me a hot pretzel if you say okay."

Emily dashed up to Marti, with Luke following.

"Unless this walk's been long enough," he said.

"No, that's okay. You can get her a pretzel, Luke. Emily, remember to say thank you."

"Thank you, Luke."

"Not 'til I give it to you, Em. Don't give out your thank-yous until your chicken's hatched."

"Huh?" But the little girl didn't wait for explanations. She took Luke's big hand in both of hers and tugged toward the corridor. "This way, remember?"

"I remember." Emily said something else to him they couldn't hear, and he looked down at her and smiled.

Rebecca's conditioned response formed another lump in her throat. She was going to swear off greeting-card ads.

"That man should have children of his own. Should have a ranch of his own, too, the damn stubborn fool. And—" From a mutter, Marti's voice shifted to one hundred percent determined. "He should have a good woman he loves to desperation, and who returns the favor."

Marti fixed her eyes on Rebecca.

Rebecca tried a chuckle. It sounded deformed. "Luke wouldn't agree. He likes his life the way it is—solo."

Marti's wave dismissed Luke's right to run his own life. "He's a fool. Man like that needs love in his life. Needs a woman by his side. Just like you need a man to love you and be by your side."

This shift to a frontal attack caught Rebecca by surprise, and she spoke before her mind caught up. "I'd have thought you'd be the last one to say that, Marti. You've done just fine without a man by your side."

If biting her tongue could have pulled the words back, Rebecca would have bitten hard enough to risk stitches. But, rather than either the righteous indignation her comment deserved, or the shuttered look of someone who'd had a sore point probed, Marti's face displayed an unmistakable blush.

"I *have* done just fine. That doesn't mean that I don't see that being in love and being loved back could make things even better. Until death do us part has a nice ring to it."

"That sort of love doesn't exist."

Rebecca felt a bit like a lab specimen that had caught the scientist's full attention as Marti asked, "How about your mother and father?"

No amusement softened Rebecca's dry laugh. "Your example proves my point."

"There must have been something between them or they—"

"Or they wouldn't have conceived me? Hardly. It doesn't take many courses on human sexuality to realize that. My mother almost certainly would have said she loved him, right up to the end. And look what it got her—a lover who deserted her when she was pregnant, an ignominious return to her family, and then a slide into the bottle. If that's what love does, no thank you."

Marti's silence at the end of this diatribe made Rebecca acutely aware of how shrill she'd sounded.

"I didn't mean to burden you, Marti, with—"

Marti waved off the stumbling words. "Let me get this straight, you think your parents had a sort of fling, and as soon as your father found out your mother was pregnant, he walked out?"

"I shouldn't have —"

"No time for that now. My flight's going to be called soon. We don't have much time. Yes or no?"

The other woman's urgency took her aback, but Rebecca had no hesitation in saying, "Yes."

Marti gave one gusty sigh, then began quickly shuffling the large envelopes in her lap. "This changes things. I'd intended to simply start you off with the journal until I returned, but—" Marti broke off to listen to the first announcement of her flight boarding. She looked around. "There isn't any more time."

"I don't—"

"Hush, and listen. You're going to have to adjust your thinking. The timeline and who did what and—there they are."

Rebecca followed her gaze to where Luke was striding toward them holding Emily, one of her arms hooked around his neck. Her smile widened as she spotted Marti.

"I'm going to spend this last little time with Emily. You take these, and look through them." She put the envelopes into Rebecca's hands, which automatically closed around them. "They should explain most of it, and when I get back, we'll have a nice long talk."

"Mama! I ate the whole thing. It was sooooo good."

Marti held out her arms and Emily went into them. Mother and daughter moved a few steps away, their intimacy, connection and love creating a zone of privacy amid the hubbub.

All passengers were ordered to board the flight, and Marti, with tears in her eyes but a determinedly cheerful voice, told

Emily goodbye and that she loved her. As Marti handed over her ticket, then headed out of sight down the gangway, Rebecca felt Emily's small hand grasp hers.

She looked down in surprise to see the little girl waving with her other hand and smiling as she called "Bye-bye, Mama," even though her mother was out of sight. Rebecca's gaze snagged on Luke, standing just beyond Emily.

He was glaring.

If he were anyone else she might have thought he was jealous that the little girl who knew him so much better had taken her hand at this emotional moment. She dismissed that thought before it even fully formed. So what was his problem?

"Let's go," he growled. "We've got a long drive back."

"Not yet." She tightened her hold on Emily's hand. "We should let Emily watch the plane take off."

Not waiting for an answer, she led the child to the wall of windows.

Crouching to Emily's level, Rebecca listened to the girl prattle on about the planes, the sky, the pretzel Luke had bought her and how Matthew didn't get to eat a pretzel or come to an airport.

"See that, Emily? The plane's starting to back away now. Your Mama's on her way."

"Mama?" the girl repeated with a frown, her gaze focusing on the slowly moving plane before them. "Noooooooo," she said on a soft, drawn-out breath.

Rebecca saw the instant that Emily made the full connection between the huge plane easing away from the terminal and the disappearance of her mother down the gangway. Before that, Marti had simply walked down a hallway. Now the little girl, who had never seen a big airplane before, recognized that Marti was in that *thing* and that as it moved away, it was taking her mother.

"Mama!" she wailed. She pressed her palms against the

window as if she could reach out and draw Marti back. Then she erupted in howls that should have shattered the glass.

Sympathy and horror welled in Rebecca, with guilt for triggering this response running a close third.

She tried to draw Emily into her arms. The five-year-old stiff-armed her with no abate to the volume of her cries. Rebecca could only pat her on the back.

A glance over her shoulder confirmed that everyone was staring at the scene, and most of the stares were decidedly annoyed.

"Shh, Emily. Hush," Rebecca urged. "Don't cry. Your Mama's coming back. She won't be happy if she heard you were crying."

"Don't tell her that."

Luke's growled order would have suited a grizzly bear. Emily turned to it like a choir of angels, throwing herself against his legs. He picked her up and held her. She wrapped her arms around his neck and rested her cheek against his shoulder, sobbing noisily.

Without even looking at Rebecca, he turned and started down the long corridor toward the exit.

She felt like part of an unwelcome parade as other pedestrians in the concourse backed away from them. As tempted as she was to leave a gap between herself and Luke and his high-volume passenger, she matched her pace to Luke's long but seemingly unhurried strides. Her cheeks felt prickly with the heat of embarrassment at the stares they drew.

They had nearly reached the point where the string of gates joined the core that housed ticket-counters and baggage claim areas, when a cultured voice sliced through Emily's sobs.

"Rebecca? Rebecca Dahlgren."

For one weak second, Rebecca closed her eyes against reality. Where was a good, wide, deep sinkhole when you desperately needed it? The next second she opened her eyes and faced Claudia Bretton-Smith, her grandmother's bitterest rival, and closest ally against people who were not "one of us."

"Hello, Claudia. How are you?"

"Terrible, I had a dreadful flight from San Francisco— you would think first class would mean something. And then, to make me stop here and change planes— The chairman of the board is going to hear about this."

If the voice alone had not been sufficient to pitch Rebecca back into her life in Delaware, the timbre of disapproval certainly did the trick.

"But you—I hardly recognized you in that—" Claudia's hesitation dripped of disapproval "—wardrobe."

The woman offered one perfectly rouged and powdered cheek, and Rebecca dutifully air-kissed it, careful not to make any contact with the designer suit that might muss it. She'd been accused more than once as a child of committing that sin.

Claudia Bretton-Smith was thin. And with her ardently red hair, and overly pale complexion, she created a memorable figure. "Worse than a scarecrow," Antonia had once said after Claudia scored a coup over her in their social wars.

"This wardrobe suits my work needs here," Rebecca said mildly.

"Oh, my dear, I should hope not. It is suited only to manual labor." She couldn't have sounded more appalled if she'd substituted *prostitution* for *manual labor*.

Rebecca gave up that unwinnable fight.

"Claudia, may I introduce Luke Chandler and his charge, Emily Susland. Luke, this is Mrs. Bretton-Smith," Before Luke could say anything—from Claudia's cold head-to-toe assessment of him she made it clear *she* was not going to say anything—Rebecca added quickly. "We have been seeing Emily's mother off on a trip. Marti Susland and Luke are clients of mine."

Claudia didn't so much as flick a glance toward the distraught child, but her attitude toward Luke shifted. "I see. So, you are with the historical site commission, Mr., uh, Chandler?"

Historical preservation was the currency of the prime rivalry between Claudia and Antonia, and Rebecca wanted it clear that neither Luke nor Emily were potential chits in that game.

"No," Rebecca interceded. "This is an entirely separate contract—with an extensive cattle ranch in Wyoming."

"Ah, you own a cattle ranch."

This time, Rebecca heard both speculation of wealth and the willingness to forgive as eccentric the attire the woman's cold looks to that point had found reprehensible.

"Claudia, if you have a flight to catch—"

"Then perhaps you know—"

"Foreman, not owner." Luke's blunt words topped all others.

Claudia underwent an instant reversion—jettisoning *eccentric* to snatch up *reprehensible* again.

Damn. If only Luke had been quiet, she might have been able to make Claudia Bretton-Smith see…

Impossible. All of it. Luke would never adjust himself an inch to affect what Claudia Bretton-Smith thought. Claudia would never understand or accept Luke Chandler, never mind by way of a hurried explanation in the middle of an airport with Emily howling. And Claudia would never, *never* pass up the opportunity to score points off Antonia by describing this scene to her.

"I see. I should hope, Rebecca, that your dealings are with the owner of this ranching establishment. And I see no need for you to dress like this—this hired hand."

"Luke is not a hired hand—"

"Sure I am." And didn't care what Claudia Bretton-Smith thought of that. "And I need to get back, get Emily home and do my work. Good day, Ma'am."

Rebecca was held suspended between the man striding easily away with the still-sobbing child and the woman whose face had settled into lines of cold disapproval.

"Really, Rebecca, I would have thought better of you. And what Antonia would say about an appearance that I could only call inappropriate is something about which I am unprepared even to hazard a guess. I can venture that she would say, as I do, that your current company is entirely unacceptable."

"*Unacceptable!* You have no right to—you know nothing about—you can criticize my clothes, but... No! No, you can't do that, either, because you don't know anything about it. You don't know anything about *anything*."

"You—Rebecca Dahl—"

"I have to go. I hope you have a good flight, Claudia," Rebecca lied, with another air kiss toward the woman's cheek. "Give my best to everyone back—" *home* wouldn't pass her lips "—in Delaware. Got to run now."

Not waiting for Claudia's response, Rebecca made that *run* a near reality. Even so, she didn't catch up to Luke until they'd nearly reached the pickup. Emily's sobs had downshifted to intermittent, interspersed with hiccuping breaths and spells of rubbing her eyes with her fist.

With no conversation, Luke buckled Emily into her seat in back, and got behind the steering wheel. Rebecca climbed into the front passenger seat, surprised to find the forgotten manila envelopes still in her hands.

As they started their return to Far Hills, she stared at the envelopes without making any move to open them. It seemed a long, long time ago that Marti had handed them to her.

She replayed the past hour over and over—her strange conversation with Marti, Marti's departure, Emily holding her hand and Luke's fierce expression, Emily's outburst, her futile efforts to quiet it, Luke's response, the meeting with Claudia Bretton-Smith. Her own eruption.

They were nearly to the Wyoming border when she burst out, "All right! I was wrong about having Emily watch the plane take off."

"Hmphf."

She translated that grunt with little difficulty as *Damn right, you were wrong.*

"But you were terrible with Claudia. You did your best to make it sound like you're no more than a hired hand."

"I am."

"Bull—" Rebecca bit off the word with a glance to the backseat. Emily, exhausted by her tears, was asleep. Rebecca still lowered her voice. "Even I know enough to see Far Hills couldn't run without you—not the way it runs now."

"Even if that's true, you think anything I'd have said would make it matter to that friend of yours?"

"She's not my friend."

He ignored that. "Honey," he started in his most exaggerated drawl, "if I'd been a horse at auction, she had me headed for the glue factory from the second she clapped eyes on me."

"She was awful. She always has been. But you could have *tried* to win her over, instead of making it so clear you didn't care what she thought of you."

"I don't."

"No, of course not. The great Luke Chandler doesn't care what *anyone* thinks of him. Why should you? You don't need anyone, you don't want anyone's good opinion. Your own good opinion of yourself is enough for you!"

"That's the only one I got to live with."

There was something in that sentence—maybe not the

words, but the tone—that gave Rebecca the unshakable feeling that she was hearing only the tip of an iceberg that rested—hard, cold, immense and dangerous—under his surface. Her irritation evaporated as she groped to understand what was behind his words.

"If you only have your own good opinion, you're going to have a very solitary life."

"Better solitary than let a pack of other people's opinions run your life, so you forget to do what's right."

"Surely there's some middle ground between solitary and right?"

"Yeah? Have you found it?"

It was a definite jab, and she felt it, because she'd spent her whole life seeking the good opinion of other people, yet she'd lived a mostly solitary life.

At the same time, the sharpness in his tone had given her another glimpse of his iceberg. It also warned her to steer clear of it. She'd already gone a hard round with Claudia. She was definitely not prepared for an even harder one with Luke.

"You want me to drive for a while?"

He flicked a look toward her, perhaps surprised at her change of subject.

"No need."

"Luke, there's no sense in you driving all the way back."

He shrugged. "I did all the way down."

"That was because Marti wanted to concentrate on Emily, and I—" No, she wasn't going into that.

"Maybe later."

"But—"

"I'm hungry."

Luke lifted his head to check the backseat in his rearview mirror. "Hey, there, Sleeping Beauty."

Instead of the little girl's usual giggles at Luke's comments, a sniffle was his answer. Rebecca turned around warily.

"I'm hungry *and* I have to go to the bathroom," the child said with decision.

"Talk about a double threat," Luke muttered, and Rebecca had to stifle a chuckle. "Okay, Em, we'll get off at the next exit."

Rebecca knew a moment of panic when she was designated to take Emily to the chain restaurant's bathroom, but the little girl marched into a cubicle on her own and asked for no help. She even washed her hands without prodding.

Emily was subdued as she ate half her burger, which left Luke to polish off the other half in addition to his own. She brightened some when Luke let her order a butterscotch sundae for dessert. She couldn't finish that, either, and again Luke stepped in.

"Now I see why you let her get dessert even after she didn't finish lunch," Rebecca said as they headed out to the truck.

His mouth twitched. "Never thought that no-dessert rule made any sense—sure never made me eat anything I didn't want."

"Not all children are as stubborn as you are."

He slanted her a look. "I prefer strong-minded."

She snorted her opinion of that.

The silence as they continued north had a different quality now. At first Emily chatted to them, then hummed and sang to herself. After a stretch of silence, Rebecca turned around to see the child sleeping again.

To her surprise, she dozed, too, lulled by the rhythm. She woke when the movement of the truck changed, realizing Luke was pulling in to a gas station and the sun was nearly gone.

She stretched hard. Luke glanced toward her.

"You up for driving some?"

"Sure."

"Or…"

"Or what?"

"It's been a long day, and it'll be late before we get in. If you're beat, we could stop overnight."

Bells went off in her head—the scary part was they were not alarm bells.

Stop overnight. Her and Luke. In a hotel. No one would know…except her and him and a five-year-old.

"Oh, let's push on. I have so much to do tomorrow."

"Sure." He got out to fill the gas tank.

He sounded as if it didn't matter one way or the other to him.

She got out quickly, nearly forgetting—again—the elevation of the truck's seat. She drew in the cooling air and stretched more in preparation for her stint behind the wheel.

"Should we wake Emily? Give her some dinner now?"

"You ever hear the expression about letting sleeping kids lie? She'll let us know when she's hungry. In no uncertain terms."

"That's dogs—let sleeping dogs lie."

"They only used that because they hadn't heard Em in full howl."

They exchanged a smile over the truck bed as she came around to the driver's side. Who would have thought she would find any aspect of that fiasco to smile over—ever, much less so soon?

"It *was* incredible, wasn't it?

"You should have heard it right next to your ear."

She concentrated on driving the truck—so much larger than she was used to—as they got back on the road.

"What's this?" Luke's longer legs had found the envelopes she'd stowed on the floor.

"Some reading material Marti gave me. I think it's on the ranch's history. I meant to read while it was light, but…"

"You were too busy being irked at me."

"Exactly."

She caught the grin curving his lips before he pulled his hat down over his face.

Dark was coming fast as a line of clouds blotted out the last sunlight. But the road was easy, wide and nearly empty.

Luke slept for only a half hour. He didn't change his position, so she wasn't sure how she knew he was awake, but she did.

An hour ago, driving through, not stopping overnight had seemed the so-much-wiser course. She hadn't banked on the surprising intimacy of the growing darkness and stillness surrounding them, the child sleeping in back, the man beside her.

"So, tell me about yourself, Luke."

"What's to tell you haven't already asked?" He tipped his hat back and sat up. "I'll ask. Have you ever left home?"

"Of course. I went to college in another state and I lived on campus." Concessions won after long and careful campaigns.

"And after?"

"I have a set of rooms in Dahlgren House. Over the generations, many Dahlgrens have done that."

"Dahlgren House, huh?" Before she could defend that seat of the Dahlgrens, he was saying, "That's what you'd planned to do when you left college? Go back and live in your old room?"

"Oh, I had some thoughts of an apartment with college friends in New York, but Grandmother is getting older, though she would never admit it, and she's all I have." She gave a rueful laugh. "Besides, you know what it's like when you go home after you've been away, and your family starts working on you...."

There was a quality to Luke's silence that made her ask, "I know you've been on your own, but you go see your family now and then, don't you?"

"No. Left to start college and haven't been back since."

"Your family didn't... You worked your way through college?"

"Yeah. Took five and a half years. Bet you went through like clockwork, four years right on schedule. So you could go right back to being under your grandmother's—"

Thumb, her mind filled in.

"—wing."

He'd tricked her into that thought. Hadn't he?

"You're no different, Luke. Why'd you come back to Far Hills if it wasn't to get back under someone's wing?"

"A job. I can leave any time."

"Right." She gave it full force of sarcasm with no apparent effect on him. "Like you haven't settled right back where you were as a kid, just like I did."

"So you *are* still living at home."

"No," she said with precision, "I am living three-quarters of a continent away. And renting an apartment from Helen Solsong."

"Same difference."

"They're nothing alike."

"I meant living under somebody's wing."

"Oh. Of course. You know, I think it's time to stop for dinner."

"Okay. You hungry, Em?"

"Yeah."

Surprised, Rebecca looked in the rearview mirror, and saw the girl was wide awake. How long had she been listening? How long had Luke known she was awake? Why hadn't he let her know Emily was listening? And what made her think she'd ever understand why he did what he did?

* * *

Rebecca finished her survey of the offerings along the back wall of the Far Hills Market, turned to her left to start up the outside aisle and came face to face with Luke.

I'm not ready, she thought.

Will I ever be?

It didn't matter, she supposed, because he was right here in front of her blocking her path, not thirty hours after he'd dropped her off.

Not thirty hours after she'd taken her overnight bag from him and started to climb the stairs, only to turn and watch the truck back out of the driveway into the street, then drive away, leaving her with a totally unexpected sense of emptiness. She'd stood there holding her bag, until she realized she was shivering.

She'd told herself at least she'd have some time to get over this strange feeling, maybe even enough to figure it out, before she'd see Luke again.

Wrong.

She'd discovered her refrigerator—which only required a couple pieces of fruit, a hunk of cheese and some eggs to look full—was as bare as her cupboards. After a breakfast of three crackers, she decided to pick up groceries before heading to the historical site commission.

"'Morning, Rebecca." Luke's voice came deep and slow.

That's how the words would sound to a woman waking in his bed.

"You aren't supposed to be here. You should be at the ranch."

His brows raised. Before he could say anything—and Rebecca could only be grateful, because she immediately remembered him telling her he'd be bringing Emily in to the baby-sitting co-op each morning—another voice intruded.

"Luke Chandler, stay right there. I have something to say

to you." Fran Sinclair was barreling down the aisle toward them.

"I was just going," Rebecca said. "Excuse me, I'll…"

Not without his cooperation, she wouldn't. And his level stare declared he wasn't in a cooperating frame of mind. Rebecca couldn't get past him without nearly full-body contact. She wasn't going to risk that.

The older woman frowned at him. "Luke, you're embarrassing Rebecca. Let her pass, then I'll say my piece."

He didn't budge. "I got nothin' to hide. From anyone."

Fran huffed in exasperation. "You rub everybody's nose in that attitude of yours."

"I go my own way, not bothering anybody else. Like always."

"Not like always. Not while you're taking care of Emily. I promised Marti I'd keep an eye on things and I'm telling you that your life is going to have to change temporarily, if you're going to do right by Emily."

"I'm doing right by her."

"By your way of thinking, I don't doubt it for a second. But your way of thinking's not the only one that counts right now. You're going to have to make changes. For starters, where were you yesterday morning?"

"That's my business." For an instant Rebecca thought she saw a flash of the boy Fran had described when they'd all had lunch together, a boy who'd firmly shut his mouth against the medicine that could cure him.

"And I'm telling you it's not just your business anymore. Where were you?"

After a moment, he growled, "Same as every morning. Working."

Fran raised her arms then let them drop in exasperation. "That's just what I mean. That is *just* what I mean. Did you even know it was Sunday?"

"So?"

"So, Marti takes Emily to church and Sunday school on Sundays."

"Missing a couple won't kill her."

"No, but it gives people fuel for saying you're not a proper person to be caring for a little girl. And you should have known that there's folks in this town watching you like a hawk for a couple of reasons—" Fran's eyes flickered toward Rebecca, and she knew that if Emily was reason one, she was reason two. "There's already folks asking questions about you taking care of Emily. And not just fools and busy-bodies. Good, caring folks who don't know you from Adam, except for nods now and then, and rumors, because of course you've never taken the trouble to let folks get to know you."

"I don't—"

"Don't start with me, Luke. I know full well your theory on not caring what people think of you. But you're responsible now for more than you for the first time in your life."

A pain so raw and deep burst across Luke's eyes that Rebecca had to bite down on her lip to keep from crying out.

"You have a responsibility to Emily." Fran clearly had missed that flash of pain. "And I don't just mean feeding her and keeping her healthy. She's going to be unsettled with Marti gone, you know, and the more normal you keep things, the better."

"I…" He swallowed, and a muscle along his jaw jumped.

"You hadn't thought of that. Well, let me tell you, Luke, you're going to have to think of a whole raft of things you haven't come close to thinking about before, and you're go-ing to have to do it fast and do it right."

For the first time in her experience, Rebecca saw him both silent and apparently chastised. Fran's voice, still brisk and brooking no disagreement, was no longer scolding as she went on.

"If work keeps you from bringing Emily to church next week, call and I'll come get her. Or you can probably fix something with Kendra or Ellyn. Go on and get back to that work you're so loyal to. Just see that you get some rest. You look tired. And you, Rebecca—" Rebecca jumped as the formidable woman's attention fixed on her. "Stop by some time and I'll give you a cup of coffee to make up for being caught in this."

She turned and steamed off, with no hint of a doubt that her instructions would be followed.

Luke didn't move for several seconds, apparently watching Fran's departure. When he abruptly spun around toward Rebecca, they were face-to-face, not quite touching, but with the awareness that a deep breath, a shift of weight could change that. He stared down at her, his eyes turbulent.

"You got something to say, too?" he demanded.

"Have a nice day?" she offered lightly.

He made a sound low in his throat, almost a growl, but some of the darkness lifted from his eyes.

"See you, Rebecca."

And then he was gone.

Rebecca's shoulders dropped and her muscles loosened as her breathing gradually settled into its normal rhythm. At least she thought it was her normal rhythm. It seemed a long time since she'd been in that state called "normal."

Chapter Eleven

"Tell us the legend, Luke. Please?"

Meg Sinclair pinned her wide-eyed, hopeful, trusting gaze on the foreman that Saturday night. Rebecca wondered if he thought he had any chance of withstanding that look, especially combined with the ones from Meg's brother, Ben, as well as Matthew and Emily.

Not that she wasted any sympathy on Luke Chandler. He'd pulled his version of the guileless look and innocent request on her late yesterday afternoon when he'd come into the office with Emily.

They'd fallen into a pattern this week, with Rebecca working at Fort Big Horn in the mornings, then arriving at the ranch office. Each afternoon, Luke wandered in at some point to ask if Rebecca would mind keeping an eye on Emily for a bit while he did something or other that wasn't safe for her to be around.

Sometimes Emily colored, sometimes she cut out unseasonal snowflakes, other times she drew pictures. She chattered about the co-op, her friends and what they did. References to Marti were a continuing theme. Rebecca enjoyed the time with the little girl, even though it pushed her departure time so late that she hadn't done any library research all week.

Well, that wasn't the only reason she hadn't made it to the library. She'd been fascinated by the first item she'd pulled from the envelopes Marti gave her—a photocopy of the journal of Charles Susland's second wife, Annalee. Although the old-fashioned handwriting made it slow reading, the tales of the wealthy young woman from Cincinnati adjusting to a raw cattle ranch in Wyoming—as well as a husband who apparently had only rough edges—kept Rebecca reading late into the nights.

Still, she'd made progress with her quest because when she'd arrived at the ranch office Monday afternoon there had been three large cartons of old records stacked on the floor. Neither she nor Luke mentioned their sudden arrival.

Rebecca used the time Emily was with her to search those records. She'd spread out from names that indicated Indian heritage, yet still hadn't found anything hopeful when Luke came in close to suppertime Friday to retrieve Emily.

Luke's eyes flickered over the folders, but he didn't mention them. Instead, he'd brought up an entirely unexpected topic.

"Looks like the weather'll hold through tomorrow night."

"Oh?"

"Full moon, too. Good for a night ride and a campfire. Ever been?"

"To a campfire? I suppose so, I don't recall a specific—"

"You should come," he'd interrupted firmly. "It's a Far Hills tradition. We'll ride out before sunset. Have some supper, and sit around the fire awhile. Did it all the time as kids."

"Kendra and Daniel and Ellyn and Grif, they'll be coming?"

"No. They got plans to see a movie in Sheridan." He seemed a little sheepish. Did that mean the two of them alone...? "Suppose you'd rather see a movie."

She loved movies. Stacked up against this, though, there was no choice. A ride under a full moon, a campfire with the darkness holding them close....

"A night ride and a campfire sound better than a movie to me." But she had to know. "So who all would be going?"

"You and me, Emily, Meg, Ben, Matthew. Payback for Kendra and Ellyn for their help this week."

And that's when she'd seen that he was recruiting her as another baby-sitter.

Not that she minded. This was better. Much, much better. She liked the kids, and having them around eased that fluttering panic she'd felt when she'd thought he was asking just her. Yes, panic was what she'd felt.

In fact, with the kids on hand now she even felt comfortable enough to widen her eyes at him in the firelight and say, "Yes, Luke. Tell us the legend."

Night before last, she'd read Annalee's account of the tale she'd first heard from Evvie Richards—Leaping Star asking for Charles's help, his refusal and her response. It was clear Annalee had believed wholeheartedly in the curse. It would be interesting to hear Luke's version.

"You all know it. I'm not going to—"

"Please, Luke," said Emily.

He sighed, but he also pushed his hat back, and began to tell the story of the Indian woman who'd given her heart to a hard man named Charles Susland.

In the firelight, Luke also looked to be a hard man, the flickering light removed what little softness his face had and left only the bedrock of bone structure. But as Grandmother said, little things give someone away. What gave Luke Chandler away were a thousand small indications of his caring—about the ranch, about his friends, about Marti, about Emily.

Later, as Luke carefully extinguished the fire and they prepared to head back, Rebecca was still thinking about the legend and tonight's teller of it. If Leaping Star had come to Luke…no, he would not have sent his family to a reservation in the first place, he would not have placed his ambitions above those he loved.

The moon was bright and the trail familiar and clear. They rode back at a careful walk. Luke had insisted Matthew ride with him and Emily with Rebecca. The fact that neither protested indicated how sleepy they were. The fact that a swell of warmth bloomed under Rebecca's ribs at that mark of Luke's trust in her riding indicated how sappy she'd become about his opinion. She knew she was a good rider. She didn't need his approval.

"Rebecca?" Emily's drowsy voice came softly out of the night, and Rebecca's momentary flare of belligerence went out like a kerosene lantern turned down.

"Hmm?"

"Will you be my aunt?"

"I…um, that's not how it works, sweetie. Aunts come with your family, you don't ask someone to be an aunt."

"Special families can be made special ways," the little girl argued, and Rebecca suspected she was hearing a quotation from Marti. "At first I just had Mama, and Matthew and Kendra were my cousins. And then Daniel came, so he's my cousin now, too. And Grif—he's a cousin. And since he married Ellyn, that adds Meg and Ben. I've got lots of cousins now." She sounded like a miser counting her gold. "Luke's sort of my uncle, only just us know that, so I don't call him uncle. Just Luke, but he still is."

If Rebecca didn't know better, she'd think those instructions might have come from someone who didn't want any adults to hear the child innocently call him uncle and misunderstand the situation.

"But I want an aunt," Emily was saying, her voice growing softer and slower.

"We'll talk with your Mom when she comes back, okay?"

No answer came. Sleep had won this discussion.

Chester's motion created a rhythmic rocking. Around them the night chorus sounded of crickets, a distant owl, the horses' hoofs and breathing, the stir of trees and bushes under the breeze. No human voices intruded on the chorus; in the darkness no sign of human effort showed itself.

If she'd had someone to lean against, Rebecca suspected she would have fallen asleep as peacefully as Emily.

An image of leaning back against Luke's broad chest, his arms wrapped around her, his thighs bracketing hers, his groin pressed against her derriere, flowed through her nerve endings like a charge of electricity.

They crested a hill then, and saw the lights and buildings of the home ranch. They were back to civilization, back to reality. And such notions were best left in the moonlit wildness of the open country.

Luke brought his horse next to hers as they entered the barn area. Matthew was turned partly sideways, leaning heavily against Luke's arm and clearly asleep.

"Stay put," Luke quietly ordered her. Meg and Ben were already leading their horses to where they could unsaddle them.

With impressive ease, Luke dismounted, still holding Matthew. He placed the boy atop a nearby bale of hay, then came around to her side.

In that instant, as he raised his arms to take Emily, still sleeping, from her, their eyes locked.

She felt as if she'd found a way to live two moments in

time at once. This one, and the moment in the Denver airport when Emily had taken her hand, and she'd looked up to see Luke glaring at them. Now she understood. He'd been fighting then what was happening now.

For, reflected in his eyes, she could see the picture they made. Her holding the dark-haired child who could be mistaken for her own. The child with a cheek pillowed against her breast, her arms softly guarding Emily's sleep. It was not only his vision that reflected to Rebecca, it was his reaction. The slow drop of his Adam's apple as he swallowed hard. The audible breath he pulled in. The tightening of the muscle along his jaw.

The gruffness of his voice finally broke the moment.

"I'll take her."

There was no way not to have contact as he reached for the sleeping child. His arm against her ribs, brushing slightly against her breast.

There was no way to stop her body from reacting. She could only fight to keep the reaction from overwhelming her mind, searching for something—anything—to keep mind and body occupied.

Luke had detailed Meg and Ben to care for the horses, and they clearly took that responsibility too seriously to let anyone else take part. So Rebecca settled on taking the leftover supplies from their hot-dog and marshmallow roast into the kitchen. While she put away food and washed up the few items that needed it, she caught faint sounds from the second floor, where Luke was putting Emily and Matthew to bed.

It was disturbingly cozy to hear those sounds and to imagine Luke Chandler playing the role of father.

She wiped hard at the counter.

"You keep rubbing that one spot and I'll be explaining to Marti why there's a gully in her counter."

Rebecca spun around to find Luke leaning against the doorjamb.

"I was…thinking."

"You didn't need to clean up." He crossed the room, and lifted the coffeepot with a quirk of questioning brows.

"Yes, thanks. I didn't mind cleaning up. Emily and Matthew are asleep?"

"Out like lights."

She took the coffee mug he offered and leaned back against the counter, at right angles to the position he took. "I noticed you didn't tell them about the rest of the legend out there."

He kept the mug at his mouth, raising his brows over the top.

"The part in Annalee's journal that says it has to be resolved in five generations. Or didn't you know?"

"Sure, I knew. I figure if you don't believe in it, why ruin a good story for some kids with an unhappy ending. If you buy the legend, it's out of their hands anyway. Meg and Ben aren't Suslands by name or blood, Emily's adopted and Matthew is sixth generation. Besides…"

"Besides what?"

His lips pressed together an instant before he answered with a lightness she didn't entirely believe. "Marti's got this theory that there's only a third of the curse left to wipe out. She figures Daniel coming to find Kendra and their son, and all the work he's done for kids, offsets old Charles deserting his and Leaping Star's kids. Then Marti would tell you Grif coming back to Far Hills, making a life with Ellyn and the kids, and sticking around to make sure the area does okay when the army base closes makes up for Charles turning his back on people who'd helped him."

"So that leaves the part about Charles turning his back on Leaping Star."

"Yep."

"But…are there other Suslands?"

"That's what I've been saying to Marti—there aren't any more. So even if there were a curse, the Suslands are stuck with it—at least a third of it."

Rebecca would hate to think of any of the Suslands cursed in any degree. With the feel of Emily's trusting warmth against her still fresh in her mind, Rebecca particularly rebelled against the idea of a curse looming over the child. She had enough to contend with. Some long-term, and some more immediate.

"Luke, what are you going to do about church tomorrow?" Rebecca asked abruptly.

"Haven't decided yet."

"Oh, Luke, you better—"

"You could take her."

"What?"

"You go to church, don't you?"

"Yes, but—"

"So, I could drop her off and pick her up when it's over."

"People might wonder… I mean—"

"What will people think." Despite the flatness of his tone she felt flame race up her neck and into her cheeks. "Hell, Rebecca, they'll probably think you're trying to butter me up so I'll tell Marti what a good job you're doing."

"I already have the job, so—"

He clunked his empty mug on the counter. "Then they'll think we're sleeping together."

Sensations—remembered and imagined—flooded her nervous system, swamping everything else. She knew that the image of sleeping with Luke was as clear on her face as the north star in the Wyoming night sky. The only solace was she could see the image in his eyes, too.

He turned away, putting his cup in the dishwasher.

"Never mind. Maybe Ellyn'll take her. I'll figure something."

He dropped the subject then—both the explicit one about Emily's churchgoing, and the one he'd raised with his comment about what people might be thinking.

Meg and Ben came in shortly after, and they set up a game of hearts until their mother and Grif came to get them just as Rebecca was leaving, so they wouldn't have been able to talk about it anyway.

Still, it irked her that he'd turned off the subject as easily as a spigot. Especially since it had haunted her every waking and sleeping minute.

Come Sunday morning, it still irked her enough that she should have reveled in his knuckling under to Fran's orders—at least to the extent of appearing in a crisp white shirt and creased jeans and sitting in the back pew at church with Emily beside him. Beneath the impassive veneer of his expression, Rebecca caught a hint of something she told herself was discomfort. Because if it was vulnerability, she wouldn't have been able to stop herself from going to him.

Maybe that explained what happened later.

Helen insisted on walking back with her to the house. Luke sat in his pickup, parked under a tree, obviously waiting to take Emily home after Sunday school. Helen started fussing in her usual way.

"...and all I can say is I can only believe it was the prayers of the righteous that kept the roof of our church from falling in when That Man walked in. Why, everyone knows he's *dated* enough women to form a harem, and as for him and Marti Su—"

"Oh, for heaven's sake, Helen! Did you listen to a word of what Reverend Mickel said about tolerance, about charity, about not judging others? A single word?"

Rebecca strode away with the woman spluttering behind her, and the smoke from a burning bridge smelling stronger every second.

*   *   *

The office door opening was a godsend. Rebecca had been dying to talk to someone about her morning discoveries in the journal of Annalee Susland.

Having it opened Tuesday afternoon by Luke was even better—because of his interest in the ranch's history, of course.

"Luke, this is so fascinating. The supplement to the *Banner* was interesting, but this... Marti wasn't able to use even a third of her research in the special section— What's wrong?"

"Just got a call from Fran."

"Fran? But—Emily—?"

"She's okay." He took his hat off, ran a hand through his hair as he seemed to consider his words. "She's not hurt. Fran said to get there right away. And plan on bringing Emily home."

"I don't understand. What—?"

"I don't know. I gotta go now."

"Luke, is there anything I can do?"

He stopped with his hand on the door. "Kendra and Ellyn are at work. If I have to talk to Fran, and Emily's upset..."

"Do you want me to come with you?"

"I know it bothers you how it might look to folks, but Emily..."

"Of course I'll come." She snagged her purse and stood. "Let's go."

He looked at her for another heartbeat then gave a curt nod. It warmed her the way no thank-you note ever had.

The drive to town was fast and silent.

As Luke pulled the truck under the shade of the big cottonwood near the street, Fran appeared at the basement door, holding Emily's hand.

"Stay here." Luke had the door open and one long leg out before he half turned and softened the order. "Okay?"

"Yes."

He started across the parking area. Emily broke away from Fran and ran to him. Luke's stride lengthened and in another two seconds, he'd scooped up the little girl whose sobs were audible to Rebecca. Not as loud as in the airport, still as heart-rending.

Luke glared at Fran, who looked grim.

"Get her settled in the truck, then come talk to me," she said.

Settling Emily was no small task. She didn't want to release Luke. She didn't want to be strapped into her car seat. She didn't want to be alone in the backseat. Finally, Rebecca moved into the backseat, holding the child in her lap.

If Fran had looked grim, Luke looked like a prime candidate for an executioner's job as he backed out of the truck to head for their meeting.

Impulsively, Rebecca reached out, resting her hand on his arm while she held Emily with the other arm and rocked her.

"Luke, listen to what Fran has to say. She's on your side—and Emily's."

He was lucky he had enough hide left to sit on the way Fran had blistered it.

On his side? He'd hate to meet Fran if she *wasn't* on his side. Fran on his side was even worse than Helen Solsong slithering over to his truck Sunday morning and blathering on about things that were none of her business.

"Luke?" Rebecca said softly as he turned the truck toward Far Hills Ranch.

"Later."

She glanced toward the backseat, then at him. "Okay."

Emily's eyes were still puffy, but her mood had improved by the time they got home. She went off to dig in her sandbox while he and Rebecca sat on the kitchen steps.

"I understand if you don't feel this is any of my business, Luke, so if you don't want to tell me—"

"I haven't been lectured to like that since I was eight years old."

"What did Fran lecture you about?"

"My language. Lifestyle. Attitude. You name it."

No matter how much you might want to, you can't go around this life pretending that what you do doesn't affect other people and vice versa, Luke Chandler. So get that ostrich head of yours out of the sand.

"But why? You've always been like this, haven't you?"

"You mean a bum who deserves that kind of lecture, so why'd Fran choose now?"

"You know I didn't mean that." That prim dignity of hers used to make him want to shake her. Sometimes it made him want to kiss her. Right now, for no logical reason, it eased some of the sting from Fran's words. "I'm just trying to make sense of this. And what it has to do with Emily and the baby-sitting co-op. While you were talking to Fran, Emily was crying about Jason's mommy saying she couldn't go back there."

He nodded. "Willa Arnold. One of Helen and Barb's satellites."

"Why would this woman not want Emily back there, and why on earth would Fran listen?"

"Fran says Em's been repeating things I say. Seems Jason took one of the more colorful ones home and used it on his mother."

"Oh, dear."

"Never thought that kid had the smarts to learn something like that, much less hit a bull's-eye in applying it to Willa."

"Luke," Rebecca admonished. "What are you going to do?"

"Do? Nothing." He'd decided that from the minute Fran started lighting in to him. "Keep Emily home. The boys'll have to pick up some of my work. It'll be okay as long as Marti's not gone too long. Maybe Ellyn and Kendra'll help.''

''The baby-sitting co-op—''

''That's up to Marti. She can beg to get back in if she wants. Not me.''

An apology might go a long way, Luke, Fran had said.

''I was going to say the co-op's been one piece of stability for Emily with her mother gone, one routine that hasn't changed. Besides, she has friends there, and she'll miss them.''

''She'll be fine here. It's just temporary.''

Unless Fran held good on her threat, which she usually did.

There's no way on earth you can make her stop imitating you, so change your ways for good or that child won't be coming back here, Luke.

She's Marti's kid, not mine. I'm not responsible for—

Oh, yes you are. You might think you're rolling through life with no attachments—you'd be a fool, but you might think that. But even a fool would have to see that other folks have gotten attached to him. And that means you can hurt them, whether you mean to or not.

''If there's anything I can do to—''

''No. Thanks. Nice of you to help today.'' The color in Rebecca's cheeks darkened and he wanted to brush the back of his fingers against the satin of her skin. Instead, he stood. ''I know you've got other work to do, and so do I.''

Even without looking at her directly, he caught the flicker across her face, as if she'd winced.

You can hurt them, whether you mean to or not.

This time he'd meant to. A little hurt now to prevent bigger hurt later. Like vaccination shots.

''Of course. I hadn't meant to hold you up.''

''No problem.''

She left in a hurry then. He didn't try to slow her down any, but he watched the trail of her little car until all the dust stirred by her passing had settled back to earth.

"Emily Susland!" he called. "We need to get some things straight, you and me."

Emily or Fran? Which talk had been harder?

Luke lay on his back in the main house guest room he was occupying while Marti was away. His head rested on his crossed wrists, which let him see out the window to the night sky.

Fran had inflicted more wounds. Talking with Emily, his wounds had been self-inflicted.

Why do you *say them if they're bad words?*

She'd stumped him with that one. He could say, because they were true, which they were. But how to explain she shouldn't repeat them because they hurt other people's feelings, when he obviously didn't give a damn about those people's feelings, had eluded him.

He'd heard himself saying he was going to work real hard at not saying them anymore. And he hoped she would, too. And they would remind each other if they slipped.

She'd solemnly agreed, and he'd felt something lift off his chest. Fran was right; Em shouldn't have to grow up to be a hermit like him.

If that meant working on minding his maverick manners so she could be happy as part of the herd, he'd do it. He might even apologize after a spell. Making an effort to polish up his reputation.

Like Rebecca had said all along.

Rebecca... *You can hurt them, whether you mean to or not.*

Fran's words rattled around in his head.

He was hurting Rebecca, whether he meant to or not.

And it wasn't by using a few rough phrases.

He'd seen how that friend of Rebecca's grandmother had reacted to him in the Denver airport. He knew enough of the world to know she objected to more than his jeans and boots. She'd been willing to overlook those when she'd thought he might be a big shot. No, what she objected to went too deep, was too much a part of him to ever change. Even if he wanted to. Even if he were willing to remake himself for a woman. Any woman. For Rebecca.

It couldn't be done.

He'd known from the first that no good could come of the two of them. Despite some mocking twist of chemistry that produced the sizzle between them that could only burn, not warm.

And then there was the Dahlgren factor.

"She's way above you, you know," Helen had said to him through the open truck window Sunday morning.

He'd considered closing it when he'd seen her coming. He'd seen Helen yapping in Rebecca's ear as they'd headed toward Helen's house. And he'd seen Rebecca finally say something in return. Rebecca strode off, and Helen huffed in place for a minute or two before wheeling around and coming at him.

"She's a Dahlgren. A Dahlgren of Delaware. She might have forgotten it for now, but she won't be forgetting it for long. They've got more money than you can imagine. And don't be thinking you'll latch on. I can guarantee, Luke Chandler, that Antonia Dahlgren won't let that happen. She'd cut Rebecca off without a dime. Just associating with you would hurt that young lady—if someone took the time to tell Antonia Dahlgren what's going on."

There'd been more of the same before Helen tired of an audience that responded to none of her stings.

Now, as much as he hated to admit it, a few had lodged under his skin.

With only himself to consider, he'd tell Grandmother Dahlgren to go to hell.

But he wasn't blind, and he wasn't deaf.

Sounds like you should tell Grandma to take a flying leap, too, he'd advised Rebecca early on.

I would never do that. My grandmother is all I have.

All Rebecca's rules were ties she thought bound her to people who gave her what she needed—a sense of belonging. He might think she'd be better off cutting the ties like he had, but it wasn't his call.

What was his call was to make damn sure he wasn't the cause of her becoming estranged from her only close relative.

He'd try to change for Emily. For Rebecca, the best he could do was leave her alone.

Rebecca had finished the old journal earlier Saturday evening, and had spent the past two hours comparing entries to the detailed family chart Marti had included in the packet.

During the week and even earlier today, she'd worked long hours at Fort Big Horn, followed by longer hours at the library. But now the library was closed, and Vince had chased her out of Fort Big Horn's headquarters.

That left her to her own devices. Reading about Annalee's sorrows had put her own in perspective.

So Luke had been at his most unapproachable the past several days. So the ease—even a kind of closeness—that had been growing in fits and starts between them seemed to have disappeared in an instant. It wasn't as if there'd ever been anything serious or enduring between them...except the desire she felt for him. That was both serious, and she feared, enduring. His distance didn't stop her heart from jumping at the sight of him. Didn't stop her hands from aching to touch him. Didn't stop her lips from craving his. Didn't stop her dreams.

Opposite all those feelings balanced the harsh reality of Annalee Susland's life as recorded in her journal.

The first son Annalee had borne Charles had died of diphtheria as a child, another had died at birth. Of their three surviving children, a daughter had died in childbirth, a son in an insane asylum and another son had been shot by bank robbers. The next generation had fared no better.

Rebecca could see why the legend of the curse had taken hold. The Suslands had had a fair measure of material success, but when it came to living long, healthy, happy lives, they had definitely missed out.

She was studying Marti's notes on the current generation of Suslands—birthdates, college degrees, marriages and such—when she realized there was another packet of papers left, neatly held together in a banker's clip as the others had been, with a blank page on top.

What could be left? She lifted the blank page and started reading.

Chapter Twelve

The TV news and the ranching magazine Luke held were losing the battle against the urge to nod off, when a bark from Bailey, one of the ranch dogs, jolted him awake. He heard a vehicle approaching. It pulled to a stop outside his door, and the dog's bark shifted from warning to greeting.

Luke opened the door before the knock fell, startling Rebecca. She was still only half as surprised as he was.

"What the hell?"

He'd spent four nights and four days reminding himself of the need to be as distant as he could be with her working in the office and him tied to the house taking care of Emily. The times he couldn't maintain physical distance he'd relied on curt coolness, but the temperature of his dreams didn't drop a single degree. And some of the dreams came when he wasn't asleep.

Now she stood on his doorstep.

"Oh. I didn't know if you'd be here. I thought you might

be at the main house with Emily, or out with…someone. But I saw a light, and no lights at the main house, so I took a chance—''

She was pale. He saw that right off.

''Kendra's got Emily overnight. She's going with them to church in the morning, and Kendra said this would be easier. I wouldn't just lock her up in the main house and come over here or go out on some hot date, if that's what you're thinking.''

''Of course not. I didn't mean to question your—''

''What are you doing here, Rebecca?''

''I…'' She drew in a deep breath. It sounded uneven. ''I've been reading those papers Marti gave me. All the papers. I finished the journal, then some notes about the Suslands, and all the tragedies and accidents that hit so many members of the family, right from the start and all the way through to Kendra and Grif. There was this other packet of information. It said, Leaping Star–Charles Susland Descendants.'' She shook her head. ''That made no sense. There weren't descendants, because their children had died. That's what Annalee said, that's what the legend said—that's what the curse was all about.''

She shivered, reminding Luke she still stood on the front porch. He drew her inside and shut the door against the night chill, even though he felt none of it. Opening the door to Rebecca Dahlgren took care of any chill he'd felt, despite wearing only a T-shirt and jeans after his post-work shower. He was hotly, tightly aware that he wore absolutely nothing else.

''Sit.'' Pressure on her arm dropped her into a corner of the sofa. He took an afghan from the sofa back and drew it around Rebecca's shoulders. She'd worn only an open-collared shirt and some sort of thin, loose pants. ''You need coffee.''

''No.'' She wrapped both hands around his wrist as he

started to pull back, and held on. "I'd never sleep if I had coffee now. I'm not sure I'll sleep anyway, but with coffee there's not a chance. I had to talk to someone. I had to tell them... If Marti had been here... I couldn't think of anyone—"

Else. She might as well have spoken the word. If she could have thought of someone else to talk to, she wouldn't have come to him. But she hadn't. She hadn't thought of Kendra or Ellyn, she'd thought of him.

He didn't like the warmth that gave him. This whole thing was dangerous. He should send her on her way, hustle her out of here—

She looked up at him, her eyes wide and confused.

He conceded to the pressure of her hold and sat beside her.

"Tell someone what?"

"*I'm* Leaping Star's descendant. Hers and Charles Susland's."

"*What?*"

"I know, I know! It's crazy, isn't it? But Marti's research has been so careful. She must have known about this all along. But she never said a word. Why wouldn't she say something? Unless she didn't want me to know. But she gave me the papers, and she'd have to know I'd spot it. I mean it's there, so clear—see this? Look!"

He skimmed over the pages she scrabbled to pull out of an envelope, less interested in what they said than what they said to her.

"It says Runs at Dawn, their youngest daughter, the one the legend says was about to die when Leaping Star asked Charles for help, didn't die after all. And she had children, and one of those children had children, and then it comes down to—here, see that name? Clark Pryor, who had one child, a daughter with Suzanne Dahlgren. Clark Pryor was my father."

So she had some of her answers...

She said it much too calmly, her eyes much too wide. "Was?"

"He died six years ago."

...and would never have many others.

"It explains a lot, don't you think? My looks. My grandmother not telling me—she doesn't understand anything that's different... But my mother must have...I mean there must have been something between them. His name was once on my birth certificate. See?" She reached one arm from under the afghan and pulled another sheet of paper from the pile, this one a copy of a birth certificate. "My mother used his last name then—there was even a birth announcement in the newspaper using those names. *Mr. and Mrs. Clark Pryor are pleased to announce...*

"Why would she use his name if they weren't married? But if they *were* married why would she have gone back to Dahlgren House and lived like a recluse in disgrace? There are so many questions."

She shivered again, and he drew the ends of the afghan tighter around her, holding them in place.

"It says—here, this sheet in Marti's handwriting—he was three-quarters Crow Indian, all except his father's father—that's where the name Pryor came from. With his being dead, I'll never have a chance to know about that side of my...my heritage."

"It says no other children, but he might have family—other family."

Her eyes came to his face. Deep, dark. "Yes, he might. Family...I'd...I'd like to know about the Crow Indians, too. I'd like to learn about all of it. I've always felt like I've had this gap in me. Now at least I know some of what the gap is. But..."

"But?" he nudged after a silence.

"But all the time there's this other feeling—I know this

sounds strange, but I can't get the thought out of my head— maybe it explains why I never felt *right* in Delaware, and then coming here… I know it's not like it is for you. I don't know anything about ranching or cattle or Wyoming, but Far Hills feels…right. I never had someplace to belong."

"You belong here."

"Thank you, Luke." Her hand covered his, still holding the afghan. "I know what Far Hills means to you, and for you to say—"

"You're a Susland, same as Kendra or Grif, so of course you belong here." He could try to cover his tracks, but that wasn't what he'd meant. He knew it. He was damned afraid she knew it.

"Am I? I don't know. Even if all of Marti's research is right, my father didn't want me in the end, and Charles Susland didn't want Runs at Dawn at the start, so what does all that mean? Am I really a Susland? Or a Pryor? Or a Dahlgren? I don't know. And my mother and father…? I don't know anything. "

"Don't cry."

It was like telling the clouds not to rain. And it was equally useless to tell his arms not to wrap around her, not to pull her tight against his chest, not to stroke her hair and rub her back while she sobbed.

He touched his lips to her hair, feeling the silkiness and breathing in the soft, fresh scent. He remembered that scent from the other times he'd held her. It wove through all his dreams of her hair spread on his pillow.

She gave one shuddery gulp, then a second before she backed off. One more uneven exhale came before she finally looked up.

"I'm sorry, Luke. I'm so sor—"

"Are you starting that damned apologizing again?"

She blinked and sniffled, but her color was coming back to normal. The afghan had slipped off her shoulders, pulled her top to one side, leaving honey-silk skin visible, down to where a faint curve gave promise of the soft, sweet flesh below.

Without moving his left arm from around her shoulders, he leaned across her to the table at the end of the sofa and snared a box of tissues. He dropped them in her afghan-tangled lap.

"Thank you." She blew her nose decisively, then delicately mopped at her face before putting the box aside. "Thank you for everything, Luke," she said in a stronger voice. "Coming here like this, I never meant—"

"I know. If you'd had someone else to go to you would have."

He meant it to be light, but he heard the edge. So did she. She looked up, her eyes wide, dark and so deep a man could drown in them with one wrong step.

"I didn't mean to—"

"Shut up, Rebecca. Just shut up. You're getting out of here now. Right now."

He had enough control to say the words softly. Enough control to pull the ends of the afghan up over her shoulders again. Not enough to keep the surge of heat when the side of his fisted hand brushed her bare skin from pushing a hissing breath out of him.

Their eyes met. He knew what must be in his—all the things that shouldn't be. In the next heartbeat he swore he could feel her breasts tightening, the tips of them forming points that brushed against his chest, sending stabs of desire directly to his groin.

"Luke."

He thought she reached for him. It wouldn't have made more than a split-second of a difference, because he was folding her tight against him and dropping his mouth onto hers.

Maybe he was trying to scare her. Maybe himself.

He kissed her with no brakes on what he wanted from her. He spelled it out, with powerful strokes and demanding touches.

His hands were on her everywhere, impatient of clothes, sweeping them aside without bothering to take them off. Her hands were less bold, but still on his bare skin, under his T-shirt, urging him as he yanked it off.

She was partly across his lap, where she could surely feel the urgency of his need, and they were both sliding deeper into the sofa's cushions with each touch. He filled his hands with the soft, smooth warmth of her breasts. Then gave them to his mouth, while his hands explored lower, deeper. Her pants and panties slid down one hip under the stroke of his hands. She was hot, damp, welcoming.

If this didn't stop *now,* he was going to take her right here on the sofa. He had to get her out of here.

He made himself stand, and pulled her up with him. They stood there, holding onto each other's arms, maybe a foot of space between them. Both breathing hard.

She had to leave.

He took her face between his palms and made sure they were looking eye to eye to tell her so.

"Don't expect any stopping to come from me, Rebecca."

"Okay."

A small word in a soft voice, but no hesitation.

He wanted to swear. He wanted to whoop and holler.

He took her wrist and towed her through the living room, into the bedroom, to the bed. He flung the covers back with his free hand, not caring or noticing which layers he caught and which he left. He took the hem of her top and pulled it up over her head, at the same time releasing the bra he'd unhooked earlier, so there was only her honey flesh before him now. The way he'd dreamed since that day it had rained and she'd peeled those few discreet layers off in the old truck.

He paused to kiss each nipple, but no more, as he slid her pants and panties down in one sleek motion, pressing his lips just below her belly button as he helped her step free.

Then he laid her on his bed.

He followed, halting with one knee between her legs to take her hands and lead them to the waistband of his jeans. He had to know.

Her hands fumbled, but didn't falter. He watched her concentration as he drank in the sight of her below him. Then the snap came loose and the zipper lowered, freeing him. The sound of her pulling in a breath upped the ante to the point that if she touched him now... He caught her hands just in time.

"Not yet."

He hardly recognized his own voice. He shoved off the jeans, grabbed a condom from the bedside table, and put it on. It took all the concentration he had.

When he came back to her, he saw the shyness rising up in her again. She put her hands over her breasts, and started to draw her legs together. He covered her with his own heat and desire, kissing her—slow, deep explicit. He felt her hesitation ebbing, felt her answering.

"Put your hands on me, Rebecca. Touch me."

Almost before the words were out, he felt her touch on his shoulder and back.

He knew how to please her. He wanted to do that. He wanted to know her, all of her, but they were rocking against each other. So close.

Now.

The word might have come from her. Might have come from him. It surrounded them. He made it a reality, pushing slow, unrelenting into her sweet, sleek heat. Her hands pressed him tighter against her for an infinite second of absolute stillness as he rested fully inside her.

That infinite second turned to motion, time expanding and

collapsing with each stroke of their bodies against each other, with each other. Pumping, straining, he gripped her hips, trying to bring them closer together than reality allowed. There was no way to bring these two separate bodies closer, to join them more than one inside the other. One surrounding the other.

And then it happened. Infinity shattered, scattering reality into tiny shards with it. They fused, merged, shimmered. Exploded.

Rebecca concentrated on the rhythm of Luke's breathing. It was the only thing her senses could understand.

His breathing was nearly steady when he abruptly rolled out of the far side of the bed and went into the bathroom. A shudder passed through her, an astonishing aftershock of sensation that rippled through her core.

She blindly reached out, finding a loose corner of something and pulled the top sheet over her body. As if she could hide from herself. As if a sheet could hold out the sensations—or was she trying to hold them in?

The door to the bathroom opened. She closed her eyes. Her mind still saw his powerful, naked body—her body still felt it.

He sat on her side of the bed, the dipping of the mattress pulling her eyes open against her will. He touched a cool, damp cloth to her forehead, then under her eyes, still swollen from her earlier tears. He wiped gently across her cheeks, following the new tracks from tears wrung from a body that hadn't known, had no idea of its own potential.

He tossed that cloth on the beat-up table beside the bed and picked up another cloth. With his free hand, he pulled the sheet off her. While she was still gasping at that, he crawled over her to the empty side of the bed, and pulled the sheet back over both of them.

Slowly, he slid the warm, damp cloth down her far side.

When the track of his touch lowered and slanted toward her core, she started to squirm. He stilled her with a "Hush." He enraptured her with his gentle thoroughness.

He brought her to a slow, sweet climax with his hands and his mouth and his patience.

When she woke much later, in the deepest dark, and reached out, he was there.

They made love again. Taking time to explore, to test experiences, to memorize responses. Taking it easy. Slow. Right up until the end when there was no chance of taking it slow.

He woke to daylight before she did. No surprise. He was a ranch riser, she wasn't.

He didn't move right away. That was different. Usually in the mornings, he rolled out of bed as soon as his eyes opened, cutting the temptation to burrow deeper and let the pre-morning dark ripen toward light.

This time he neither rolled out nor burrowed in. He simply lay there, feeling her against him, feeling the rise and fall of her breathing, and its flutter across his ribs. Remembering the sensations of being inside her. Wanting them again.

That probably was natural. He rarely wakened with a bed partner—not once since he'd returned to Far Hills—so rarity provided a reasonable explanation. He supposed even what had happened last night fell under the category of reasonable, given the pull between the two of them. They'd tried to ignore it and that had just let it get stronger. But they'd settled that now.

As long as it didn't happen again.

He wasn't fool enough to think that nothing had changed. But he'd sorted out what was best, and that hadn't changed.

What also hadn't changed was what could happen if certain folks found out she'd spent the night with him.

* * *

Rebecca woke in full awareness of where she was, what she'd done and who she'd done it with. She also woke to the smell of eggs and toast, and hungrier than she could ever remember feeling.

She searched the floor for her discarded clothes. She found her panties and her shoes. Period. Luke's T-shirt, though, was available. With her panties it was almost decent.

She trailed the smells out of the bedroom, and spotted Luke through the open doorway to the compact kitchen. He was at the stove with his back to her—his bare back—with his jeans, apparently not closed, hanging loosely on his hips.

Suddenly not sure how to proceed, she halted, idly fingering items on the bookshelves along the living-room wall.

Well-worn paperback spy thrillers. Thick tomes with obscure titles where an occasional "Irrigation" or "Animal Husbandry" indicated they had to do with ranching. CDs with a bent toward country, with a strong dash of Latin. And then, on a lower shelf, old vinyl albums. She bent down to look more closely. Every one classical, mostly Chopin.

She pulled one out and saw looping feminine handwriting at the top right-hand corner: Polly Albright. The next one had the same name in the same handwriting. And the third. She checked five more, spotted around the collection. It was unanimous.

Straightening, she moved to the kitchen doorway. He was emptying a carafe of water into a coffeemaker. Around the sour-tasting lump of unfamiliar jealousy and all-too-familiar uncertainty, Rebecca forced out a light tone.

"Who's Polly, and why do you have all her records?"

With the water carafe suspended over the top of the coffeemaker, he held still, except for a tremor in a muscle under his shoulder. The quick, sharp *hiss* of a drop hitting the heating element seemed to bring him out of suspended animation. He put the pot in place. Then, not turning, he said without emotion, "A cousin, and because nobody else wanted them when she died."

"Oh." His answer was so unexpected, her single syllable sounded the way she felt—as if she'd been hit in the gut. "I'm sorry."

He shrugged. It convinced her of pain rather than indifference. And that brought his answer into focus.

"She was the one who introduced you to Chopin?"

"Yeah, she loved all that stuff." He snagged his work shirt off the back of a chair, pulled it on, and started buttoning it, still with his back to her.

"Was she a musician?"

"Piano." He shoved the shirt's tails into his waistband and zipped his jeans. "Look, I—"

Seeing the door between them starting to close, she hurried to get through it. "What happened, Luke?"

He slammed it anyway. "She died. I got her records. Look, I got work to do. There're eggs on the stove. Help yourself to coffee, anything else you want."

She didn't move. He slid his feet into boots left by the back door, pulled on the denim jacket and took his hat from a shelf. Fully armored, he paused, then glanced over his shoulder toward her for the first time.

"No need to hurry. Take your time."

His final mumbled "See you" was almost covered by the sound of the door softly closing. No need to slam this one— that would have been redundant.

A large, unfamiliar car with Wyoming plates was in Helen's driveway, blocking Rebecca's access to her usual spot. So Rebecca parked in the street.

The walk up the driveway felt like a thousand-mile hike. Going up the stairs put an ascent of Mount Everest to shame. She just hoped that when she crawled into her own bed her mind and memories would be quiet long enough that she could sleep.

The doorknob turned under her hand.

She'd locked it, hadn't she?

She pushed the door open, and faced two women, one standing, one seated. Both looked disapproving, only one also looked avidly interested—that was Helen Solsong.

The other one was Antonia Folsom Dahlgren.

Chapter Thirteen

"Grandmother! What are you doing here?"

"I am here to find out what *you* are doing."

"I... I..." A memory of Luke's body over hers, his face intent, his eyes hungry, flashed not only through her mind but across her nerves and into the core of her being. The heat of it should have made her blush, the intimacy of it should have made her stammer more. It didn't. "I'm working."

"With your grandmother looking for you last evening," said Helen, "I thought it my duty when you didn't come home to call her this morning, and she came right down from Sheridan."

Rebecca swung around to Antonia. "You arrived last night?"

"Yes. You were not here," she cast a cold eye around the apartment, "so I returned to Sheridan, which is the closest community with even adequate accommodation. You may go now, Helen."

It was not only a dismissal, it was dismissive. Helen cast another look at Rebecca, then reluctantly left.

"Would you like coffee?" Rebecca's move toward the kitchen area ended abruptly with the answer.

"No. Banks is preparing coffee downstairs—"

Rebecca knew Antonia wouldn't have traveled alone. Until she heard the name of the Dahlgren driver, she hadn't realized how much she was hoping Helmson might be on hand.

"After you make yourself presentable, we will attempt to obtain an acceptable meal. Wear your gray suit."

Rebecca didn't move. "It's wonderful to see you, but this is not the best time. My work for the historical site commission—"

"Since the other project you have taken on is outside your career path, you can take time from that to spend with me. Why you would associate with a farmer when you could be Mrs. Simon Locksdale if you made the least effort, I cannot fathom."

"Grandmother," she said with all the patience she could muster, "Simon is not interested in marriage to me. He's gay. And my client is Far Hills Ranch, one of the state's oldest and most successful."

"We shall discuss this after we have eaten. With your whereabouts unknown I have, naturally, not eaten since yesterday."

Rebecca doubted that. Still the jab of guilt—unreasonable as it might be—at being away while her grandmother looked for her, spurred her toward the bathroom.

The mirror brought her up short. Her clothes were rumpled, her hair was mussed, and her mouth swollen. Despite the jarring note of their parting, she looked to be exactly what she was—a woman who had spent a spectacularly satisfying night in Luke's bed.

* * *

She had to be out of training.

Where once Rebecca would have smoothly deflected Antonia's dictums, she found herself bridling that long, long Sunday. Although she said nothing, it dulled her edge in maneuvering her grandmother. Antonia made it clear—without stooping to saying it—that there was precious little she approved of at the historic site, in the town of Far Hills, probably in the state of Wyoming and perhaps west of Delaware. The encounter with Vince was the worst.

They found him in his office, catching up on paperwork. He was friendly and open. Antonia was cool and distant. He explained the historic background of the old fort. She indicated that an outpost on a latter-day frontier could hardly be interesting to someone who sat on the boards of museums dedicated to the founding of the country.

As Rebecca steered slowly down the gravel road from the site, trying to avoid the worse pits and dips, she glanced at her passenger. Antonia sat upright, her low-grade expression of distaste upgrading to a grimace with each jounce. Rebecca'd insisted on driving to avoid Banks. Now it didn't seem such a good idea.

Rebecca had been waiting for the right time to share Marti's discoveries. Antonia wouldn't understand why Rebecca cared—the Dahlgrens were enough for anyone of sense. But at least, Rebecca had hoped, she would accept it. Now she wasn't so sure.

Luke had driven past Helen Solsong's house twice. Once on the way to his meal of crow with Fran Sinclair, and once afterward.

No sign of Rebecca's car either time, only a luxury rental that hadn't been rented long enough to pick up much Wyoming dust.

He should give it up. He'd thought he'd do this one thing

for Rebecca, try to ease things some while still making it clear last night was a mistake. At least for her.

He'd reached the stop sign when he saw Rebecca's car coming from the right, ready to turn into Canyon Street. An older woman sat in the passenger seat. With the cars abreast, his eyes met Rebecca's, hers widening to surprise with just enough of something else to make him turn the truck and follow her back to Helen's.

Rebecca went around to the passenger door to open it. Either her passenger was feeble or expected service. One look at the upright carriage and tight mouth of the woman who was easily pushing seventy, and he opted for choice number two—Grandma Dahlgren expected service.

"Grandmother, this is Luke Chandler. He's—" He saw caution chase confusion across her eyes. He didn't blame her. He didn't know how he'd describe her, either. "—the foreman of the Far Hills Ranch, where I'm working on the computer system. Luke, this is my grandmother, Antonia Dahlgren."

He cupped the front of his hat in his palm and tipped it all the way off his head with a polite, "ma'am." He resettled the hat with the brim higher than usual and met Antonia Dahlgren eye to eye.

"Grandmother surprised me with a visit. She flew into Sheridan last night." She glanced at him, then away. *Last night* surged through him like a mountain stream in spring's first burst. Fast, powerful, unexpected. "We've had a full day seeing the area and Grandmother's eager to get back to Sheridan. It's been a long day."

She sounded the way she had when she'd arrived. Stilted, careful, picking her words. She'd been reminded of her world, and she'd slid right back into it.

"Hope you enjoyed the day, ma'am," he heard himself saying. "You should be proud of your granddaughter. Rebecca's been working real hard at the historic site."

"It hardly deserves to be called historic," Antonia Dahlgren said. "Our family had been here several centuries before those newcomers began to move across this wasteland."

Luke said nothing. He could have said plenty, the mildest being that only a witch would dismiss her granddaughter's hard work. His silence seemed to make Rebecca even more uneasy. Before she could step in, though, her grandmother spoke again, having clearly read his silence for lack of understanding.

"The Dahlgrens," she explained, "were among the earliest settlers in this country. An important force in politics and culture and commerce long before that *fort* was begun."

"Settlers?" Luke repeated. "You mean those latecomer Europeans? Because the other side of Rebecca's family tree probably has you beat by a thousand years."

So much for holding his tongue.

Rebecca flushed, a surge up her neck and across her cheeks. It offset the tired paleness of her skin.

"I hadn't had a chance to tell you yet, Grandmother," she started without looking at her relative. "I happened across some material that sparked my professional curiosity, and I found a possible connection here to my father's family."

The lies were interesting. But not nearly as riveting as the sight of Antonia Dahlgren going as pale as Rebecca had gone red. But she wasn't going to say anything in answer to Rebecca's announcement. Leastwise not in front of him. And Rebecca seemed to have said her fill. That left him.

"That's why I stopped by, Rebecca."

"Oh?" she said brightly, but without making make eye contact.

"A man I know's over at the café. He's Crow. He's willing to talk to you if you want."

"Really?" One word, and the stiff surface fell away.

"Oh, Luke, yes, I'd love to. I was hoping…but so quickly! When?"

"Tom's there now. I could drive you."

"I suggest," started Antonia, with no hint of suggestion about it, "you give this matter consideration, Rebecca. You are rushing headlong into another of your enthusiasms."

"I'm simply gaining information. I am not committing myself."

"It is too late for you to meet strange men. I do not share your impetuous optimism. This is foolhardy."

"I am not being impetuous." She spoke without heat, but he could practically see the starch seeping back into her.

Antonia's facial muscles tightened. Luke suspected she wasn't used to Rebecca contradicting her. But maybe Rebecca hadn't ever wanted something as much as she wanted this.

"I'm going to see this man, Grandmother." Her voice was strong, "I'll talk to you tomorrow morning."

She kissed the air near the woman's cheek, then headed for his truck. He tugged his hat, murmured a "ma'am," and followed.

As she hesitated inside the door of the café, she felt a directing hand at the base of her back. A fleeting, would-be impersonal touch. Except it couldn't be impersonal. Not after the way she'd felt that hand last night at the same spot on her bare skin.

She barely heard Luke ask Nan to bring three pieces of pie and she almost missed his nod to a dark-haired man seated at the counter as he guided her to a booth in back. She slid into the booth, and Luke followed, his side brushing against hers. She was still fighting her response, when the dark-haired man slid into the seat opposite.

Tom Brackel nodded across the table as Luke performed

the introductions, ending, "Rebecca's got some questions for you, Tom."

"If you don't mind," she added.

"Go ahead," Tom offered.

"Because of my work at Fort Big Horn, I've been reading background on the tribes—especially Crow, Lakota, Cheyenne."

"Some books are good. Some make us laugh."

"Oh." She wished she knew which was which, but she focused more narrowly. "I don't know if Luke told you…I have information that the man who was my father was three-quarters Crow. But I read membership in the tribe is from the mother?"

"Yeah. But if you've got other relatives enrolled in the tribe, say the mother of your father, they can enroll you."

"If he had relatives, they might be on the reservation?"

"Maybe. Crow Agency is just up I-25. You could check."

The waitress brought the pie, and the conversation shifted to some mutual acquaintance of Luke and Tom's, then slid toward their days working together on a Montana ranch. After a while, she realized Luke was steering it back to Tom's younger days. This time his friend told a little more about being Crow.

"To enroll in the tribe," Tom went on, "you'd go before the enrollment committee, to see if they'll accept you. You have to be at least a quarter Crow. Sounds like you've got the blood."

"Would the committee teach me about the history and the customs and the life?"

"No. Maybe some of your father's clan would. Or the community college—Little Big Horn Community College— has classes on things like that, Crow language, too. You know Crow's mostly used on the reservation?" He waited for her to shake her head. "Most folks speak English, too. We get used to shifting from one to the other."

She leaned forward. "When could I come to the reservation?"

"You could drive up any time, but if you want me to try to find some of your father's clan…?"

"Do you think you could?"

"Maybe." He sketched a shrug. Then his eyes went to Luke. "I can try. I'll call."

"Thank you, Tom." Rebecca blinked fast against sudden tears.

"We'd best get going," Luke said smoothly. "Long day."

Rebecca wondered if he meant the carryover from last night, or her day with her grandmother. She didn't want to think about that too closely, as they went out to the truck.

"Didn't he approve of me?" She'd teethed on disapproval, knew its shades and moods. But she'd been left unsure if that was what she'd sensed from Tom. "He hesitated each time before he spoke. I wondered if…" if Luke had twisted his friend's arm into coming to talk to her.

"That's his way. A lot of Indians I've known do that. Tom's grandmother says silence is as much a part of conversation as words." He glanced toward her. "She's the only other person I've ever heard use that phrase, *my heart fell to the ground.* She's Crow, too."

Had she inherited the phrase from her Crow ancestors, along with her dark hair and eyes? A phrase her mother had heard, adopted and unknowingly taught her daughter.

He pulled to a stop in front of Helen's house, which no longer sported a rental car in the driveway. He didn't turn off the engine.

"You, uh, could come up for coffee if you'd like."

"Better not. Gotta pick up Em at Kendra's."

"Good night, then." She opened the truck door, then

looked over her shoulder. "With Grandmother here, I probably won't get to Far Hills for a few days."

He nodded.

"But if something comes up, if you need me…I mean to help with Emily or…anything, just call. And, Luke," she added quickly, before he could say he couldn't envision needing her, "thank you. Thank you so much for arranging for me to talk to Tom. And for coming with."

"No problem."

Luke couldn't remember another time he'd been glad to hear the phone ring. Most often it meant something more that needed doing around the ranch or, worse, an intrusion on his privacy. This time it interrupted what he'd been doing too damned much of—thinking.

The four days since dropping Rebecca off at her apartment had been hell. He hadn't seen her or heard from her. He'd heard *of* her—more than he'd wanted to. Especially the rumor that Rebecca planned to go back to Delaware "for a while."

His usual therapy of working himself into a stupor hadn't been available because of watching Emily. Added to that, the girl had asked when Rebecca was coming back about fifty times a day.

He'd been more than happy to say yes when Ellyn offered to take Em for the night and run her into town in the morning for her return to the baby-sitting co-op—everyone thought it best if he was not on hand for that event. Trouble was, that left him alone with his thoughts, and they were crappy company.

"Hello."

"Luke, it's Ellyn. We, uh…I thought you should know…"

"What? Something wrong?"

"It's just…when we drove back just now from picking

up Emily, I saw Rebecca's car parked where the road curves to Dry Creek. She's not in it. I would have checked more, but with it getting dark and having the kids…''

He was pulling his jacket on while he juggled the phone. "I'll go."

"Good, good. And Luke, if you need something, if there's anything we can do, you will call, won't you?"

"Yeah."

"What are you doing, Rebecca?"

She hadn't heard Luke coming, yet she wasn't startled. Did that mean she'd expected him at some level? Or that her instinct for self-preservation was too preoccupied with other matters to notice a man approaching her in the dark in the middle of nowhere?

"Thinking."

"You couldn't think somewhere more civilized?"

A tip of his head indicated her suit. She'd peeled off her nylons and traded her pumps for flats before walking out here, but the skirt would never be the same after sitting on the ground.

She gave a wry nod toward the stars emerging as twilight faded. "The thinking light's better here."

"Mind if I sit down?"

"It's your ranch." He sat beside her on the bank of the empty creek bed, not quite touching, but close enough for her to pick up his heat. "I was trying to find the creek where we had the campfire. They say water's good for helping you think things through, and I liked that creek, with the rocks and everything. But this is where I ended up. Where *did* I end up, Luke?"

"Dry Creek."

She snorted. "Figures. So much for my wilderness skills."

"What happened, Rebecca?"

She didn't answer right away, though she knew she would. Apparently he knew it, too, because he let the silence ripen.

"I was in Sheridan. I showed Grandmother the papers Marti found—the ones about me, about my father's family. I didn't expect her to be interested, but it was worse than that."

All this nonsense about your father's family. You don't know these people. They're not like us.

No, I don't know these people, Grandmother. Perhaps when I do, I won't choose to have any more to do with them. Until I do know them, I can't make that choice.

Rebecca, it would be foolish of you to pursue this. As a Dahlgren—

But I'm not a Dahlgren. At least I wasn't born a Dahlgren. Not according to this birth certificate.

"I...I couldn't believe what I said to my grandmother. I'd never spoken to her like that." Her attempt at a chuckle sounded odd. "I think I expected the earth to open up and swallow me."

"It didn't."

"No, it didn't. I was so...I just don't understand how she could have not told me. All these years and she never told me."

"Told you what?"

"My parents were married, and she knew it. The marriage was annulled. I don't know what went wrong, but they did love each other enough to get married. Maybe—"

"You can drive yourself nuts with maybes."

"That's just it, Luke. I didn't have to have all these maybes. Mother died before I was old enough to ask, but if I could have found Clark Pryor, I could have asked him. Grandmother admitted she knew who he was and where he was all that time. I can understand when I was a child, but later? If she'd told me when I was twenty-one, I'd have had a year, maybe two to know him, to ask. Now I'll never know. The two biggest things in my life—being illegitimate and not knowing who my father was—and my grandmother had the information, and never gave it to me. She would never have told me—never—if it hadn't been for Marti.''

"Your grandmother was probably doing what she thought was best for you."

She shook her head. "What she thought was best for the Dahlgren name."

She'd said it. The thought she'd never even let form in her brain before. She'd said it, and lightning hadn't struck.

"So you came out here to think about that?"

"I didn't want to go back to my apartment. Helen probably has listening devices planted for thinking." He didn't crack a smile at her sorry joke. "I drove around," she shrugged, not wanting to admit how strongly she'd been drawn to this land, how she'd resisted, until she couldn't resist any longer, "and I ended up here."

"You could have come to me instead of sitting in a pasture."

"I didn't want to bother you."

"Rebecca, you've bothered me—" He stopped, reached down to scoop up a handful of rocky earth from the bank, then started again, the drawl thickened with self-mockery. "I don't take women to bed every time they show up at my doorstep wanting to talk. You'd probably have been safe."

"That's what I was afraid of." The words were out before she could think to stop them. With her gaze pinned on his hand, she plunged on. "I didn't want to show up on your doorstep in tears again. If we ended up making love, I'd feel like a charity case, and you'd regret it the next morning. And if we didn't, I'd feel even worse."

He threw the dirt down, verbally sent regret to eternal damnation, stood, and with less fuss than she could have believed, drew her up next to him.

"C'mon."

"Luke!" she protested as he started her toward the road.

He spun back, his face intense. "You don't say something like that if you don't mean it, Rebecca."

"I mean it, but—"

"You are no charity case. Never will be. I've wanted you in my bed from the minute you stepped out of that car the first day, one long leg at a time under that stupid skirt. If you want to talk, we'll talk. But if you want to be in my bed, I'm not wasting any more time here."

Chapter Fourteen

Rebecca had some time for second thoughts as Luke hurried her back to her car. She certainly had time for second thoughts as she followed his pickup to his house. But the second thoughts didn't hit until he held the door open and she had to decide which direction to take.

Living room to talk? Or bedroom to...not talk?

She stopped dead by the back of the couch.

He dropped his jacket and hat on a chair by the door, never taking his eyes off her, then came to stand just in front of her. She leaned back for the couch's support.

"It's your decision, Rebecca."

"You scare me."

"Makes us even."

"I scare you?"

"Don't look so pleased about it."

"It would be an achievement to scare Luke Chandler. Especially for someone like me."

"Someone like you?"

"Prissy, prim—all the things you've said about the way I dress. I've never been a very...uh, sensual woman."

He cut the gap between them in half, and multiplied her heartbeat by four. When he slowly raised one hand to her throat, her pulse rate squared.

"How you dress and what you are are two different things." He stroked down and out, catching the lapel of her jacket, then sliding under it to her shoulder, carrying the material with his movement. Slowly, his other hand repeated the motion on the opposite side. He dropped the jacket just off her shoulders. When she would have freed her arms he made a sound that commanded stillness.

His mesmerizingly slow hands came back to her throat, to the high buttons on her blouse. One button came open, and her heart jolted. A second. A third. She looked down, watching the movement of his tough, scarred hands in fascination. The side of his hand brushed down her skin as he worked, as erotic a touch as she had ever felt.

"I wanted to do this that first day," he murmured as he reached the final button.

She wanted nothing more than to let a shiver release the tension of nerves under her suddenly too-tight skin.

He brushed down her skin exposed by the hanging material of her blouse in feathery touches, his eyes watching the progress. When he reached her skirt, he stepped in close, his hands going to the tab at the back of her waist. She felt the strength of his response against her abdomen. Her own response escalated as his movements brought the sensitized tips of her breasts against his chest.

She pulled her arms free of the jacket. The zipper on her skirt slid down, and his hands cupped her hips as he eased the garment off over her half-slip. The skirt dropped to the floor and she stepped out of it, along with hesitation.

Without haste, she unsnapped his shirt and tugged the

T-shirt beneath free. His scent of open air, sage and man came stronger as she feasted her palms on his chest. She dragged it into her lungs, into her soul with fast, deep breaths.

Standing there with her blouse swinging open, the press of his body sliding the slip against her bare legs, she felt immeasurably sensual.

"Luke…let's…the bed…"

"We're not going to make it to the bed."

He was right.

After a side trip to the kitchen for sustenance, they finally made it to his bed.

Now wearing his T-shirt, Rebecca straddled Luke's lap as he leaned back on pillows. She took the brownie he'd been eating out of his hand.

"Haven't you had enough to eat yet?"

Shifting to put the brownie on the bedside table caused the T-shirt's too-big neckline to slide off her right shoulder and down her arm. As she moved back over him, it drew back up for an instant before sliding off the other shoulder.

"You got something else in mind?"

She leaned forward, letting the tips of her breasts brush his chest through the thin fabric.

"Mmm, hmm." She reached over to the table again, with a repeat of the T-shirt neck's tantalizing slide, this time bringing back a foil packet.

He groaned, but took the packet. "I've created a monster."

"Created?" She sounded indignant. "I wasn't a total innocent, you know."

"Damn near."

She sat back slightly as he finished putting on the protection, the intimate friction drawing another groan from him, as well as a less voluntary response.

"That's not true. I'd made love before and—"

He'd never been the jealous kind, but he didn't want to hear this. Didn't want to hear it at all.

"Like this?"

He brought his torso up. At the same time he caught that sliding neckline with two fingers and dragged the right side down to her elbow, revealing one smooth, russet-tipped breast. Before she could react, he ran his tongue up from the bottom curve to that already-pebbling tip, circled the sweet texture, then put his mouth over it and drew on her. She jolted, her back arching. He used his hand on her hip to harness the motion into aligning their lower bodies. He nearly swore as he encountered her panties. He pushed up against her anyhow, and felt an answering shimmer.

He lifted his head to state, "You never made love like this."

Her head had fallen back, her eyes closed. But now she straightened and opened her eyes to meet his.

"No." Her voice was dark, sweet smoke. "Never like this before."

Something hit him then. An instinct, an awareness…the edge of a fear. He'd felt it a few times in the backcountry, and he'd never ignored it. It had kept him alive.

It said to get the hell out of this situation.

Then Rebecca put her hands on his head and arched her back again, offering what he could not refuse, and he forgot fear. He opened his mouth over her nipple, experiencing the texture and taste with his tongue, testing it gently with his teeth.

She shifted against him…. No, they were both moving, trying to find each other. But her damn panties—

The sound of fragile fabric giving way to a pair of hands used to wrestling calves, tractors and barbed wire made her jump. He dropped the remnants and used both hands on her hips to bring her where he wanted her, *needed* her.

"Luke, what—? Ah!"

He sucked on her with a matching rhythm, and knew she was close. And he'd be right behind.

No, not yet. He wasn't ready for this to be over so fast.

He forced himself to still, to hold her hips motionless at the same time he drew back from her nipple, twisting and falling back to lie flat. Sharp, shallow breaths gave him an instant of control.

He looked up, the sight of her, lips parted, eyes molten, breast damp and swollen, caused another surge, and she moaned with it, the sound translating into a roll of her hips against him, the motion hidden by the hem of the T-shirt.

But he would not let her hide anything. Not now.

He jerked the bottom of the T-shirt up to her waist. In an instant, she'd taken hold of the gathered fabric and pulled it over her head, releasing it to float out of their universe off one extended hand.

He ran his big hands from her waist to the delicate skin over her hips, to the even more delicate skin lower, until his thumbs brushed at where they were joined. At her gasp, he looked up to her eyes.

She breathed in slow and long, then let it out. Then he watched her gaze drop, watched the moment she looked at where his body entered hers, felt it in the roll of muscles tightening around him.

"Luke…"

When their eyes met this time, they held. Held as he slowly lifted his hips. Held as she slowly rolled against him.

Held as the individual motions melded into one unified quest. Held as the deliberateness gave way to desperation. Held as the desperation exploded into triumphant cataclysm.

Held until she crumpled onto his still-heaving chest and into arms that tied her there.

"Luke…" Her whisper of his name was barely a movement of breath against his burning skin, yet struck through bone, and into his marrow.

Spent, satisfied, stifling the urge to hold her so tight that she blended into him molecule by molecule, he knew what the fear had been warning him about.

Never like this before.

The words didn't apply just to Rebecca and her limited experience, and they had nothing to do with sex. They had to do with her, with the sound of her voice, the scent of her skin, the vulnerability of her heart and the depth of her soul.

They had to do with making love.

Never like this before.

The third time they made love was slow and sweet. Then slow and not so sweet. She'd crested one peak and was climbing fast toward the next, and he knew this time he wouldn't be able to stop himself from tumbling over with her.

That's when she said it. Twice.

"I love you. Luke, I love you."

He'd heard women say it before. Some of them, he supposed, even thought they meant it beyond the moment it was spoken. This was the only time he'd been tempted to believe it.

He smoothed her hair back, touched his lips to the sweet dampness on her forehead, then claimed her mouth with his own, as they reached that crest together, and dove, with only each other to hold onto, into the wild, thrilling, soul-searing plunge that brought them back slowly, so slowly, to earth, to his bed, to their bodies joined and tangled.

He held her, pretending to sleep, until she truly did. Only then did he ease out of the bed, deal with necessities, then return to the bed. He shouldn't have. It was near enough to dawn that he could have gotten up, started his day, pushed what she'd said down deep where it could maybe be forgotten.

Instead, he crawled back into the bed, took her back in his arms and carefully settled her sleeping body against his.

I love you. Luke, I love you.

Come daylight he'd have to deal with those words. Have to make it clear he didn't hold her to them. She had a life to go back to in Delaware. She had a rich grandmother who could give her a comfortable, safe life—an easy life. All the things a footloose ranch foreman couldn't ever hope to give someone.

Especially not a footloose ranch foreman like him.

I love you. Luke, I love you.

It was just what he'd spent years trying to avoid. Having someone love him. Rely on him. Count on him to save them. Because he could fail again. Just like with Polly. He couldn't risk failing Rebecca. He couldn't risk *her* that way.

But for these last minutes of safe darkness, he'd stay here, holding Rebecca and hearing those words.

I love you. Luke, I love you.

And knowing that if he hadn't kissed her, he would have answered.

I love you, Rebecca.

"Tom Brackel found some of your father's people. I'll drive you up after lunch. Kendra's got Em for the afternoon."

Rebecca stared at Luke. He'd walked into the ranch office and made his announcement at nine-thirty Saturday morning with no preamble. She'd heard his words, but processing them all at once seemed to be beyond her.

Or maybe it wasn't *these* words she was having trouble processing, but images. Images, and emotions. And remembered words.

When you go back East…

It's like you've been saying, your grandmother's your family. She wants you home—that's not hard to understand.

Luke had started his campaign of hints and expectations Friday morning. At least this time he hadn't simply walked out. And she didn't run home.

She spent Friday on the ranch, first comparing availability and costs for the computer system she'd selected, then riding out with everyone in the afternoon to move the same herd as before to new grazing. Then came a strained dinner with Antonia in Sheridan. She'd returned to the ranch and stayed with Luke in the guest room of the main house that night. With Emily down the hall, they'd slept more than made love for the first time in their nights together—and Rebecca thought she'd never slept better.

She'd been able to spend that time at Far Hills because she'd submitted the first phase of her work for the Fort Big Horn project and, true to Vince's prediction, they needed to wait for approval.

That had given Antonia more ammunition in her campaign to have Rebecca return to Delaware with her on Monday "while the project is in hiatus, although, really, anyone could complete the project now that you have laid the groundwork."

Antonia would have been shocked to know she had an ally in Luke.

When you're back home at Dahlgren House, you won't be running out of hot water.

You'll be able to do just about anything you want when you get back to Delaware.

Luke might have both hands on her back ready to push and Antonia might be pulling, but she was not going back East. Certainly not any time soon. Maybe never. No matter what.

Sure, she was scared, but she wasn't stupid. She knew what this was about.

I love you. Luke, I love you.

Even as she'd said the words, she'd known he wouldn't

want to hear them. But she'd needed to say them. She'd needed him to hear them, even though his reaction had given her an answer she didn't want.

"Rebecca? You hear me?"

"Tom found people who are willing to meet me?"

"Yeah. Members of your father's clan. His mother, her people."

"My grandmother." Judging from Luke's sharpened look, Rebecca knew her attempt to smile had failed.

"Thought you'd want to meet her."

"I do. It's...it'll be a little odd. I mean, since I never met my father."

"We'll leave here twelve-thirty."

"There's no need for you to—"

"I'm driving you."

He wouldn't be budged. And she didn't mind giving up trying. Luke might not want her and her love in his life permanently, but he hadn't pushed her out of it yet.

The door of the small, weathered house with the bench under the curtained front window opened slowly.

Rebecca appeared, then paused to say something to those inside.

He'd been sitting out here for forty-five minutes, feeling as nervous as a calf face-to-face with a mountain lion. Tom had said it would be better to let Rebecca meet the clan members on her own, and not to let the first visit go too long.

She paused a moment longer, then headed down the path toward the truck. Her face was neutral, controlled, with none of the flashes of emotion he'd come to expect in her.

She got in the truck and sat very still, facing forward. He wanted to pull her across the smooth seat, wrap his arms around her and hold her. Her very stillness prevented him from doing that. That and the elderly woman and middle-aged man standing in the doorway, watching them, their faces as neutral as Rebecca's.

"You ready?"

"Yes, thank you."

Once the truck was rolling, she turned her head to look out the side window. He waited until they were on I-25 to ask, "How'd it go?"

"All right."

The words were even and flat. But something about them stirred a need to see her face. He hunched over the wheel, trying to get an angle without success. It didn't take long using the remote control to shift the right-hand side mirror to see tears tracking down her face.

Cursing under his breath, he checked the other mirrors for traffic, then pulled off to the shoulder, turning off the engine and taking hold of her upper arm all in one motion.

He pulled her around to face him more roughly than he'd intended so he grasped her other arm to steady her as he demanded to her wet and startled face, "What the hell happened?"

"Noth—" She gulped once, then sobbed.

He wasn't sure if he'd intended the noise that came from his throat to be a word, but he knew he intended to have her in his arms. Her face pressed against his shoulder, one of her arms around his waist, the other bent between them, and both of his arms held her firmly against him. He slowly stroked her back, her shoulders, her head as the sobs came.

Some favor he'd done her. What the hell did he think he was doing meddling in this? Calling Tom, bringing her up to the reservation like this? The storm of crying was as brief as it had been unexpected.

"Wait 'til I get my hands on Tom," he muttered as she gulped again.

"No, Luke, you don't... I'm *glad* I went."

"Something must have happened," he said grimly. "Did somebody say something to you?"

"No, really." She leaned back and met his eyes. "They were very polite. They didn't say much."

"Didn't look like they greeted you with open arms."

"I wouldn't have expected them to. I'm a stranger."

Maybe she hadn't expected, but she'd hoped. He'd seen it and heard it when she'd asked Tom about membership in the tribe, about learning the culture. She wanted someplace she belonged.

One side of her mouth lifted. "Besides, I'm not the type most people greet with open arms."

The hell she wasn't. But he'd demonstrated his weakness in that regard enough, no need to say it out loud, too.

"Then what was this about?" A shift of his shoulder indicated his damp shirt.

Her eyes followed the gesture. Ruefully, she used her fingers and palm to smooth out the moist and rumpled fabric.

"Would you believe happiness?"

"Happiness?"

She pulled back enough to free the arm between them, and he saw that she held a small snapshot of a young man with long, dark hair in jeans and a T-shirt.

"It's Clark Pryor. They gave me his picture. From shortly before my mother met him. It's the first time I've seen him."

He stroked her hair. "Your father."

She drew in a shaky breath. "My father. His mother— my grandmother—gave this to me. I know I don't belong there yet. I'm not a member of the family or the clan or the tribe. They have no reason to accept me." Her voice dropped to an almost awed note. "But there's a chance."

Luke had been kicked in the chest by plenty of calves he'd been wrestling and by a horse or two he'd been trying to shoe. This felt like all those times rolled together.

She'd been saying it all along, how much it meant to her

to be accepted by people, by a group, by a family. But he hadn't heard it full volume 'til now. Probably because he'd seen the dark side of being part, and preferred the safety of being apart.

But even he could see what it meant to her.

She leaned back farther in his arms. He knew the touch was coming. He let it come. Her fingers on his jaw, so light and warm and soft it seemed like it should be able to heal that old scar. He let his eyes drop closed, and for that moment, he accepted her touch and her words.

"And I have you to thank."

But acceptance ended. It had limits. And conditions. That's what he'd learned long ago. And that's what had taught him not to care about acceptance.

He retreated from the touch first, not opening his eyes until he'd twisted back to face the truck's dashboard, giving the key a hard twist in the ignition.

"Luke...?"

"Time we get back. I've got work."

He dropped his foot heavy on the accelerator.

"Luke. What's wrong?"

The question was soft, but the way she said his name told him she wasn't going to let this pass without an answer.

"Just don't go looking for anything from those people."

She stiffened beside him. Even though he'd broken the connection and was looking straight ahead, he knew that. He should have been glad.

"You mean because they don't have the means the Dahlgrens do?"

Saying yes would push her away. He should say yes.

"Is that what you want from them?"

"Of course not. If that's what I wanted..." she'd knuckle under to her grandmother. "I hope, someday, I'll be accepted by them. That's what I want. Family," she finished softly.

His curse was succinct. "That's exactly what I'm saying. You get all doe-eyed and misty thinking they're family because you share some blood. Blood, a name—*family*. None of it makes any difference. None of it's anything to count on. So don't go making that mistake. And don't blame me for driving you up here if you do make that mistake—because you're just the type who will—when it blows up in your face."

The silence left him plenty of time to wish he didn't know she was studying him despite keeping his attention firmly on the wide, straight road. It also left plenty of time to curse himself a half dozen times for not keeping his mouth shut.

"This has to do with Polly, doesn't it? Your cousin who died."

Bull's-eye. And it felt like it had gone right into his chest.

"You must have been very close to her," she said so softly she could have been talking to herself. "Polly didn't grow up on the ranch, though, did she? I would have heard about her from the others. She wasn't part of the group of you that spent summers."

"No. Later."

"After your father stopped being foreman at Far Hills."

"Yeah. My uncle—my mother's brother—had a development firm down in Denver, and he offered my dad a vice presidency. He needed someone who knew ranchland to talk ranchers and farmers into selling their land so Uncle Jim could subdivide it and rake in more money." He tried to keep it neutral. "So we moved."

"To Denver," she filled in.

"I hated it from the first day."

"It never got any better?"

"For me, no. My parents were thrilled, though. Every time Dad and Uncle Jim pulled off another big deal, there'd be some new thing they'd buy—fancy clothes; bigger TV; more expensive car; and if the deal was big enough, we'd move to a better address. I wasn't in any school long enough to make real friends even if I'd wanted to. But Polly…''

"Polly?" she prompted.

"She was a year younger than me."

"She taught you about music," Rebecca prompted again.

"She wasn't trying to improve me or anything. She was sharing what she loved. And she listened to me, when I talked about Far Hills—about ranching. God knows we didn't have anyone else to share with, either one of us. She had a brother and sister who wanted all the new, expensive stuff even more than their parents did, and she had a set of cousins on her mother's side that were just like the rest of them. We'd go to these family parties—always with a slew of potential clients or helpful contacts—and Polly and I would spend the whole time in her room or my room, hiding out."

"What happened, Luke?"

"I grew up. She grew up. I escaped to college. And one day I got a phone call that something terrible had happened, and it was vital that the family stand together, otherwise the scandal could *hurt business.* Polly had killed herself, and that's what they were worried about—business."

"Oh, Luke." Her fingers rested lightly against his sleeve. He felt warmth from the touch on his skin, into his flesh, muscle and bone, through his blood. Deeper and deeper, like a rock falling into an old, hollow well.

"Don't feel sorry for me. Feel sorry for them, the miserable—" He swallowed the profanity, but not the anger. "No, don't feel sorry for them. They deserve the worst. They've spent their whole lives worried about what someone else is thinking, even when they should have been thinking of Polly. But you can feel sorry for Polly, because that cost her her life."

Chapter Fifteen

Under her fingertips she could feel Luke's tension, like a headstrong horse that might bolt any second. Fighting against the urge to bolt was his stubbornness. And something more. Something she prayed she wasn't imagining. Something whose existence she would never know for certain if she didn't test it now.

She forced all the questions swirling in her head into one quiet sentence.

"How did it cost Polly her life, Luke?"

"They knew she'd had these...thoughts. They didn't do a damned thing. They were too worried about what people would think. God forbid that the family would have to admit to being anything but perfect—big smiles and shiny cars and new houses. Couldn't have someone depressed ruining that snapshot. Couldn't have someone saying she hurt too much to keep on living. Not when she had everything money could buy. A teenager's moods—that's what they called it."

"Maybe they didn't really know, Luke. Maybe they were too close to see it." A need to explain, to excuse them pushed the words out. She wasn't sure she believed them.

A phrase in Luke's voice came back to her then.

You can drive yourself nuts with maybes.

"Counselor at Polly's school told them. Hell, *she* told them. She told—" the last word seemed to be wrenched from his gut "— me."

If she mishandled Luke's rare trust now, would he ever let her see inside him again?

"Luke, let's pull over. Please."

He complied, then sat facing straight ahead, silent.

"When did she tell you, Luke?"

"All the time. She'd talk about…endings. About the relief of not trying anymore. I told her not to talk crazy." His mouth twisted, and he grunted in self-derision. "Great advice, huh? Hell, what did she need a psychiatrist for when she had me, right? That's what my idiot uncle said. *Keep it all in the family. Much better that way.*"

"You told your uncle you thought Polly should see a psychiatrist?"

"I should have made sure she did."

"Luke, you were what? Eighteen? Seventeen? What—?"

A slice of his hand cut off her explanation. "She called me. Three days before—" his throat worked, but he wouldn't spare himself "—Polly killed herself, she begged me to come back that weekend. Begged me. But I was having too much fun. I told her no."

"You can't know that you could have changed anything, Luke. You said she'd been talking about killing herself even when you were around, so how could you possibly have known she really would?"

He spun on her, skin drawn tight over the bones of his face. "I should have known."

The first heartbeat she was frozen. The second she recognized his rage. She'd felt it. She knew it. It was the rage that tore at her soul sometimes that she hadn't been able to make things different. That she had failed.

She reached to touch his cheek. He turned away, so her hand came to his rigid shoulder.

"They didn't even call me until the next day. Too busy getting their cover story out. About a tragic, undetected heart defect that interacted with some cold medicine. Like anybody cared. Like anybody they knew gave a good damn about Polly, living or dead."

He let out a short breath, drew in a long one. His shoulders dropped. She could almost see the sorrow settle around him.

"And then, after they finally got around to calling me, they said I didn't need to come home, because it was going to be a very quiet service. Private. *Because that's how Polly would want it.*"

The bitterness in his words stung Rebecca's own throat, making it hard to swallow.

"By the time I hitchhiked back it was over. Raw dirt over a grave, that's all I saw. Until I went to my uncle's. They were all there, my parents, her parents—all of them and their business associates. I shouted some things at them. They started hustling me out, saying I was embarrassing the family." He rubbed his right palm over his left knuckles. "That's when I punched the glass door out.

"They backed off then. Afraid of another loony in the family, I guess. Hitchhiked back to school with a bloody towel wrapped around my hand.

"So, I lied before. I did go back once after I left for college. One time."

The rest of the trip back to Far Hills was strained.

Luke wouldn't talk about his cousin any more. Not about

her death, not about his estrangement from his family. Especially not about his emotions on either subject.

That left Rebecca to her own uncomfortable thoughts.

The most uncomfortable was the one that in a sense, Antonia Dahlgren's actions matched those of Luke's family. Faced with an uncomfortable situation they had done their best to make the problem conform to socially acceptable parameters. For Polly's family that had meant ignoring the seriousness of her symptoms and passing them off as teenage moods. For Antonia that had meant ensuring that her *problem* became a social asset instead of a liability by training her granddaughter to do her bidding.

No, no she was being too harsh. Polly's tragic suicide and Luke's pain naturally made her own reactions more highly charged. She had to be fair to Antonia. To be reasonable.

And that's where the other uncomfortable thought came in as they turned off the highway onto Far Hills Ranch land. Could it be that *she* was doing the same thing the adults in Luke's family had done—trying to preserve the facade of a family's image by ignoring what was really happening?

"Something's up."

Rebecca looked up as they drew to a stop near the main house. A half dozen vehicles of various descriptions were parked in the area. She recognized Kendra's, Daniel's, Ellyn's, Grif's and Fran's.

"Luke! Luke!" Emily came tumbling out the back door, charging toward the truck.

She knew Luke's short exhalation was relief as he recognized Emily's excitement and joy. He scooped up the girl who trustingly leaped toward him.

"Slow down, Em. Slow down. You're all noise and no sense," he was saying when Rebecca joined them at the front of the truck.

"Mama's coming home!"

"Now that's cutting to the chase," Kendra said with a laugh as she followed Emily at a more sedate pace.

"I'm a big sister," Emily announced. She spotted Matthew, and wiggled to get down. As she ran toward him, they could hear her bragging. "I'm a big sister, and you're not!"

Luke turned to Kendra, "Marti's lined up her return? When?"

"Try six o'clock tonight."

"She was supposed to call from China. Is the baby—"

"Fine. Marti said the baby's fine. She said she wasn't sure when they would leave until they were actually on the plane. Then she and the baby rested up a day in Los Angeles, and saw a U.S. doctor—and apparently Robert was there to greet them," she inserted with a significant lift of one eyebrow. "We had a nice long talk. She called Grif and Ellyn, too."

Kendra's gaze came to Rebecca for a moment, then back to Luke before she continued. "They're flying into Sheridan and Robert will rent a car and drive them down, with an expected arrival around six. We thought we'd spiff up some, make sure the nursery's ready, put up balloons and such. Besides, we didn't think you'd have the refrigerator stocked for what Marti's lining up tonight, so we're fixing some things."

Luke looked wary. "What?"

"Oh, lasagna, and that taco dip everyone likes and some—"

"Not the food. What's Marti lining up?"

"I don't know exactly, but she says she's got some things to tell us. She wants everyone here tonight, including you, of course," she said to Luke. Then she turned to Rebecca. "And she asked especially if you could come, and she said she particularly hopes that you'll bring your grandmother."

Antonia was once more at Rebecca's apartment when she arrived.

"I'm glad to see you, Grandmother." Rebecca smiled, forcing down objections to Antonia invading her private space. "We've been invited to Far Hills Ranch tonight. It's a welcome-home supper for Marti Susland—I've told you about her—and the baby daughter she's just adopted in China."

A controlled wave of Antonia's hand dismissed that as unimportant. "Where have you been today, Rebecca?"

"I have professional obligations and—"

"You went to meet those people at an Indian reservation. And that man took you."

A small town and Helen Solsong were a lethal combination for secrets. Rebecca moved to the dresser to retrieve clean underwear, a soft yellow long-sleeved T-shirt and her best jeans.

"Yes, I met some of my father's relatives. Luke was kind enough to drive me to the Crow reservation. And now I'm going to take a shower and change clothes for the supper at Far Hills."

"I have no interest in a hoedown at some ranch. As for today, you are being extremely foolish."

"I am going to continue to see my father's relatives as long as they accept my visits. But right now I am taking a shower."

She closed the door on Antonia's glare.

The automatic motions of showering and changing let her mind shift into a strange, empty hum. It was only as she combed her hair into a chignon that anything as solid as a thought formed.

Luke liked her hair down.

She dropped the pins on the shelf below the mirror, listening to the soft pings with satisfaction, and turned to the door.

Antonia cast a brief, disparaging glance over Rebecca's attire, then went right to the point.

"I had a higher opinion of your good sense, Rebecca. You had demonstrated that you are a more reasonable individual than your mother, and here you are following the same path she did. If you will remember that even in the end Suzanne came to see that a man like your father would not have fit in with her life, you might spare yourself difficulty."

Fit in with her life? What life? Drinking herself to death in her room?

"You must recognize that this man, this ranch foreman, would be entirely out of his element in your life as a Dahlgren of Delaware. It is foolishness to give a man such as him any opportunity to embarrass us."

She could tell Antonia that Luke wanted nothing to do with the Dahlgrens of Delaware, wanted no part in her life. She couldn't get out the words.

"*You*, not *us*. I would never be embarrassed by anything Luke Chandler did. His manners aren't based on what people think of him, but on what he thinks of himself. And when he does think of other people, he's not wondering what they're thinking of him, he's worrying about how they feel. That's a true gentleman. That's a true man."

"You are spouting nonsense," Antonia Dahlgren intoned coldly.

"Grandmother, I am going to Far Hills Ranch." She picked up her keys. "If you want to come, fine. If you don't, then I will see you tomorrow."

Rebecca had a raging headache.

The dispute at her apartment had planted the seed. It had budded during their silent drive to the ranch.

They arrived as Marti was preparing to put little Sarah to bed, so she had a chance to ooh-and-aah over the baby. An opportunity Antonia pointedly did not avail herself of. That didn't stop Marti from approaching her.

"We're so glad you could come, Mrs. Dahlgren."

"You have interfered in my granddaughter's life, Ms. Susland. I am here to see that your interference encroaches no further upon us."

"Grandmother!" Rebecca's headache burst in to full bloom.

"No, it's all right, Rebecca. Your grandmother should say what she thinks, and so will I. I don't see that I interfered at all. I opened a couple of doors, Rebecca chose to walk through them. I made sure she got word of the job at Fort Big Horn. *She* applied—and the committee vote was unanimous that she was the best candidate. I gave her the research I'd found on her family, but she'd already been looking. I just had an advantage because I started from the other end, so the tracks from Clark Pryor to her weren't as well hidden as they were when she tried to trace back from her to her father."

Antonia stiffened, but Marti was going on.

"The one thing Rebecca might find fault with me on is not telling her at the start that I knew her connection to Far Hills Ranch." Worry shaded her eyes as she faced Rebecca. "I wanted you to get to know us as people before you got hit with family. And I wanted you to get to know the ranch without all that history hanging over you. If that was wrong, I'm sorry."

Rebecca took both her hands. "No, Marti, it wasn't wrong."

"Good." She smiled. "Now, if you'll excuse me, I'm going to put my baby to bed."

"Rebecca—"

"No more, Grandmother. Please. We'll talk later."

The fact that Luke spent this entire time leaning against the door frame with his arms crossed over his chest and his eyes watching everything did not help the state of Rebecca's head. She tried to smile at something Ellyn said and thought her head might split.

"Listen up, everyone," Marti called as she returned to the room. "Before we eat, I want to let you all know about some decisions I've made."

The room quieted as if on cue, with none of the usual jokes or teasing. Robert Delligatti moved unobtrusively to Marti's side.

"I wanted you all here because we're family."

Rebecca felt her cheeks heating at that. Luke, just in her line of vision as she faced Marti, gave a twitch of his shoulders she would have bet was involuntary. No one else moved. Least of all Antonia, who'd gone as stiff as granite.

"With a second child now and other, uh, interests," Marti exchanged a look with Robert that sent glances rocketing among Kendra, Daniel, Ellyn and Grif, "it's time to make some changes here at Far Hills Ranch. You all know my father left the ranch divided in five shares. One for each of his daughters, plus one share to whoever's actually running the ranch. Each of my two older sisters left her share to her only child, so Kendra and Grif each have a share. I·have three shares—my own, one I inherited from my half-sister Amy, and one for running the ranch."

Rebecca suspected this explanation was for her benefit since clearly everyone else already knew—but why explain it to her?

"But I'm not really running Far Hills anymore," Marti was continuing briskly. "Luke is. And that's not going to change. If anything, with another baby and all, I'll be doing less. So I'm signing over one share to Luke."

Joy jolted through Rebecca as she turned to him. This was so right, so perfect—but his glowering focus never wavered from Marti, who was already going on.

"I'll always keep my share of Far Hills, but the other share—Amy's—that's one I've been holding in trust. And now it's right that it go to Rebecca."

None of her lifelong lessons in controlling her emotions had prepared Rebecca for this moment.

"Me? I can't—no. It's not…that's not right."

"Oh, yes it is," came Kendra's voice from behind her. Ellyn patted her arm. "It is right."

"You're family," Marti pronounced. "And Luke—"

"No."

"Luke—"

"It's right Rebecca should have her share, but I'm not blood. I—"

"Your blood's in this ranch, Luke Chandler," argued Marti. "I've seen you spill it. Along with your sweat and tears."

And your heart and your soul.

"I'm leaving anyhow. I was just waiting till you came back from China."

"Luke, you can't!" Rebecca cried. "You can't leave here. If it's because I'd have a share…"

"It has nothing to do with you." She would have believed him when she first met him. Now she knew it was a lie. "It's time to move on. Try another place. Been here too long. Gettin' routine."

Rebecca tried to reach for him, but a grip on her arm drew her the other way at the same time the others closed in around Luke, arguing with him.

"Let go, Grandmother, I have to talk to Luke. Make him see sense."

Antonia drew her through a doorway into the family room. "Rebecca, stop this display at once."

"Luke can't leave. He's—"

"Do you think he's leaving for nothing? Do you think he didn't want a piece of Dahlgren money before you could be free of him?"

The absolute coldness of her grandmother's voice brought Rebecca around to face her. Antonia nodded.

"Now do you understand what I've been saying about a man like him? He's just like your father. A man not worthy of a Dahlgren. A man more than willing to take advantage when a foolish woman lets her emotions rule. But I'm not foolish. I kept my head, as I did with your father. I pay what needs to be paid to keep the Dahlgrens free of men like that."

"You...you paid Clark Pryor to leave Mother?"

"It was necessary. They had been living in an appalling apartment. And when I cut his job off—even in this godforsaken area, where they pretend not to have heard the Dahlgren name, Dahlgren money carries weight."

"You had him fired?"

Antonia clearly didn't hear the horror in her voice. "Which should have been more than sufficient to bring Suzanne to her senses. Instead, she was prepared to take you and follow him to the reservation. Even after I had his brother's job cut off, so there was no one to support the family, even then she was going to take you. A Dahlgren raised on a reservation!"

"But...this was all after I was born? They *were* married!"

"Having it annulled wasn't difficult after I finally got Suzanne from that man's clutches."

"*You* had it annulled? You broke her heart. You broke your daughter's heart."

"Suzanne was weak. She let her emotions rule her. Even when I showed her he'd taken the check after two years—"

"Two years? You starved him and his family for two years, then you dangled money in front of him? Why didn't you leave them alone? Leave *us* alone? You took away my father, you took away my mother, you took away my name—all for what?"

"Do not speak that way to me. You had that other blood in you, but I worked hard to overcome that. If her father hadn't interfered with Suzanne, I would have succeeded a generation earlier, but with you I had no interference. I raised you as a true Dahlgren. And you showed promise of living up to that name, of overcoming your birth before you came here. You must see now that I was right—I *am* right. This man is just like your father. Sooner or later, the money is all they want.''

''Are you trying to tell me that Luke's leaving Far Hills because you've *paid* him?''

''As I said, I've taken care of it.''

''No.'' A calm she'd never felt before flowed through Rebecca. ''No. Nothing on this earth would convince me that you or anyone else could buy Luke Chandler. I believe in him, whatever doubts I've had about myself.'' She shook her head. ''I can't count how many times I've said I had no one but you, and I was right, because I didn't even have me. That was the price I paid to have you, Grandmother. But I've learned—that price is too high.''

''Rebecca—''

''You should leave. There are many things I'm grateful to you for and, perhaps someday…but now, just go.''

Rebecca stepped back into the kitchen. Beyond the knot around Luke, she spotted a competent no-nonsense face.

''Fran? Fran, would you please drive Antonia to town? Her car and driver are at my apartment. She needs to leave and I…I need to stay here.''

Such simple words to change a lifetime.

''This is a mistake, Rebecca—''

She spun around to Antonia. ''Then it's *my* mistake. My mistake to make. My mistake to live with. Not yours. Please go. We don't want to make a scene.''

The bitterness behind those words was lost on her grandmother. All of her life had been about not making a scene. And the words worked now as Rebecca needed them to. Antonia Dahlgren drew herself erect, and stalked out. Fran squeezed Rebecca's shoulder, then followed.

Rebecca didn't stop to think what she was doing or what she might say next. She followed her heart, and headed straight to Luke.

The group around him made way for her, as Grif finished up what sounded like a lecture—as only a colonel in the army can lecture—"Don't be a stubborn fool, Luke."

Luke didn't reply. He was watching her. She met his eyes, and this time she saw clearly what was in them.

"Go after her, Rebecca. As long as I'm not around, she'll accept the idea of you having a share of the ranch. You can make that work. Don't do something you'll regret."

"It's more important right now that I do something I *won't* regret, Luke."

A flicker of uncertainty crossed his eyes. "You don't know what you're up against, Rebecca. You've been protected by the Dahlgren name, the money. You don't know what the world's like without that."

"About time I learned then."

"Rebecca." He sounded exasperated. She figured that was good. "Think about what you'd be giving up. The house and cars and clothes and comfort and…and everything. You won't have those things."

Tears stung her eyes and she didn't know if they were from his misguided nobility or fury.

"I'd horsewhip you for that, Luke, if I weren't convinced that only a man in love would give up what he wants most in this world to try to give a woman what she doesn't want anymore."

"Ah, ahem, yes," said Robert. "Time we all go outside, don't you think?"

Rebecca never remembered how Robert managed to steer everyone else out of the kitchen, but it seemed to her that he accomplished it between one breath and the next. When the door clicked closed, leaving the two of them facing off in the kitchen, she spoke again.

"You don't deny it." She felt like she was walking a high wire. No net. No experience. Just Luke's eyes, pulling her across, foot by foot.

"That's not the point—"

"You don't deny that you're a man in love. That *you* love *me*." Just saying the words…it was like the open umbrella high-wire walkers used to catch the air, to give them balance and lift.

"Your grandmother can give you—"

"No, Luke, she can't. She doesn't give. She barters. I didn't understand that before I came here. All my life, I felt…then you and everyone else at Far Hills showed me that love is freely given, not something to be earned by following a set of rules."

"I can't give you what you're used to."

"I don't want what I'm used to. I want better. I want you."

"I won't ever care as much as you do about what people say. And there'll be plenty to say you're a fool, to say I came after you for the name, the money."

Odd how a stray phrase could settle into a heart, could calm it and thrill it at the same time. *I came after you.* Luke Chandler came after her. He'd wanted her. He'd chased her. He truly did love her.

"Luke, I don't need a government warning label. I know what I want. I know what I'm getting into. You've taught me a lot. About ditches and cows and horses. You've taught me about myself. Things I never knew. And you taught me about sticking up for what—and who—I believe in, no matter what people might say. There's nothing and no one I believe in more than you."

One tear slid down her cheek. Silent, like the ones she used to see her mother shed as she sat on the side of her bed, mourning.

"All my life I feared being like my mother, making the

same mistake she did. I used to think that mistake was fall-ing in love with the wrong man. But it wasn't. It was not staying with the man she loved. I'm not making that mis-take.''

She saw the sheen in his eyes before he pulled her tight against him. She'd reached the far end of the high wire, and found her safe haven. No longer lost.

''Ah, Rebecca. You're making a lousy bargain, but I'll be damned if I let you go now. I'm holding you to your word.''

She was smiling as he brought his mouth down on hers, smiling as their bodies molded together, the response strong and immediate. Still smiling, though a little wobbly, when he ended the kiss to speak with his lips nearly brushing hers.

''You're wrong about what I want most in this world.''

With the proof pressed against her stomach, her smile stretched wider. ''Oh? Want to explain that to me?''

He growled. She felt as if the smile had wrapped around her heart.

Luke tucked her against his side and headed purposefully for the door, only to find everyone huddled on the doorstep.

''We had to stay close because of the baby monitor,'' Kendra said, deadpan.

''So, is it all clear for us to come back in?'' Daniel asked, that devilish glint in his eyes.

''Yep. Because we're leaving.'' Luke kept both of them moving toward his house.

''But all this food—'' started Marti, then caught herself and laughed.

''We'll leave a care basket on the doorstep later,'' Ellyn called out after them.

''Much later,'' Grif amended with a chuckle.

''Thank you!'' Rebecca shouted over her shoulder. ''You know manners don't hurt, Luke,'' she chided with a grin, as they took the steps up to his porch. ''Especially not when someone's offering the fuel that will keep up our strength.''

With the door still wide open, he pulled her into his arms and kissed her long and deep. When they finally came up for air, she heard what sounded like cheers from the direction of the main house.

"Good point," Luke said, his voice husky. "Thanks!" he shouted.

Then he slammed the door closed behind them, and proceeded to demonstrate what he wanted most in the world.

Epilogue

There was one more thing to do before they all headed up to view the plaque Marti had had made for Leaping Star's overlook. The Thanksgiving Day turkey was in the oven. Fran was looking after baby Sarah, and the rest of them were ready to load into the four-wheel-drive vehicles to drive as close as possible before they followed the path Rebecca and Luke had taken one summer night.

There'd been talk about riding up. But with Kendra two months from her due date, with the day's full schedule, and with the chancy weather forecast for the rest of the weekend, they'd decided to do it this way.

Come Monday, Marti and her girls would be heading out with Robert for an extended stay in Washington, D.C. If it worked out—and Rebecca expected it would—Marti would soon be living in Washington, with trips back to visit Wyoming.

"After all those years Kendra and Grif visited for summers at Far Hills, we'll just reverse roles,'' Marti had said. ''Emily and Sarah will always have the ranch, just like Kendra and Grif did.''

Yes, things were definitely working out to Marti Susland's satisfaction, Rebecca thought. With one exception.

''Luke Chandler, you are going to sign this,'' the ranch owner said.

''No.''

Rebecca had stayed in the background until now, but they'd been going round and round and making no progress. She stepped close to where he stood before the desk. ''What's this really about, Luke?''

He resisted another two breaths before making eye contact with her, then stubbornly staring out the window where the others were visible. But he finally spoke.

''I won't have anyone saying you were taken in by a fortune hunter, going after a share of the ranch.''

After an instant of stunned silence, Rebecca said, ''I don't believe it. You do care what people think!''

''I won't have them saying you were taken in,'' he repeated doggedly.

''Not a very good fortune hunter,'' Marti pointed out, ''since you'd have done a good sight better for yourself if you hadn't helped the girl get herself disinherited by the Dahlgrens.''

Rebecca smiled slightly at that, but her attention was all on the man in front of her.

''I won't have people saying that I romanced you because I knew you'd get a share of Far Hills. That you maneuvered to get me this share—'' his hand tapped the legal document on the desk between him and Marti ''—because I was pulling your strings.''

''Is that Helen and Barb's latest fabrication? I can't believe you're letting that bother you.''

''I won't have them saying you're a fool to be with me.''

"I won't let what anybody's saying stop us from what's right." She'd said the words deliberately, and she saw their effect on him now. He was stubborn, this man she'd been living with for two months, but he wasn't immovable.

"You're going to sign this document accepting that share for running the ranch. You're going to run this ranch like the great rancher you are. And there's nothing you can say that will keep me from putting my share behind you, because I know nobody could love this place more than you do."

He parted his lips, but she stepped up closer to him, close enough for his body to react and his mouth to snap shut. "And if you're worried about people thinking I was fooled by a fortune hunter you'll just have to prove them wrong by showing the whole world you love me for me and not for my share of the ranch. You'll have to treat me very, very well."

"I'll treat you—" he bit off that growl to look around for Marti, but she must have slipped out, because the next thing Rebecca knew, his body was against hers and his mouth was over her lips.

"I know some of you don't believe in the legend of Leaping Star, or in what she told Charles Susland all those years ago on this spot."

"You mean the curse," interposed young Ben Sinclair.

"I don't think of it as a curse," said Marti, seriously. "I don't think she was telling him that she was going to make that happen. I think she was telling him that with a man like him as head of the family, *he* was going to cause bad things to happen. And a lot of bad things did happen to his family. A lot of bad things."

Robert silently handed her a handkerchief.

"But," she continued strongly after wiping her eyes, "that's past now. Whether somebody believes in the legend or not, they'd have to see that things are right on Far Hills Ranch.''

Rebecca watched the older woman's face as she looked around their group. First Kendra, her hand resting atop the swell of her pregnancy, while Daniel used one arm to encircle her waist and the other to steady Matthew on his shoulders. Next, Grif and Ellyn, arms looped around each other, with Meg on one side of them and Ben on the other. Then her, tucked securely against Luke's side. And Robert standing beside Marti, with his hands on Emily's shoulders.

Things were perfect at Far Hills, though not so beyond the haven of Rebecca's new home. Antonia had cut all ties with her granddaughter. Rebecca was taking a slow and cautious approach with her Pryor relatives, which seemed to suit them, too. She had worked out more of Antonia's role in her parents' breakup. How she had persuaded Suzanne to return to Delaware ''for a while'' with baby Rebecca because the Pryor men had lost their jobs. How she had then had Suzanne declared an unfit mother, holding Rebecca hostage to keep Suzanne from leaving. And how she had had Clark Pryor arrested twice when he tried to see his family. But also how he had never given up trying until Suzanne had died and the spirit went out of him, too.

She had learned a great deal about her Crow heritage, including that Pryor family history had also passed down the legend of Leaping Star and Charles Susland and their role in it. A legend Clark Pryor had told his young wife, and had used as an example in a letter to her of how unlikely it was that her mother would ever accept him.

''You turn away from your children, so your blood will be alone. You turn away from my people, so your blood will have no home. You turn away from me, so your blood will be lost. Only when someone loves enough to undo your wrongs will the laughter of children live beyond its echo in Far Hills.''

The words of the legend hung long in the air after Marti spoke them. She cleared her throat and spoke in her usual tone.

"But we have loved. And old wrongs have been undone." Again, her gaze went from Kendra and Daniel, to Grif and Ellyn, to Rebecca and Luke. "And Leaping Star can rest now."

Marti pulled the cloth off the simple marker that Luke's men had set into a boulder at the side of the overlook, and everyone moved to get a closer look.

Everyone except Rebecca and Luke.

"You know," he said, "some folks think this is crazy, putting a plaque up here, where nobody'll see 'cept us."

"Tough."

Luke tilted his head, surveying her with a grin. "You trying to tell me you don't care what people say?"

"Some," she admitted. "I care more about Marti, and everyone at Far Hills, and you—especially you. And I've gotten better at shutting out the voices of *people*."

"That so?" His tone was still light, but she saw something deeper in his eyes. "Well, maybe we should get married so you don't have to work so hard at shutting out those voices."

"Maybe we should get married?" she repeated, her breath coming in short puffs. She and Luke had not been apart since that night Marti'd come back from China. He'd made it clear in so many ways that he expected them to remain together. But he'd never said anything. He'd never said *marriage*. And neither had she.

"Yeah. You're still learning to defy all those conventions, so I guess we shouldn't tax you too hard just yet."

Despite the hammering in her chest, she had to ask, "Is that the only reason?"

"No. The other one's because I love you. And because if you weren't here, Far Hills would be just another stretch of dirt.'' His gaze touched her lips, her throat, her forehead, her cheeks, then came back to her eyes. "So what do you say? Will you marry me?''

"I say yes.''

The kiss they exchanged was an announcement of a sort, but they followed it up with the words to tell their friends— their family—that they would be getting married.

Excited talk of dates and arrangements followed, interspersed with laughter—the laughter of adults and children alike, carrying over the land of Far Hills Ranch, rolling on and on. And never ending.

* * * * *

SILHOUETTE®
SPECIAL EDITION™

AVAILABLE FROM 19TH APRIL 2002

BECAUSE OF THE TWINS… Carole Halston

That's My Baby!

Bachelor Graham Knight was unprepared for instant daddyhood. But as warmhearted Holly turned his three-year-old twin terrors into precious darlings, he knew only she could make him say 'I do'.

THE CATTLEMAN AND THE VIRGIN HEIRESS
Jackie Merritt

The Stockwells

Amnesia victim Hope LeClaire had found heaven—in the arms of her rescuer Matt McCarlson. Except, as a Stockwell, Hope was Matt's enemy. Could they find happiness?

THE LAST MERCENARY Diana Palmer

Soldiers of Fortune

For mercenary Micah Steele rescuing Callie Kirby from a dangerous desperado was safer than trying to combat his desire for her. Was the last mercenary finally ready to claim a bride?

AND THE WINNER—WEDS! Robin Wells

Montana Brides

Champion driver Austin Parker just had to seduce the only woman who wasn't chasing him—Frannie Hannon. But would he take Frannie as his bride once he learned she was expecting his child?

TEXAS ROYALTY Jean Brashear

Sweet revenge on the princess who broke his heart, that's all Devlin Marlowe wanted. With a single word, Dev could crumble Lacey DeMille's world. But then he saw her again…

COWBOY'S BABY Victoria Pade

Virgin Kate McDermot had returned from Las Vegas married and pregnant. But knowing Brady would feel trapped by fatherhood, she'd grant his freedom. Except her 'temporary husband' was looking more permanent every day…

0402/23a

2 FREE

books and a surprise gift!

We would like to take this opportunity to thank you for reading this Silhouette® book by offering you the chance to take TWO more specially selected titles from the Special Edition™ series absolutely FREE! We're also making this offer to introduce you to the benefits of the Reader Service™—

★ FREE home delivery
★ FREE gifts and competitions
★ FREE monthly Newsletter
★ Exclusive Reader Service discount
★ Books available before they're in the shops

Accepting these FREE books and gift places you under no obligation to buy, you may cancel at any time, even after receiving your free shipment. Simply complete your details below and return the entire page to the address below. *You don't even need a stamp!*

YES! Please send me 2 free Special Edition books and a surprise gift. I understand that unless you hear from me, I will receive 4 superb new titles every month for just £2.85 each, postage and packing free. I am under no obligation to purchase any books and may cancel my subscription at any time. The free books and gift will be mine to keep in any case.

E2ZEA

Ms/Mrs/Miss/Mr ....Initials....................................
                                                          BLOCK CAPITALS PLEASE
Surname ....
Address ....
....
....Postcode................................

Send this whole page to:
UK: FREEPOST CN81, Croydon, CR9 3WZ
EIRE: PO Box 4546, Kilcock, County Kildare (stamp required)

Offer valid in UK and Eire only and not available to current Reader Service subscribers to this series. We reserve the right to refuse an application and applicants must be aged 18 years or over. Only one application per household. Terms and prices subject to change without notice. Offer expires 31st July 2002. As a result of this application, you may receive offers from other carefully selected companies. If you would prefer not to share in this opportunity please write to The Data Manager at the address above.

Silhouette® is a registered trademark used under licence.
Special Edition™ is being used as a trademark.